THE CHALICE OF THE GODS

BOOKS FROM THE WORLD OF PERCY JACKSON

RICK RIORDAN

PERCY JACKSON
AND THE OLYMPIANS

THE CHALICE
OF THE GODS

DISNEP • HYPERION

Los Angeles   New York

First Edition, September 2023
1 3 5 7 9 10 8 6 4 2
FAC-004510-23215
Printed in the United States of America

This book is set in Venetian 301/Fontspring
Designed by Joann Hill

Library of Congress Cataloging-in-Publication Data
Names: Riordan, Rick, author.
Title: The chalice of the gods / Rick Riordan.
Description: First edition. • Los Angeles ; New York : Disney-Hyperion, 2023.
• Series: Percy Jackson and the Olympians • Audience: Ages 8–12. • Audience:
Grades 4–6. • Summary: Percy Jackson's hope for a normal senior year is shattered
as the gods present him with three quests, beginning with the retrieval of Zeus's
goblet, in order to get the necessary three letters of recommendation for college.
Identifiers: LCCN 2023011433 • ISBN 9781368098175 (hardcover) •
ISBN 9781368098274 (ebook)
Subjects: CYAC: Mythology, Greek—Fiction. • Mythology,
Roman—Fiction. • Adventure and adventurers—Fiction. • Friendship—
Fiction. • LCGFT: Action and adventure fiction. • Novels.
Classification: LCC PZ7.R4829 Ch 2023 • DDC [Fic]—dc23
LC record available at https://lccn.loc.gov/2023011433

Reinforced binding
Follow @ReadRiordan
Visit www.DisneyBooks.com

SUSTAINABLE FORESTRY INITIATIVE
Certified Sourcing
www.forests.org
SFI-01681

Logo Applies to Text Stock Only

To Walker, Aryan, and Leah

Here's to new beginnings!

CONTENTS

ONE

I GET FLUSHED

Look, I didn't want to be a high school senior.

I was hoping my dad could write me a note:

Dear Whoever,
Please excuse Percy Jackson from school forever and just give
him the diploma.
Thanks,
Poseidon

I figured I'd earned that much after battling gods and monsters since I was twelve years old. I'd saved the world . . . three times? Four? I've lost count. You don't need the details. I'm not sure *I* even remember them at this point.

Maybe you're thinking, *But wow! You're the son of a Greek god! That must be amazing!*

Honest truth? Most of the time, being a demigod blows chunks. Anybody who tells you different is trying to recruit you for a quest.

So there I was, stumbling down the hallway on my first morning of classes at a new high school—again—after losing my entire junior year because of magical amnesia (don't ask). My textbooks were spilling out of my arms, and I had no idea where to find my third-period English class. Math and biology had already melted my brain. I wasn't sure how I was going to make it to the end of the day.

Then a voice crackled over the loudspeaker: *"Percy Jackson, please report to the counselor's office."*

At least none of the other students knew me yet. Nobody looked at me and laughed. I just turned, all casual-like, and meandered back toward the administration wing.

Alternative High is housed in a former elementary school in Queens. That means kiddie-size desks and no lockers, so you have to carry all your stuff from class to class. Down every hall, I could find cheery reminders of the school's former childhood—smudges of finger paint on the walls, unicorn stickers peeling off the fire extinguishers, the occasional ghostly whiff of fruit juice and graham crackers.

AHS takes anybody who needs to finish their high school career. It doesn't matter if you are coming back from juvie, or have severe learning differences, or happen to be a demigod with really bad luck. It is also the only school in the New York area that would admit me for my senior year and help me make up all the course credit I'd lost as a junior.

On the bright side, it has a swim team and an Olympic-size pool (no idea why), so my stepdad, Paul

Blofis, thought it might be a good fit for me. I promised him I'd try.

I'd also promised my girlfriend, Annabeth. The plan was that I'd graduate on time so we could go to college together. I didn't want to disappoint her. The idea of her going off to California without me kept me up at night. . . .

I found the counselor's office in what must've once been the school infirmary. I deduced that from a painting on the wall of a sad purple frog with a thermometer in its mouth.

"Mr. Jackson! Come in!"

The guidance counselor came around her desk, ready to shake my hand. Then she realized I had six thousand pounds of textbooks in my arms.

"Oh, just put those down anywhere," she said. "Please, have a seat!"

She gestured to a blue plastic chair about a foot too low for me. Sitting in it, I was eye level with the jar of Jolly Ranchers on her desk.

"So!" The counselor beamed at me from her comfy-looking, adult-size chair. Her bottle-thick glasses made her eyes swim. Her gray hair was curled into scalloped rows that reminded me of an oyster bed. "How are you settling in?"

"The chair's a little short."

"I mean at school."

"Well, I've only had two classes—"

"Have you started on your college applications?"

"I just got here."

"Exactly! We're already behind!"

I glanced at the purple frog, who looked as miserable as I felt. "Look, Ms.—"

"Call me Eudora," she said cheerfully. "Now, let's see what brochures we have."

She rummaged through her desk. "Poly Tech. BU. NYU. ASU. FU. No, no, no."

I wanted to stop her. My temples were throbbing. My ADHD was pinging around under my skin like billiard balls. I couldn't think about college today.

"Ma'am, I appreciate your help," I said. "But, really, I've kinda already got a plan. If I can just get through this year—"

"Yes, New Rome University," she said, still digging through her desk drawer. "But the mortal counselor doesn't seem to have a brochure."

My ears popped. I tasted salt water in the back of my throat. "The mortal counselor?"

My hand drifted toward the pocket of my jeans, where I kept my favorite weapon: a deadly ballpoint pen. This wouldn't have been the first time I'd had to defend myself from an attack at school. You'd be amazed how many teachers, administrators, and other school staff are monsters in disguise. Or maybe you *wouldn't* be amazed.

"Who are you?" I asked.

She sat up and smiled. "I told you. I'm Eudora."

I studied her more closely. Her curled hair *was* in fact a bed of oysters. Her dress shimmered like a jellyfish membrane.

It's weird how the Mist works. Even for demigods, who see supernatural stuff all the time, you have to concentrate to pierce the barrier between the human world and the godly one. Otherwise, the Mist just kind of plasters over what you see, making ogres look like pedestrians or a giant drakon look like the N train. (And believe me, it's embarrassing trying to board a drakon when one rampages into the Astoria Boulevard station.)

"What did you do with the regular counselor?" I asked.

Eudora waved her hand dismissively. "Oh, don't worry about her. She couldn't help you with New Rome. That's why *I'm* here!"

Something about her tone made me feel . . . not reassured, exactly, but at least not personally threatened. Maybe she only ate other guidance counselors.

Her presence felt familiar, too—the salty tingle in my nostrils, the pressure in my ears as if I were a thousand feet underwater. I realized I'd encountered someone like her before, when I was twelve years old, at the bottom of the Mississippi River.

"You're a sea spirit," I said. "A Nereid."

Eudora chuckled. "Yes, of course, Percy. Did you think I was a dryad?"

"So . . . my father sent you?"

She raised an eyebrow, as if she was starting to worry I might be a bit slow on the uptake. Weirdly, I get that look a lot.

"Yes, dear. Poseidon. Your father? My boss? Now, I'm

sorry I can't find a brochure, but I know you'll need all the usual human requirements for New Rome University: test scores, official transcripts, and an up-to-date psycho-educational evaluation. Those aren't a problem."

"They aren't?" After all I'd been through, it might've been too early to judge on that last one.

"But you'll also need a few, ah, special entry requirements."

The taste of salt water got sharper in my mouth. "What special requirements?"

"Has anyone talked to you about divine recommendation letters?" She looked like she really wanted the answer to be yes.

"No," I said.

She fiddled with her jar of Jolly Ranchers. "I see. Well. You'll need three letters. From three different gods. But I'm sure for a demigod of your talents—"

"*What?*"

Eudora flinched. "Or we could look at some backup schools. Ho-Ho-Kus Community College is very nice!"

"Are you *kidding* me?"

The Nereid's face started to glisten. Rivulets of salt water trickled from her oyster-bed hair.

I felt bad about getting angry. This wasn't her fault. I knew she was only trying to help me because my dad had ordered her to. Still, it wasn't the kind of news I wanted to deal with on a Monday morning. Or ever.

I steadied my breathing. "Sorry. It's just . . . I *need* to get into New Rome. I've done a lot of stuff for the gods over the years. Can't I just, like, e-mail them a recommendation form . . . ?"

Eudora's eyebrows knotted. Her dress was now sloughing off sheets of seawater. A pool of it spread across the green-tile floor, seeping ever closer to my textbooks.

I sighed. "Ugh. I have to do *new* quests, don't I?"

"Well, dear, the college admissions process is always challenging, but I'm here to help—"

"How about this?" I said. "If *my father* really wants to help, maybe he should explain this to me himself, rather than sending you here to break the bad news."

"Oh. Well, that would be, um—"

"Out of character," I agreed.

Something buzzed in Eudora's hairdo (shell-do?), making her jump. I wondered if maybe she'd gotten an electric eel stuck in her oyster bed, but then she plucked out one of the shells. "Excuse me. I have to take this."

She put the shell to her ear. "Hello? . . . Oh, yes, sir! I . . . Yes, I understand. Of course. Right away."

She set the shell on the desk and stared at it, as if afraid it might ring again.

"Dad?" I guessed.

She tried for a smile. The saltwater lake was still spreading across the office floor, soaking my textbooks, seeping through my shoes.

"He thinks you might be right," Eudora said. "He'll explain this to you in person."

She said *in person* the way most teachers say *in detention.*

I tried to act cool, like I had won an argument, but

my dad and I hadn't talked in . . . a while. He usually only brought me to his underwater palace when a war was about to start. I was hoping maybe he'd give me a week or so to settle in at school before he summoned me.

"Great. So . . . I can go back to class?"

"Oh, no, dear. He means *now*."

Around my feet, the water swirled into a whirlpool. The tiles began to crack and dissolve.

"But don't worry," Eudora promised. "We'll meet again!"

The floor dropped out from under my chair, and I plunged into a churning maelstrom with a thunderous *FLUSH!*

TWO

Ψ

MY DAD HELPS OUT*
(*NO ACTUAL HELPING OCCURS)

You know you've been a demigod too long when you're flushed out of your school straight into the Atlantic Ocean and you're not even surprised.

I didn't try to fight the current. I could breathe underwater, so that wasn't an issue. I just sat in my blue plastic chair and rocketed through Poseidon's Private Plumbing System™, powered by a five-billion-gallon tsunami. Faster than you could say, *Well, that sucked*, I erupted from the seafloor like I'd been coughed up by a mollusk.

As the sand cloud around me settled, I tried to get my bearings. My nautical senses told me I was about forty miles southeast of the Long Island coast, two hundred feet down; no big deal for a son of Poseidon, but, kids, don't try this at home. A hundred yards in front of me, the continental shelf dropped into darkness. And right on the precipice stood a glittering palace: Poseidon's summer villa.

As usual, my dad was remodeling. I guess when you're immortal, you get tired of having the same crib for centuries. Poseidon always seemed to be gutting, renovating, or expanding. It helped that when it came to undersea building projects, he had pretty much infinite power and free labor.

A pair of blue whales was towing a marble column the size of an apartment building. Hammerhead sharks slathered grout between rows of coral brickwork with their fins and cephalofoils. Hundreds of merfolk darted here and there, all wearing bright yellow hard hats that matched their lamp-like eyes.

A couple of them waved at me as I swam through the worksite. A dolphin in a reflective safety vest gave me a high five.

I found my dad standing by a half-constructed infinity pool that looked over the abyss of the Hudson Canyon. I wasn't sure what the point of an infinity pool was when you were already underwater, but I knew better than to ask. My dad was pretty chill most of the time, but you didn't want to question his stylistic choices.

His clothes, for instance.

Some of the Greek gods I'd met liked to morph their appearance on a daily basis. They could do that, being, you know, gods. But Poseidon seemed to have settled on a look that worked for him, even if it didn't work for anyone else.

Today, he wore rumpled cargo shorts that matched his Crocs and socks. His camp shirt looked like it had been targeted in a paintball war between Team Purple and Team Hello Kitty. His fishing cap was fringed with spinnerbait lures. In his hand, a Celestial bronze trident thrummed with power, making the water boil around its wicked points.

With his athletic frame, dark trimmed beard, and curly salt-and-pepper hair, you'd think he was maybe forty-five—until he turned to smile at you. Then you noticed the weathered lines of his face, like a well-worn mountainside, and the deep melancholy green of his eyes, and you could appreciate that this guy was older than most nations—powerful, ancient, and weighed down by a lot more than water pressure.

"Percy," he said.

"Hey."

We have deep conversations like that.

His smile tightened. "How's the new school?"

I bit back the urge to point out that I'd only made it through two classes before getting flushed into the sea. "So far it's okay."

I must not have sounded convincing, because my dad furrowed his bushy eyebrows. I imagined storm clouds forming along the Atlantic coast, boats rocking in angry swells. "If it's not up to snuff, I'd be happy to send a tidal wave—"

"No, it's cool," I said hastily. "So, about these college rec letters . . ."

Poseidon sighed. "Yes. Eudora volunteered to counsel you. She's the Nereid of gifts from the sea, you understand. *Loves* helping people. But perhaps she should have waited a bit before breaking the news. . . ."

In other words: Now *he* had to do it, and he didn't like that.

If you've concluded that Poseidon is a "hands-off" type of parent, you win the chicken-dinner award. I didn't even meet him until I was in middle school, when (purely by coincidence) he needed something from me.

But we get along okay now. I know he loves me in his own way. It's just hard for gods to be close to their mortal offspring. We demigods don't live long compared to the gods. To them, we're sort of like gerbils. Gerbils who get killed a lot. Plus, Poseidon had a lot of other stuff going on: ruling the oceans; dealing with oil spills, hurricanes, and cranky sea monsters; remodeling his mansions.

"I just want to get into New Rome University," I said. "Isn't there any way you can . . . ?" I wriggled my fingers, trying to indicate godlike magic that could make problems disappear. Not that I'd ever seen such a thing. Gods are much better at magically creating problems than making them go away.

Poseidon combed his mustache with the tip of his trident. How he did that without cutting his face, I don't know.

"Unfortunately," he said, "those recommendation letters are the best I could do. They are the only way the Olympian Council will let you work off your debt."

Communicating underwater is complicated. I was partly translating his words from whale-song hums and clicks and partly hearing his voice telepathically in my head, so I wasn't sure I'd understood him.

"I haven't got any student debt," I said. "I haven't even been accepted yet."

"Not student debt," Poseidon said. "This is the debt you owe for . . . existing."

My heart sank. "You mean for being a child of one of the Big Three. *Your* kid."

Poseidon gazed into the distance, as if he'd just noticed something interesting in the abyss. I half expected him to shout, *Look, shiny!* and then disappear while my head was turned.

About seventy years ago, the Big Three gods—Zeus, Poseidon, and Hades—made a pact not to sire any more demigod children. We were too powerful and unpredictable. We tended to start major wars, instigate natural disasters, create bad sitcoms . . . whatever. Being gods, the Big Three still found ways to break the pact and not get in trouble. Instead, it was us demigod kids who suffered.

"I thought we'd moved past this," I muttered. "I helped you guys fight the Titans—"

"I know," my dad said.

"And Gaea and the giants."

"I know."

"And—"

"My son." The edge to his voice told me it would be best to stop listing my greatest hits. "If it were up to me, I would waive this ridiculous requirement altogether. Alas, someone"—he glanced up, *someone* being code for *my unreasonable brother Zeus*—"is a stickler for rules. You were never supposed to be born, so you are technically ineligible for New Rome University."

I couldn't believe this.

Also, I could *totally* believe this.

Just when I thought I might catch a break, I didn't. The Olympian gods seemed to think I was their personal kickball.

I relaxed my jaw to keep from grinding my teeth. "So, three recommendation letters."

Poseidon brightened. "Zeus wanted it to be twenty-five. I talked him down to three."

He looked like he was waiting for something.

"Thank you," I grumbled. "I don't suppose you could write one for me?"

"I'm your father. I would be biased."

"Yeah, we wouldn't want any bias."

"I'm glad you understand. To earn each letter, you will have to undertake a new quest. All three will have to be completed before the application deadline of the winter solstice. Each time a god writes you a letter of recommendation, give it to Eudora, and she'll put in your file."

I tried to think of gods who might cut me some slack and give me simple quests. I'd helped lots of immortals over the years. The trick was coming up with some who would *remember* I had helped them—or even just remembered my name. "I guess I can ask Hermes. And Artemis . . . ?"

"Oh, you can't go asking the gods. They'll have to come to you. But don't worry!" Poseidon looked really pleased with himself. "I took the liberty of putting your name on the Olympian quest board."

"The what now?"

Poseidon snapped his fingers and a neon-yellow flyer appeared in his hands. It was an ad with my photo and this copy:

PERCY JACKSON WILL DO
YOUR QUESTS
(IN EXCHANGE FOR COLLEGE RECOMMENDATION LETTERS)

The bottom of the flyer was cut into little strips with my home address on each one.

The photo looked like it had been taken from inside my bathroom mirror, which raised a whole bunch of disturbing questions. My hair was wet. My eyes were half-closed. A toothbrush was sticking out of my mouth.

"You already posted this, didn't you," I said.

"It wasn't a problem," Poseidon assured me. "I had my sea sprites put them up all over Mount Olympus, too."

"I am so . . ."

"Grateful." His hand settled heavily on my shoulder. "I know. I also know you weren't expecting this extra obstacle, but just think! Once you get into college, you should have a much easier life. Monsters hardly ever attack older demigods. You and your girlfriend . . ."

"Annabeth."

"Yes. You and Annabeth will be able to relax and enjoy yourselves."

Poseidon straightened. "And now I think I hear my interior designer calling. We still haven't decided whether the bathroom tile should be seafoam or aquamarine. Wonderful to see you again, Percy. Good luck with the quests!"

He thumped the base of his trident against the patio stones. The floor opened, and I was flushed right back through the ocean floor without even a plastic chair to sit in.

THREE

Ψ

WE COMPLAIN ABOUT QUESTS
AND DECORATIVE GOURDS

"You have to do *what?*"

Annabeth and I sat on the fire escape outside my bedroom, our feet dangling over 104th Street. Over the past few weeks, as summer wound down, the fire escape had become our happy place. And despite everything that had happened today, I was happy. It's hard to be sad when I'm with Annabeth.

I filled her in on my first day at AHS: the classes, the headaches, the unplanned field trip to the bottom of the sea. Annabeth swung her legs—a nervous habit, like she wanted to kick away mosquitoes or pesky wind spirits.

"That's ridiculous," she said. "Maybe I can get my mom to write you a rec."

Annabeth's mom was Athena, goddess of wisdom, so a college rec from her probably would have gone a long way. Unfortunately, the few times we'd met, Athena had sized me up with her piercing gray eyes like I was a deepfake.

"Your mom doesn't like me," I said. "Besides, Poseidon was pretty clear. I have to do *new* quests for three gods. And the requests have to come from them."

"Ugh."

"That's what I said."

Annabeth fixed her gaze on the horizon, like she was looking for a solution way out in Yonkers. Do solutions come from Yonkers?

"We'll figure it out," she promised. "We've been through worse."

I loved her confidence. And she was right. . . . We'd been through so much together already, it was hard to imagine anything we couldn't face.

Occasionally, somebody would ask me if I'd ever dated anybody besides Annabeth, or if I'd ever thought about dating someone else. Honestly? The answer was no. When you've helped each other through Tartarus, the deepest and most horrifying place in the universe, and you've come out alive and stronger than you were to begin with . . . well, that isn't a relationship you could ever replace, or should ever want to. Yeah, okay, so I wasn't even eighteen yet. Still . . . no one knew me better, or put up with me more, or held me together as much as Annabeth, and I knew she could say the same about me—because if I were slacking as a boyfriend, she would let me know real quick.

"Maybe they'll be small quests," I said hopefully. "Like picking up garbage on the highway on Saturday or something. But this is an *I* thing and not a *we* thing. I don't want to drag you into it."

"Hey." She rested her hand on mine. "You're not *dragging* me into anything. I'm going to help you get through high school and into college with me, whatever it takes."

"So you'll write my essays?"

"Nice try."

We sat in silence for a minute, our shoulders touching. We were both ADHD, but I could've stayed like that for hours, perfectly content, appreciating the way the afternoon sunlight glinted in Annabeth's hair, or the way her pulse aligned with mine when we held hands.

Her blue T-shirt was emblazoned with the gold letters SODNYC. That sounded like an insult, but it was just the name of her new high school: School of Design, New York City.

I'd asked her about her first day already. After starting to tell me about her architecture teacher and first big homework assignment, she'd abruptly cut herself off with "It was fine. What about you?" I guess she knew I would have more to tell, more problems to solve.

That didn't seem fair to me—not because she was wrong, but because I didn't want to put her second. The thing about great problem-solvers is that they often don't let others help them with their own stuff.

I was getting up my nerve to ask again, to make sure no gods or monsters had visited *her* during her day and given her quests, when my mom called from inside. "Hey, you two. Want to help with dinner?"

"Sure, Sally!" Annabeth pulled her legs up and climbed through the window. If there was anyone Annabeth liked helping more than me, it was my mom.

When we got to the kitchen, Paul was chopping garlic for the stir-fry. He wore an apron one of his students had given him for an end-of-year present. The quote on the front read "A RECIPE IS A STORY THAT ENDS WITH A GOOD MEAL." —PAT CONROY.

I didn't know who that was. Probably a literary person, since Paul taught literature. I liked the quote, though, because I liked good meals.

Annabeth grabbed a knife. "Dibs on the broccoli."

Paul grinned at her. His salt-and-pepper hair had gotten a little longer and curlier over the summer, and he'd taken to shaving only every couple of days, so he looked, as my mom put it, "pleasantly roguish."

"I cede the chopping board to the daughter of Athena," he said with a little bow.

"Thank you, kind sir," Annabeth said, equally formal.

My mother laughed. "You two are adorable."

Paul winked at Mom, then turned to heat up the wok. Ever since last spring, when Paul had tutored Annabeth in some impossible English project, the two of them had bonded over Shakespeare, of all things, so half the time when they talked to each other, they sounded like they were acting out scenes from *Macbeth*.

"Percy," my mom said, "would you set the table?"

She didn't really need to ask, since that was my usual job. Five mismatched pastel-colored plates. I got the blue one, always. Paper napkins. Forks. Glasses and a pitcher of tap water. Nothing fancy.

I appreciated having a simple ritual like this—something that did not involve monster-fighting, divine prophecies, or near-death experiences in the depths of the

Underworld. Setting a table for dinner might sound boring to you, but when you have no downtime in your life *ever* . . . boring starts to sound pretty great.

My mom checked the rice cooker, then took a bowl of marinated tofu from the fridge. She hummed as she worked—some Nirvana song, I think. "Come as You Are"? From the glow on her face and the sparkle in her eyes, I could tell she was in a good place. She moved like she was floating, or about to burst into some dance moves. It made me smile just seeing her like that.

For too long, she'd been an overstressed, underemployed mom, heartbroken after her short affair with the god of the sea and constantly worried about me, her demigod child who'd been hounded by monsters since I was old enough to crawl.

Now she and Paul had a good life together. And if I felt a little sad about having one foot out the door just when things were getting better, hey, that wasn't my mom's or Paul's fault. They did everything they could to include me. Besides, I *wanted* to go to college. If I had to choose between being with Annabeth and . . . well, *anything*, that was no choice at all.

Paul dropped a clove of garlic into the wok, which sizzled and steamed like a sneezing dragon. (And yes, I've seen dragons sneeze.) "I think we are ready, milady."

"Incoming." Annabeth dumped the stir-fry mixture into the oil just as our doorbell rang.

"I'll get it," I said, and ran to let in our fifth for dinner.

As soon as I opened the door, Grover Underwood shoved a basket of fruit into my hands. "I brought strawberries." His nose quivered. "Is that tofu stir-fry?"

"Hello to you, too," I said.

"I love tofu stir-fry!" Grover trotted around me and made a beeline for the kitchen, because Grover knows what's good.

My best friend had allowed his appearance to go a little wild, which is saying something, since he is a satyr. His horns and his curly hair were having a race to see which could be taller. So far the horns were winning, but not by much. His goatish hindquarters had grown so shaggy he'd stopped wearing human pants to cover them, though he assured me that humans still saw them as pants through the obscuring magic of the Mist. If anyone looked at him strangely, Grover just said, "Athleisure-wear."

He wore his standard orange Camp Half-Blood shirt, and still used specially fitted tennis shoes to cover his cloven feet, because hooves are noisy and hard for the Mist to cover up. I guess the explanation "athleisure-wear plus tap-dancing shoes" didn't work so well.

My mom hugged Grover and gushed over the basket of strawberries as I put them on the kitchen counter.

"They smell wonderful!" she said. "Perfect dessert!"

"Last crop of the summer," Grover said wistfully.

He gave me a sad smile, like he was ruminating about how this had been *my* last summer at camp as well. Once demigods graduate high school, if we live that long, most of us transition out into the regular world. The thinking is that by then, we are strong enough to fend for ourselves, and monsters tend to leave us alone because we're no longer such easy targets. That's the theory, anyway. . . .

"Now we have to get ready for gourd season," Grover continued with a sigh. "Don't get me wrong. I love decorative gourds, but they're not as tasty."

My mom patted his shoulder. "We'll make sure these berries don't go to waste."

The rice cooker chimed just as Paul turned off the burner on the stovetop and gave the steaming wok one last stir. "Who's hungry?"

Everything tastes better when you're eating with people you love. I remember each meal my friends and I shared in the galley on board the *Argo II*—even if we were mostly just chowing down on junk food between life-and-death battles. These days, at home, I tried to savor every dinner with my mom and Paul.

I spent most of my childhood moving from boarding school to boarding school, so I never had the whole family-dinner thing growing up. The few times I was home, back when my mom was married to Smelly Gabe Ugliano, supper together had never been appealing. The only thing worse than Gabe's stink was the way he chewed with his mouth open.

My mom did her best. Everything she did was to protect me, including living with Gabe, whose stench threw monsters off my trail. Still . . . my rough past just made me appreciate these times even more.

We talked about my mom's writing. After years of

dreaming and struggling, her first novel was going to be published in the spring. She hadn't made much money on the deal, but hey, a publisher had actually *paid* her for her writing! She was presently wavering between elation and extreme anxiety about what would happen when her book came out.

We also talked about Grover's work on the Council of Cloven Elders, sending satyrs all over the world to check out catastrophes in the wilderness. The council had no shortage of problems to deal with these days.

Finally, I filled in Grover about my first day at school, and the three recommendation letters I was supposed to get from the gods.

A look of panic flashed across his face, but he suppressed it quickly. He sat up straighter and brushed some rice out of his goatee. "Well then, we'll do these quests together!"

I tried not to show how relieved I was deep down. "Grover, you don't have to—"

"Are you kidding?" He grinned at Annabeth. "A chance to do quests, just the three of us? Like old times? The Three Musketeers!"

"The Powerpuff Girls," Annabeth suggested.

"Shrek, Fiona, and Donkey," I said.

"Wait a minute," Grover said.

"I'm fine with this," Annabeth said.

Paul raised his glass. "The monsters will never know what hit them. Just be careful, you three."

"Oh, it'll be fine," Grover said, though his left eye twitched. "Besides, it always takes a while for word to get around among the gods. We've probably got weeks before the first request comes in!"

FOUR

ψ

I TAKE A HIMBO FOR SMOOTHIES

The first request arrived the next day.

At least I'd gotten through all my classes this time. I survived math, kept my eyes open through English, had a nap in study hall (favorite class ever), and got to meet the swim team in seventh period. The coach said our first swim meet would be on Thursday. No problem, as long as I remembered not to breathe underwater, swim at Mach 5, or come out of the pool totally dry. Those things tended to get me strange looks.

It wasn't until I was on my way to meet Annabeth and Grover at Himbo Juice after school that I got accosted by a god.

I was sitting on the F train when someone's shadow fell over me. "May I join you?"

I knew instantly I was in trouble. Nobody talks on the subway if they can avoid it, especially to people they don't know. No one *ever* asks if they can join you. They just wedge themselves into whatever seat is available. And besides, the car was almost empty.

The guy in front of me looked like he was about twenty. He had short-cropped black hair, large brown eyes, and coppery skin. He was dressed in ripped jeans, a skintight black tee, and various bits of gold: rings, earrings, necklace, nose ring, wrist bangles. Even the laces of his boots glittered gold. He looked like he'd just stepped out of an ad for some Madison Avenue boutique: *Buy our jewelry and you will look like this dude!*

I caught a whiff of cologne: something between clove and cinnamon. It made my eyes water.

He said something again.

"What?" I asked.

He gestured to the seat next to me.

"Oh. Uh—"

"Thank you." He plopped down in a cloud of too-sweet-smelling fragrance and looked around the train at the six other riders. He snapped his fingers, like he was calling a dog, and all the people froze. Not that you could really tell any difference.

"So." He spread his manicured fingers on his kneecaps and smiled sideways at me. "Percy Jackson. This is nice."

"Which god are you?"

He pouted. "What makes you think I'm a god?"

"Lucky guess."

"Hmph. And I went to all this trouble to blend in. I even put on *clothes*."

"I appreciate the effort. Really."

"Well, you've ruined my big reveal. I am Ganymede, beloved cupbearer to Zeus, and I need your help. What say you, Percy Jackson?"

The train came screeching into my stop. Annabeth and Grover would be waiting.

"Do you like Himbo Juice?" I asked the god.

I'd had all kinds of meetings with gods before, but this was the first time I'd ever taken one to a smoothie bar. The place was packed. Fortunately, Annabeth and Grover had scored our usual booth in the corner. Annabeth waved me over, then frowned when she saw the golden guy trailing behind me.

"We put in our order already," she said as we slipped into the seat across from them. "I didn't know you were bringing a friend."

"Order for Grover!" said the server at the counter. Like most of the dudes who worked at Himbo Juice, he was huge and ripped and wearing a tank top, and his smile was blindingly white. "I've got a Fiji Fro-Yo, a Salty Sailor, and a Golden Eagle!"

"An eagle?! Where?" shrieked Ganymede, trying his best to hide under the table.

Annabeth and Grover exchanged a confused look.

"I'll get the drinks," Grover said, and he jogged over to the counter.

"The Golden Eagle is just a smoothie," Annabeth told Ganymede, who was still hunched over and quivering.

Cautiously, the god straightened up. "I . . . I have some unresolved trauma about eagles."

"You must be Ganymede," Annabeth guessed.

The god frowned. He looked down at his shirt. "Am I wearing a name tag? How did you know that?"

"Well, you're gorgeous," Annabeth said.

That seemed to cheer up the god, though it didn't do much for my mood.

"Thank you," he said.

"And Ganymede was supposed to be the most beautiful of the gods," Annabeth continued. "Along with Aphrodite, of course."

Ganymede bobbed his head like he was weighing the comparison. "I suppose I'll allow it."

"You used to be mortal," she went on. "You were so beautiful that Zeus turned into an eagle and snatched you away, brought you to Olympus."

Ganymede flinched. "Yes. Long ago, but it still stings. . . ."

Grover reappeared with a tray of smoothies. "I got you a Mighty Mead," he told Ganymede. "Hope that's okay. What did I miss?"

"He's a god," I said.

"I know *that*," Grover said. "He's Ganymede."

"How did you—?" Ganymede stopped himself. "Never mind."

"We were just about to hear why Ganymede came to find me," I said.

Grover passed around the smoothies. Salty Sailor for me, obviously—just a hint of salted caramel with apples and bananas. The Fiji Fro-Yo was Grover's. The Golden

Eagle was Annabeth's: turmeric, ginger, coconut milk, and a bunch of brain-food-type stuff, as if she needed any help in that department.

Ganymede thoughtfully stirred his Mighty Mead, occasionally eying Annabeth's smoothie like it might grow claws and snatch him into the heavens. "I saw your ad on the bulletin board," he began. "It . . . it also seemed too good to be true."

"Thanks?"

"And all I have to do to reward you is write a letter of recommendation?"

I bit my tongue to keep from making several comments: *Tips are appreciated. Actually, our surge pricing is in effect.* "That's the deal. And what is it *I* have to do?"

"*We,*" Annabeth and Grover corrected me in unison.

Ganymede squeaked his straw in his smoothie lid. I hated that sound. "I have to be sure this is *completely* discreet," he said, dropping his voice and peering around nervously, even though none of the other patrons were paying us any attention. "You cannot tell anyone else. Is that understood?"

"Discreet is what we do," said Grover, who had once blindly dive-bombed Medusa in a pair of flying shoes while screaming at the top of his lungs.

Ganymede sat up a little straighter. "How much do you know about my responsibilities on Mount Olympus?"

"You're the cupbearer of the gods," Annabeth said.

"Must be a sweet job," Grover said dreamily. "Immortality, godly power, and you just have to serve drinks?"

Ganymede scowled. "It's a horrible job."

"Yeah, must be horrible." Grover nodded. "All that . . . drink-pouring."

"When it was just at feasts," Ganymede said, "that was one thing. But now ninety percent of my orders are deliveries. Ares wants his nectar delivered on the battlefield. Aphrodite wants her usual with extra crushed ice and two maraschino cherries delivered to a sauna in Helsinki in fifteen minutes or less. Hephaestus . . . Don't get me started on Hephaestus. This gig economy is killing me."

"Okay," I said. "How can we help?"

I was afraid he'd subcontract his delivery business to me, and I'd end up bearing cups all over the world.

"My most important symbol of office . . ." Ganymede said. "Can you guess what it is?"

I figured this must be a trick question. "Since you're cupbearer of the gods, I'm going to guess . . . a cup?"

"Not just any cup!" Ganymede cried. "The chalice of the gods! The goblet of ultimate flavor! The only cup worthy of Zeus himself! And now . . ."

"Oh," Annabeth said. "It's missing, isn't it?"

"Not missing," said Ganymede miserably. "My cup has been stolen."

FIVE

Ψ

EVERYBODY HATES GANYMEDE
BECAUSE HE'S SO PRETTY

Ganymede put his face in his hands and started to weep.

I looked at Annabeth and Grover, who both seemed as unsure as I was about how to comfort a crying god. I patted his shoulder. "There, there."

That did not seem to help.

One of the Himbo Juice employees came over, his smile crumbling around the edges. "Is the smoothie not okay, sir? I can make you something else."

"No." Ganymede sniffled. "It's just . . ." He gestured weakly at our juice drinks. "I can't stand seeing so many cups. It's too soon. Too soon."

The employee flexed his pecs nervously, then made a hasty retreat.

"You know," Grover said, "the kids at Camp Half-Blood make some great arts-and-crafts projects. They could probably fashion you a new goblet."

The god shook his head. "It wouldn't be the same."

"Or you could look into single-serving cups made from recyclable material."

"Grover," Annabeth chided. "He wants his special cup."

"I'm just saying, single servings might be more hygienic. All those gods sipping from the same goblet—?"

"You said it was stolen," I interrupted. "Do you know who took it?"

Ganymede scowled. For the first time, I saw godly anger glowing in his eyes—a sign that this guy had more to him than just good looks and bling.

"I have some ideas," he said. "But first, you have to promise that this remains confidential. The goblet makes drinks taste good to the gods. But if a *mortal* got hold of it . . . one sip from it would grant them immortality."

Suddenly my Salty Sailor didn't taste so special. My first thought was about all the random people who might find that cup, take a drink, and become immortal. The evil-eyed lady who served fish sticks at the AHS cafeteria. The dude who screamed at me to buy ice cream every time I passed his Mr. Happy Treat on First Avenue. The Wall Street broker who always cut in line at the coffee shop and assumed every order was his.

Based on my past experience, the last thing this world needed was more gods.

My second thought was: Why do the gods keep losing their magic items? It was like a job requirement for them: I) become a god, 2) get a cool magic thing, 3) lose it, 4) ask a demigod to find it. Maybe they just enjoyed doing it, the way cats like knocking things off tables.

My next thought: "If it's so powerful, why would you trust us to get it back?"

Ganymede stared at me. "I couldn't trust anyone

else! You've already turned down immortality once, Percy Jackson."

He said this as if I had done something completely inexplicable, like ordering blueberries on a pizza. (Although come to think of it . . . that could work.)

And, I mean, yes, I did turn down immortality once. Zeus had offered me a minor godship after I saved Mount Olympus from the Titans a few years ago (certain rules and restrictions may apply). But I'd chosen systemic change instead. I'd asked the gods to stop ignoring their demigod kids.

Turns out that's another way the gods are like cats. They're not so great at learning new tricks.

"Okay," I told Ganymede. "Totally confidential."

"And these others?" Ganymede gestured to Grover and Annabeth.

"*These others* know how to keep a secret," Annabeth said. "Loose lips are never a good strategy."

"Totally," Grover said.

"They're my best friends," I said. "You can trust them as much as you can trust me."

Which, come to think of it . . . was kind of open to interpretation, but Ganymede relaxed his shoulders. He wiped his tears away with his gold-ringed fingers.

"Fine," he said. "I suspect someone on Olympus is trying to embarrass me, make me look bad in front of Zeus. If he finds out I lost my cup . . ." The god shuddered. "No. I have to recover it."

"You have enemies?" I asked. It was hard for me to

imagine how the drink server of the gods would make people mad.

"Oh, yes," Ganymede said. "Hera, for one. She's hated me since the day Zeus snatched me up to Olympus. Zeus was always complimenting me, you see—how handsome I was, how much I brightened up the palace. It's not *my* fault I have nicer legs than she does."

Annabeth grimaced. "Let's hope it's not Hera."

"No . . ." Ganymede stared into his smoothie. "Probably not. She would consider it beneath her."

I wasn't so sure about that. If messing with my life wasn't too petty for the queen of the gods, I wasn't going to rule out her stealing beverage containers.

"But there are others," Ganymede continued. "Everyone on Olympus hates me, really, because I'm a newcomer, an upstart kid made immortal. They call me a gold digger! Can you believe that?"

I tried not to stare at the twenty pounds of gold he was wearing. "You suspect anyone else in particular?"

He glanced around the shop, as if one of the himbos might have been a spy. He gestured for us to lean in.

"Before I was the cupbearer," he said, "there were two other goddesses who had my job. First Hebe. Then Iris."

Iris the messenger goddess, I had met. Every demigod calls on her from time to time to send rainbow messages—our version of video calls—but I also remembered visiting her organic health food store in California. The experience left a patchouli burn in my sinuses that took weeks to clear.

Grover slurped his Fiji Fro-Yo. "Iris seems kind of chill to be stealing chalices."

"Perhaps." Ganymede frowned. "But Hebe . . ."

Her, I didn't know. She had a cabin at camp—one of the newer ones—but she'd never been on my quest bingo card before.

"The goddess of youth," Annabeth said, probably noticing that I looked pretty clueless. "But, Ganymede, you're, like, eternally young and beautiful. Why would she want to embarrass you?"

"Oh, you don't know her," Ganymede said. "In the early days, every time I would serve drinks at the feast table, she'd mutter *Spill it, spill it* as I walked past. She's so immature."

Grover shrugged. "Well, if she's the goddess of youth . . ."

"That's no excuse! She needs to grow up!" said the three-thousand-year-old twentysomething.

"Okay," I said. "Do you have any proof she took it?"

"Proof?" He scoffed. "That's what I need *you* for. Don't you heroes dust for fingerprints, analyze DNA samples, that sort of thing?"

"You might be thinking of *CSI*. But okay, we'll start with Hebe. Then check Iris."

"Fine." Ganymede sipped his smoothie. "Hmm. Not bad. Maybe when I get fired and turned back into a mortal, I could work here."

"You'd make a great himbo," Annabeth admitted. "So how long has your chalice been missing?"

Ganymede paused to think. "A century?"

"A *century*?!" I asked.

"Or a week?" Ganymede pinched his nose. "I always get those time periods confused. Not long, anyway. So far, I've been able to fake it with my delivery orders. The other gods kind of expect to-go cups with those. But if I don't get my proper chalice back before the next in-person feast, everyone will notice. I'll be humiliated!"

"When is the next feast?" Grover asked. (Grover likes feasts.)

"I don't know!" Ganymede cried. "Zeus is unpredictable! He might schedule one in twenty years. Or it could be tomorrow. The point is, I need that goblet back before word gets out!"

He leaned forward, his expression stern. "Question those goddesses. See what they know. But *don't* offend them. And *don't* say I sent you. And *don't* give away that my cup was stolen."

"That'll make it hard to question them," Annabeth said. "Any idea where these goddesses hang out?"

I was bracing myself for him to say the North Pole or Outer Mongolia. If I had to take a leave of absence to go questing across the world, the college recommendation letters wouldn't matter. I'd never graduate high school.

"They stay close to Mount Olympus," he said to my relief. "I mean Manhattan. They should be around here somewhere." He waved vaguely, as if the whole of Manhattan couldn't possibly be too difficult to search. "Do this for me, Percy Jackson, and I will write you a letter!"

It didn't sound like much of a reward. Then again, usually gods just asked for things and promised nothing in return. Kind of like that bratty kid in *The Giving Tree*.

(Speaking of which, *never* give that book to a satyr for his birthday, thinking he might like it because it's about a tree. That satyr will cry, and then he will hit you. I speak from experience.)

"This recommendation letter will be *positive*?" I checked. "And you'll actually sign it?"

Ganymede frowned. "You drive a hard bargain, but very well! Now, away with you, before I am undone!"

He disappeared in a glittering cloud of dust. As usual with magical happenings, the mortals around us didn't seem to notice anything. Or maybe they just figured he had found the perfect smoothie and ascended to himbo enlightenment.

"Well." I sipped my Salty Sailor and scanned my companions' faces for any sign of regret. "This should be fun. Any ideas where to start?"

"Unfortunately, yes," said Grover. "But let me finish my drink first. We're going to need our strength."

SIX

Ψ

BECAUSE LICORICE

Here's a challenge: try to do a full day of school (actually, that could be the whole challenge by itself), and then, afterward, go on a quest to find a goddess, knowing that when you get home, *if* you get home, you'll still have a couple of hours of math and science homework to do.

I was feeling pretty salty as we headed downtown, and it had nothing to do with my Salty Sailor.

Grover brought us straight to Times Square—the noisiest, most crowded, most tourist-infested part of Manhattan. I tried to avoid Times Square as much as possible, which naturally meant I just kept getting sucked into it, usually to battle a monster, talk to a god, or hang from a billboard in my boxer shorts. (Long story.)

Grover stopped at a storefront I would have passed right by. For half a block, all the windows were covered in foil. Usually, that means the place is either out of business or super shady. Then I looked up at the enormous electronic sign above the entrance. I might have walked by it a dozen times before, but I'd never paid it any attention. In Times Square, all the flashy jumbo screens kind of blend together.

"No way," I said.

Annabeth shook her head. "She *really* named her place Hebe Jeebies?"

"Afraid so," Grover sighed.

"And how did you know about this place?" I asked.

His cheeks flushed. "They have great licorice ropes. You can't pass by without smelling them!"

I couldn't see anything through the windows. I definitely didn't smell anything. Then again, I don't have a satyr's nose for licorice. It's kind of like catnip for goat guys.

"It's a candy store, then?" Annabeth asked.

"No, more like . . ." Grover tilted his head. "Actually, it's easier to show you."

I wasn't sure traipsing into a goddess's lair was the best idea, but Grover pushed through the doors and we followed. Because licorice, I guess.

Inside . . . well, imagine all the cheesiest entertainment centers from the 1990s got together and had a food baby. That was Hebe Jeebies.

Rows of Skee-Ball machines stood ready for action. A dozen *Dance Dance Revolution* platforms blinked and flashed, inviting us to boogie. Aisles with every arcade game I'd ever heard of, and dozens that I hadn't, lined the vast, dimly lit warehouse, making the whole place a glowing labyrinth. (And *labyrinth* is a word I never use lightly.)

In the distance, I spotted a candy station with fill-your-own-bag dispensers and huge bins of colorful sweet stuff.

On the other side of the warehouse were a cafeteria with picnic tables and a stage where robotic iguanas played musical instruments.

There was a ball pit the size of a house, a climbing structure that looked like a giant hamster habitat, a bumper-car course, and a ticket-exchange station with oversize stuffed animals for prizes.

The whole place smelled of pizza, pretzels, and industrial cleaner. And it was *packed* with families.

"I get it now," said Annabeth, shivering. "This place *does* give me the heebie-jeebies."

"I've been here a few times." Grover's expression was a combination of anxiety and hunger . . . which, come to think of it, was his usual expression. "I've never found the other end of the place."

I looked at the happy kids running around obliviously and the parents who seemed just as thrilled to play games they probably remembered from their own childhoods.

"Okay," I said, inching back toward the front door. "I'm getting strong Lotus Casino vibes in here . . . like *low-rent* Lotus Casino, but still . . ."

I didn't have to explain what I meant. Years ago, we'd gotten stuck in a Vegas casino that offered a thousand reasons to never leave. We'd just barely escaped.

"It's not a trap," Grover said. "At least, I've never had any trouble leaving. These families . . . they come and go. They don't seem to be stuck in time."

He had a point. I didn't spot anybody with bell-bottoms or 1950s haircuts, which was a good sign. A family walked by, their arms full of stuffed-animal prizes, and left the building with no problem.

"Then . . . what's the catch?" Annabeth asked. "There's always a catch."

I nodded in agreement. I'd never walked into any establishment run by a Greek god, monster, or other immortal being that didn't have a nasty downside. The more interesting the place looked, the more dangerous it was.

"I don't know," Grover admitted. "I usually just get licorice and leave. I keep a low profile."

He frowned at me, as if worried I might do something high-profile like burn the place down. Honestly, that hurt. Just because I've been known to burn places down, blow things up, and unleash apocalyptic disasters wherever I go . . . that doesn't mean I'm *totally* irresponsible.

"And you're sure Hebe is here?" I asked.

"No, but . . ." Grover wriggled his shoulders. "You know that feeling you get when there's a god around and you can't see them, but you kind of feel like there's a swarm of dung beetles on the back of your neck?"

"Not exactly . . ." I said.

"Also," said Annabeth, "*dung beetles* is oddly specific."

Grover brushed the metaphorical poop bugs off his neck. "Anyway, I've got that feeling now. We could ask the staff if Hebe's around. If we can find someone."

We moved into the arcade. I kept my hand at my side, ready to draw out Riptide, my pen-sword, though there didn't seem to be much to fight except grade-school kids and video game bosses. I half expected the robot iguana band to charge us with banjo bayonets, but they just kept playing their programmed songs.

"Oh, my gods," Annabeth said. "Stackers. I haven't played that since . . ."

Her thoughts seemed to drift away. She'd been at Camp Half-Blood since she was seven years old, so she must have been reliving a *really* early memory. It made sense to me that she would like a game where you had to place one block on top of another. She was all about building and architecture.

As we approached the candy station, I felt a pang in my abdomen. Not because I was hungry, but because the smell reminded me so much of my mom's old workplace, Sweet on America. I used to love going there during the summer and watching her help people pick out candy. I guess it was a pretty hard job, and it didn't pay much, but my mom never failed to make people smile. They always left happy, with just the right mix of treats, which made my mom seem like a superhero to me.

Of course, she was still a superhero to me for a lot of reasons. But back when I was seven or eight, having a mom who was the candy lady felt like the coolest thing ever. She used to bring me free samples when she came home, and this place had all my old favorites: blueberry saltwater taffy, blue sour laces, blue . . . well, everything. It's amazing my tongue hadn't turned permanently violet.

Grover sniffed at the rows of licorice ropes, which came in so many colors they reminded me of Paul's tie

[43]

rack. (Paul loves wearing funky ties to school. He says it keeps his students awake.)

A group of adults walked past, giggly and teary-eyed, reminiscing about their favorite treats and games from back in the day.

"It's a nostalgia trap," I realized. "The place is selling people their own childhoods."

Annabeth nodded. Her gaze drifted around the amusement center like she was scanning for threats. "That makes sense, but a lot of places sell nostalgia. It's not necessarily a bad thing. . . ."

An employee walked past wearing a bright blue Hebe Jeebies polo shirt and matching shorts, fussing with a wheel of paper prize tickets.

"Excuse me, miss?" Annabeth touched her arm, and the employee jumped.

"What?" she snapped.

I realized she was just a kid. She had wiry black hair with pink barrettes, a pouty baby face, and a name tag that read SPARKY, MANAGER. She couldn't have been more than nine years old.

"Sorry." Sparky took a breath. "The token machine is broken again, and I gotta get these tickets to . . . Anyway, how can I help?"

I wondered if the gods had child-labor laws for their magical businesses. If so, the goddess of youth apparently didn't believe in them.

"We're looking for Hebe?" I asked.

"If this is about a refund for a defective game—"

"It's not," I said.

"Or the pizza being moldy—"

"It's not. Also, yuck."

"Depends on the mold," Grover murmured.

"We just need to speak to the goddess in charge," Annabeth said. "It's kind of urgent."

Sparky scowled, then relented. "Past the diving cliff; left at the henhouse."

"Diving cliff?" I asked.

"Henhouse?" asked Grover.

"She'll be in the karaoke bar." Sparky wrinkled her nose like this was an unpleasant fact of life. "Don't worry. You'll hear it."

She hurried off with her wheel o' prize tickets.

I looked at Annabeth and Grover. "Are we really going to search out a karaoke bar . . . like, on purpose?"

"You can duet with me on 'Shallow,'" Annabeth offered.

"You don't want that," I promised.

"Oh, I don't know." She pinched my arm lightly. "Might be romantic."

"I'm just going to keep walking," said Grover.

Which was probably the wisest choice.

We found the diving cliff: a two-story wall of fake rock where you could jump off into a suspiciously murky pool of water. A couple of kids were doing it on a loop, splashing down, clambering out, and racing back up to the top, while their parents stood nearby, engrossed in a game of *Space Invaders*.

I am a son of Poseidon, but you couldn't have paid me enough to jump into that pool. Any enclosed body of water where little kids have been playing? No thanks. Nevertheless, I took note of where the pool was, just in case I needed some H_2O to throw around.

I am a guy of limited talents. If I can't kill it with water, a sword, or sarcasm, I am basically defenseless. I come preloaded with sarcasm. The pen-sword is always in my pocket. Now I had access to water, so I was as prepared as I could ever be.

We passed the henhouse . . . which I'd thought might be a nickname for a private event space or something, like where you'd have hen parties. But no. It was an actual henhouse. Right in the middle of the arcade stood a red shack on stilts, surrounded by a chicken-wire fence. On the floor around it, about a dozen hens and some little yellow chicks were pecking at feed, clucking, and basically being chickens.

"Why?" I asked.

"Hebe's sacred animal," Annabeth said. "Maybe we should move along."

I didn't argue. The chickens were staring at us with their beady black eyes as if thinking, *Dude, if we were still dinosaurs, we would tear you to pieces.*

At last, we found the karaoke bar. It was partitioned off from the rest of the amusement center by a set of sliding mahogany doors, but that didn't stop the music from seeping through. Inside, half a dozen tables faced a sad little stage, where a squad of old folks belted out a song that sounded vaguely Woodstock-ish. The stage lights pulsed a sickly yellow color. The sound system crackled.

That didn't seem to bother the boomers, who threw their arms around one another and waved their canes, their bald heads gleaming as they wailed about peace and sunshine.

"Can we leave now?" Grover asked.

Annabeth pointed to a booth against the far wall. "Look over there."

Sitting in the booth, tapping her feet to the music, was a girl about my age. At least, that's what she appeared to be. But I could tell she was a goddess because immortals always make themselves a little too flawless when they appear in human form: perfect complexion, hair always photo-shoot ready, clothes far too crisp and colorful for mere mortals. The girl in the booth wore a pink-and-turquoise minidress with white go-go boots but somehow managed to make it look hip and not like a retro Halloween costume. Her hair was a dark beehive swirl. It occurred to me she was channeling a fashion that would remind the boomers of their own childhoods.

We approached the booth.

"Lady Hebe?" I asked.

I figured that was the safest way to address her. I was guessing her last name wasn't Jeebies.

The goddess raised a finger to silence me, her eyes still fixed on the geriatric singers. "Don't they seem happy? So *young* again!"

The boomers did seem happy. I wasn't sure about

young, but maybe *young* meant something different back in the day.

"Um, yeah," I said. "We were just wondering—"

"Please, sit." The goddess waved her hand, and three chairs appeared on the outside of the booth.

Then Hebe issued one of the most terrifying threats I had ever heard from a god: "I'll order us some pizza, and we can talk while the old folks sing protest songs."

SEVEN

BIG SHOCKER: I OFFEND A GODDESS

It was the pizza that got me.

I don't mean with food poisoning. I mean with nostalgia.

The cheese slice looked like a triangle of melted vinyl, garnished with three sad flecks of basil and served on a paper plate limp with grease. I had no intention of eating it—not after Sparky's mold comment—but the smell took me right back to third grade.

Wednesdays were pizza days. I remembered the burnt-cheese smell in our basement cafeteria, the cracked green plastic chairs, the feverish conversations I used to have with my friends about trading cards, the history teacher who was our lunch monitor, Mr. Christ. (No kidding, that was his actual name. We were too scared to ask what his first name was.)

Now, looking at (and smelling) Hebe Jeebies's glistening plastic pizza, I felt eight years old again.

"Wow," I said.

Hebe smiled, as if she knew exactly what I was thinking. "Wonderful, isn't it? Feeling young again?"

Okay, maybe she didn't know *exactly* what I was thinking. Being in third grade for me had not been wonderful. Neither had the pizza. But it was still a rush, being pulled back in time by nothing but a smell.

Grover dug in, devouring his pizza slice, his paper plate, and my napkin. I had learned to keep my hands away from him when he was in grazing mode or he might have started gnawing on my fingers.

Annabeth remained focused on the karaoke boomers. They were now belting out a slow, sad song about where all the flowers had gone. I wanted to shout, *I don't know. Why don't you go outside and look for them?*

"What a fabulous generation," Hebe said, admiring the geriatric singers. "Even now, they refuse to accept growing old." She turned to me. "And you, Percy Jackson, I assume you've come to ask a favor. Perhaps you're starting to regret turning down immortality?"

Here we go, I thought.

Every time the gods brought up my rejection of Zeus's offer, they treated it as a sign of stupidity—or worse, as an insult to godkind. I hadn't figured out a great way to explain it to them. Like, maybe if you all promised to claim your demigod children sooner, so your kids weren't living their whole lives not knowing who they were or where they came from, that would be a win for everyone?

I must have looked like I was about to bust out the sarcasm, because Annabeth intervened.

"He made the selfless choice," she said. "Because of

that, your kids got their own cabin at Camp Half-Blood. You finally got the respect you deserve."

Hebe narrowed her eyes. "Perhaps. Still, Percy Jackson, turning down eternal youth? You can't really *want* to grow old. Don't you understand how terrible that will be?"

There didn't seem to be a right answer to that.

Honestly, I'd spent most of my life wishing I *could* be older, so I could get to college, get out of the target years when monsters were trying to kill me every other day.

I didn't want to contradict the goddess, though, so I tried a careful answer. "I mean, I guess getting older is part of life—"

"This pizza is great!" Grover interrupted, probably in an attempt to save me from god-level zappage. "And the music . . ." He frowned at the boomers. "Wait a minute. . . . Are they actually getting younger?"

He was right. The changes were subtle, but their hair didn't seem so gray now. Their postures were straighter. Their voices sounded more assured, though still terrible.

"They come here to remember the old days." Hebe gestured around her. "Nostalgia is the doorway back to youth. I'm just showing them how to open it."

A shiver ran across my shoulders. The last thing the world needed was boomers aging backward, like, *We enjoyed monopolizing the planet so much the first time, we're going to do it again!*

"That's . . . nice of you," Grover tried. But from the slight tremor in his voice, I could tell he was not liking this place anymore, no matter how good the licorice ropes were.

Hebe crossed her go-go boots at the ankles. She placed her arms across the back of the booth. With her smug expression, she reminded me more of a Mafia boss than a 1960s teenager.

"Is that why you're here, then?" she asked. "You want to know the secret of youth? I imagine none of you really had a childhood, did you? Always running errands for the gods, fleeing monsters, *adulting*."

Her expression soured, as if that word disgusted her.

"Our Skee-Ball tournament usually shaves off a year or two," she continued. "Or you can redeem tickets for various elixirs at the rewards station. I'll just warn you that if you're looking for something extreme, I don't turn anyone into babies. They do nothing but cry, poop, and throw up. The real childhood magic starts at around eight years old."

Annabeth shifted in her seat. "There were no infants in the arcade. No one younger than, like, eight. Your manager, Sparky—"

"Stays in the main arcade," Hebe said. "I am *always* the youngest person in any room, you see, even if it's just by a few months. I can't stand to be out-youngued." She brushed away the idea, banishing it from her presence. "But I do prefer the teenage years."

"So you hang out in a karaoke bar," I said. "Makes sense."

She nodded. I made a mental note not to fight her with sarcasm. She was obviously immune.

"Now," she said, "if you'll tell me how young you want to be, I will tell you what it will cost."

"No," I said.

Suddenly the air around us felt colder and oilier than the pizza.

"No?" asked the goddess.

"That's not why we're here."

Hebe's expression turned from smug to "resting goddess face," which was not a good thing.

"Then why," she asked, "are you wasting my infinite time?"

"We're looking for information," Annabeth said.

"About the gods," Grover added. "*A* god. Hypothetically. I don't know . . . Ganymede, for example?"

I was tempted to shove a napkin dispenser in Grover's mouth, but it was too late.

Hebe sat forward. Her fingernails were painted Day-Glo yellow. "Now why would you ask about him?"

The boomers finished their song. After a few high fives, they replaced their mics and shuffled offstage, heading back to the arcade. Typical boomer timing: have a blast, then leave right before everything goes sideways.

Grover squirmed under the goddess's gaze. A shred of napkin clung to his goatee like a tiny ghost. "We're just conducting a brief opinion survey—"

"He sent you here," the goddess guessed. The longer

she sat with us, the younger she looked. If I'd seen her at AHS, I would've pegged her for a sophomore or even a freshman—a very colorful, vindictive-looking freshman. "Tell me, why would Ganymede do that?"

Annabeth held up her hands, trying to show our peaceful intentions. "It's not so much that he sent us—"

"He *has* been acting nervous lately," mused Hebe. "But he wouldn't send out a group of heroes unless . . ." She smiled. "Unless he's lost something. Oh, you can't be serious. He's lost the chalice of the gods?"

She laughed with such delight, I started to relax. If she found this funny, maybe that was good. I liked delighted goddesses a lot more than angry ones.

I shrugged. "Well, we can neither confirm nor deny—"

"How wonderful!" She giggled. "That upstart little witch is in *so* much trouble! And he sent you to question me because . . . ?"

All the humor drained from her face. "Oh, I see."

"We just wanted some background information," I said hastily. "You know, like who might have a reason to, uh—"

"Steal the chalice," she finished.

Annabeth shook her head. "We're not implying—"

"You think I stole it! You came here to accuse me!"

"Not entirely!" Grover yelped. "I—I came here for the licorice!"

Hebe stood. Her dress swirled with pink-and-blue paisley light. "Heroes accusing *me* of theft! The only thing I've ever stolen is time from the Fates so mortals could enjoy longer lives! I care nothing for that . . . that *usurper's* cup! Do you think I would want my old job back, waiting tables on Mount Olympus, when I have my own establishment right here with all the pizza, karaoke, and bumper cars I could ever desire?"

That sounded like another trick question. Stupidly, I tried to answer it.

"You're right," I said. "Of course that's silly. But maybe you know someone else who could've stolen it? Or if you'd let us look around so we can report back that it definitely isn't here—"

"ENOUGH!" Hebe roared. She spread her hands. "What did you say earlier, Percy Jackson? *Getting older is part of life?* Well, perhaps you should start that process over again. Maybe you'll do it *right* this time and learn some manners!"

The goddess burst into a storm of rainbow glitter that knocked me right out of my chair.

EIGHT

I WANT MY MOMMY

If nostalgia was the door back to youth, I felt like Hebe had opened that door and drop-kicked me through it.

My entire body hurt. Muscles ached in my gut and back where I didn't even know I had muscles. My brain throbbed like it was too big for my skull.

I lay flat on the floor, the carpet sticky and bristly against my arms. When I sat up, I felt both sluggish and too light, as if someone had given me a transfusion of liquid helium. Annabeth was lying on my left, just starting to stir. Grover was facedown a few feet away, snoring into the rug.

We were alive. We had not been turned into glitter or arcade tickets. Hebe had vanished. Something was wrong, though. My hands felt stubby. My pant legs were too long. The cuffs pooled around my ankles.

I didn't really understand what had happened until Annabeth groaned and sat up. She, too, was swimming in her too-big clothes. Her face . . . well, look, I would know Annabeth's face anywhere. I love her face. But this was a version of her I'd never seen before—except in a few old pictures and dream visions.

This was Annabeth the way she'd looked soon after she'd arrived at Camp Half-Blood. She'd regressed to about eight years old.

She rubbed her head and stared at me, her eyes going wide, then let out a curse that sounded strange coming from the mouth of a third grader. "Hebe *younged* us."

"BLAAAAAHHHH!" Grover sat up and rubbed his head.

His horns had shrunk to tiny stubs. His goatee was now a gone-tee. His fake feet and shoes had rolled away from his suddenly baby-size hooves, and his shirt was so big it looked like a nightgown.

"I don't feel so good." He picked a string of cheese off his face, then looked at his hooves and moaned. "Oh, no. I don't want to be a kid again!"

I didn't know if he meant the human kind or the goat kind . . . probably both. Satyrs mature half as fast as humans, I remembered Grover telling me. Which meant . . . multiply by two, carry the one, divide by . . . Nope, never mind. I'd save the math for my homework. If I ever got home again.

"Maybe we'll change back if we leave the building?" I suggested.

Annabeth stood up shakily. It was strange seeing her as a younger girl. I had an irrational fear that she would yell, *Gross! Boy cooties!* and run away from me.

Instead, she said doubtfully, "Worth a try."

We made our way back through the amusement center. When we passed the coop, the chickens looked at us with renewed interest. I didn't even know chickens *could* look interested, but they cocked their heads and clucked and flapped their wings. One of the chicks in particular, which had pink fluff around its eyes and beak, followed us along the fence, strutting and peeping.

"Wow, rude," Grover said.

"What?"

"She's threatening to tear the flesh from our bones."

I glanced nervously at the chick. "Okay, li'l killer. Calm down. We're leaving."

Suddenly, Grover rounded on me, lowered his head, and butted me in the chest hard enough to push me back a step.

"Ow!" I complained. "Dude, why?"

"Sorry, sorry!" Grover rubbed his horns. "I—I need to play. I'm practicing social dominance in the herd."

He butted me in the chest again.

"This is going to get old real quick," I said.

"Right now, I'd love to get old real quick," Annabeth said. "Let's keep going."

None of the other patrons paid us any attention. I guess we were just three more children in the crowd. I looked for Sparky, or somebody else in an employee uniform, but I didn't see anyone. I tried to keep my focus on finding the exit, but every blinking light and beeping sound caught my attention, tempting me to try the games.

It's hard having ADHD, but now I remembered how

much *harder* it had been when I was younger, before I'd learned how to channel my focus, control my fidgeting, or, for all practical purposes, even operate my own body.

Being eight years old again was terrifying. The idea that I might have to go through all those years again . . . I felt tears welling in my eyes. I wanted my mommy. I pushed down the sense of panic as best I could. The exit. Just find the exit.

No one tried to stop us. No one had chained the doors. We simply stepped back into the afternoon sunlight of Times Square. . . .

And we were still little kids.

I grabbed Grover's arm to keep him from head-butting a street performer in a Mickey Mouse costume.

"So, what now?" Annabeth asked, her voice tight. "We can't just . . . go home like this."

When Annabeth asks for advice, I know things are bad. She's always the one with the plan. Also, home for her was a dorm room at SODNYC. She couldn't exactly show up nine years younger.

"It'll be okay," I said.

She scowled at me. "You think so? Then you're a dummy!"

She put her palms to her temples. "Sorry, Percy . . . I—I can't think straight. I think Hebe changed more than just how we look."

I knew what she meant. I hadn't felt this panicky in a long time—it was like I'd eaten a combination of sugar and glass, and I would either get cut to pieces or shake apart from the inside.

"I'm not doing nine years over again," I said. "Let's go back in and find Hebe."

"And then what?" Grover bleated. "She might turn us into babies!"

"Stop it!" Annabeth said.

"No, *you* stop it. Meanie!"

"Am not!"

"Are too!"

"Guys!" I grabbed their arms and held them apart. "We can figure this out. Back inside."

I was trying to be the reasonable one. Definitely a sign of the apocalypse. I led them back into Hebe Jeebies, which was the last place I wanted to be.

Almost immediately, we ran into Sparky, who looked much more cheerful without her wheel o' prize tickets.

"Hi, welcome to Hebe Jeebies!" she said. "Do you know your way around?"

"We were just here," I said. "Except older."

"That doesn't narrow it down. . . ." She looked us over more carefully. "How much older? Fifty? Eighty?"

"Seriously?" Annabeth said.

"We asked you where Hebe was," Grover offered. "You pointed us to the karaoke bar?"

"Oh, right," Sparky said. "You three. Okay, then, have a good time."

"Wait!" Grover said. "We need to see Hebe again!"

Sparky arched her eyebrows. "What, you want to be even *younger*? When Hebe blesses you, you shouldn't get greedy. I'm sixty-five myself. It took me months of working here to get this young again!"

Of course. Sparky was another boomer—just a nine-year-old boomer.

"We don't want to get any younger," I said. "We want Hebe to put us back the way we were."

Sparky scowled. "Hold on. . . . Are you lodging an *age-based complaint*?"

I didn't like the way this manager kid/boomer was looking at me, like she was going to bury me in two-for-one pizza coupons. "Well, it's just . . . I think there's been a misunderstanding. We'd like—"

"You'd like to complain." Sparky pulled a bullhorn off her belt and announced to the entire arcade, "We have an age-based complaint!"

The crowd erupted in cheers, hoots, and jeers. Many of them grinned at us in a malicious way, like they expected a good show.

"Um . . ." I said.

"Unleash the predators!" Sparky screamed. "Let the chase begin!"

Bells clanged. Money changed hands. A few customers speculated as to who would fall first: me, Annabeth, or Grover. It didn't look like the odds were in my favor.

My pulse pounded, but scanning the room, I couldn't see any bloodthirsty predators.

"We just want to talk to Hebe!" I insisted.

Sparky pointed her megaphone right in my face and nearly blasted my eyebrows off.

"Maybe you will, if you survive the race. Have fun!" She lowered her bullhorn and strolled off.

In the depths of the arcade, someone screamed. A chair went flying. A pinball machine toppled over.

Annabeth drew her knife, which looked bigger in her small hand.

Grover yelped. "Here they come! I can smell them!"

"Smell what?" I demanded. "I don't see—"

Then I did. The chickens from the henhouse were rampaging through the arcade. Normally, I wouldn't use the word *rampage* to describe poultry behavior, but these birds were pure feathered chaos. Dozens swarmed over the game cabinets and knocked over furniture, ripping the upholstery with their claws and beaks. Some flew over the heads of the customers, strafing their hairdos. Others snapped hot dogs out of people's hands.

The Hebe Jeebies patrons didn't seem to mind. They squealed in delight as they ran from the hen-pocalypse like those crowds at bull-running events in Spain, as if they were thinking, *These animals might kill me, but at least I'll die in a really cool way!*

The hens headed straight toward us, violence in their beady little eyes.

I pulled out my ballpoint pen. "These chickens want trouble? I'll give them trouble."

Which was probably my worst heroic line ever.

Even more embarrassing—when I uncapped Riptide, it remained a ballpoint pen. No sword sprang into my hands.

"What the . . . Why?" I screamed at the pen, which didn't help with my whole unheroic vibe.

"Maybe it doesn't work for kids," Grover suggested. "You're too young now."

"You mean my sword has a *childproof cap*?"

"Hey, guys?" Annabeth said, sheathing her knife. "Argue later. Right now, I have a different plan: RUN!"

NINE

Ψ

THE CHICKENS DRAW FIRST BLOOD

If you've never had to run through an arcade pursued by killer chickens . . . you wanna trade lives for a while? Because seriously, you are *welcome* to mine.

The birds were small, but they were fast, vicious, and surprisingly strong. They stormed across the space in a wave of feathers and claws, shredding more furniture, scattering the customers, and driving up the high scores on the *Dance Dance Revolution* machines. The whole time, their unblinking eyes stayed fixed on us, their beaks and talons gleaming like polished steel.

I'd heard stories of people staging rooster fights, putting razor blades on the birds' feet for extra damage— because people do terrible things—but these hens were even scarier. They were killing machines au naturel, and they looked like they really enjoyed their job.

My eight-year-old legs were not up to the chase. I'd never been a great runner, and now I was falling behind Annabeth and Grover.

"Hurry!" Annabeth yelled back at me, like I hadn't thought of that. "Over here!" She bolted toward the play structure with big plastic crawl tubes.

I wanted to ask what her plan was, but I was already out of breath.

"Guys, grab that table!" She pointed to a high café table, the kind you'd stand around to mingle at a fancy party or whatever.

It took me only a second to understand why she wanted it. By now, we'd had enough adventures together that I was usually only a few steps behind Annabeth's thought process, rather than a few days.

Grover grabbed the top. I grabbed the pedestal base. It was heavy, and I wasn't nearly as strong as a feral chicken, but we managed to lug the table over to the entrance of the play structure. Annabeth plunged into the tunnel first, then Grover and I followed, pulling the base of the table in behind us like we were corking a bottle. The circular tabletop was just big enough to block the entrance, leaving no room for chickens.

A moment later, the flock slammed into the play structure, making the plastic tubes shudder. The chickens screamed in outrage. But for the moment, we were safe.

"How long until they figure out there are other ways into the tube?" I asked.

"Not long." Annabeth's eyes blazed with intensity. I could see how afraid she was, but I also knew she *lived* for these situations. She was at her most Annabeth when she was thinking her way out of an impossible predicament.

That was good, because we tended to have a lot of those.

"Why chickens?" I grumbled. "Of all the animals . . ."

"Would you prefer jaguars?" she asked.

"It's because of Hebe's temples," Grover said, chewing his knuckle. "The priestesses always kept hens and chicks. Roosters were kept in Hercules's temple. The birds only got together on Hebe's holy day."

"Oh, right," Annabeth said. "Hebe married Hercules when he became a god." She shuddered. "I almost feel sorry for her."

"Hold up," I said. "Grover, how do you know about the hen/rooster thing?"

"Daycare," he said miserably. "Hebe sponsors daycare centers for young satyrs. We used to sing 'Happy the Holy Hen' every morning."

Suddenly, I had a new theory about why satyrs aged half as fast as humans, but I decided this might not be the moment to discuss it.

"You're a member of the Council of Cloven Elders," I said. "Can't you ask the chickens to back off?"

"I can try." He bleated something in Goatenese.

The chickens slammed into the play structure with even more force. A steely beak punctured the plastic between my legs.

"I guess that's a no," Grover said.

"Hebe's holy day," Annabeth mused. "Baby chicks . . ."

I frowned. "What are you thinking? Some kind of distraction? I don't have any roosters handy."

"No, but there were chicks in that coop. . . ."

"So?" I yelled as another beak almost gave me a thigh piercing.

"So we need to get back to the coop. And grab a chick."

"Killer hens are chasing us," Grover said, "and you want to run to their coop and steal their babies?"

"Yes. And then run again." She raised her hands defensively. "Percy, I know you're going to say this is a terrible idea—"

"This is a terrible idea."

"—but you have to trust me. Let's go."

She crawled deeper into the play tube. I grumbled under my breath and followed. As much as I hated her idea, I had none of my own—and I *did* trust her.

The tunnel angled upward until we were crawling just below the ceiling. I glanced out one of the Plexiglas bubble windows and saw most of the flock still running around on the floor, squawking angrily. A few of the smarter birds had figured out that, hey, they had wings! Some flapped up and body-checked the play tube. Others ran along the top, pecking at the plastic, but so far they hadn't figured out how to get to us.

We stopped at a T.

"Grover, go left," Annabeth said. "Distract the flock while Percy and I go right and make a break for the coop. We'll rendezvous back at the karaoke bar."

"Do I get to say this is a terrible idea, too?" Grover asked.

"Just do your best," Annabeth said. "You're the fastest runner. You're also the only one who speaks Chicken."

"Technically Chicken isn't a distinct language," he said, "though many animal dialects sound just like Chicken. . . ."

"Dude, just yell at them," I suggested. "Do you know any fowl insults?"

"This is a family amusement center!"

"Where they are trying to kill us for complaining."

"Good point," Grover said. "I will insult the chickens." He shouldered past me and crawled down the left-hand tunnel, his hooves moving like cloven pistons.

"Let's go," Annabeth said in her best squad-leader voice. And off we went down the right-hand tube.

We slid down a bendy-straw chute and plunged into a ball pit, which wasn't great for making a quick escape. Fortunately, the chickens were preoccupied. At the opposite end of the play structure, Grover had emerged in all his insult-flinging glory and was bounding across the Skee-Ball machines, throwing the wooden balls behind him, making the hens trip and weave. I remembered some myth about a woman throwing gold apples behind her to slow down guys who were chasing her. Skee-Balls seemed to work pretty well, too.

"SQUAWK!" Grover yelled. "CLUCK! CLUCK!"

Judging by how much this enraged the flock, it must have been a scathing comment about chicks' mothers. Grover disappeared into the arcade, followed by most of the poultry mob.

"Keep up." Annabeth waded through the ball pit, holding her hands above her head like she didn't want her nonexistent rifle to get wet. Meanwhile, I kept my ballpoint pen handy, which I guess would've been super useful if the chickens had decided they wanted an autograph.

"Whatever you do," Annabeth warned, "don't hurt the hens. They're still Hebe's sacred animals."

"That's my top priority," I muttered. "Not hurting the chickens."

"I'm serious," she said. "This will only work if we don't make Hebe even angrier."

I didn't know what Annabeth's plan was, or how it would work, but you can file that under I Had No Better Ideas, which was already a pretty thick folder.

Annabeth climbed out of the ball pit and offered me a hand. I'd like to say I got out gracefully. I didn't. I shook about a dozen plastic balls out of my big pant cuffs and scraped a half-chewed cheeseburger off the bottom of my shoe. I wondered what else might be slowly turning into fossil fuel at the bottom of that ball pit . . . probably a bunch of demigods who had dared to lodge age-based complaints.

"Coop," Annabeth said, and took off running.

Even as an eight-year-old, she had more single-mindedness than I ever would, which might have bothered me if I'd had the bandwidth to focus on it.

We found the chicks in the coop, right where we'd left them. They didn't look happy about missing out on the chase. When Sparky had unleashed the predators, she'd apparently triggered a control that rolled the chicken-wire fence down exactly halfway—low enough for the adult hens to jump over, but too high for the baby chicks to clear. I guess this was Hebe's version of an amusement-ride sign: YOU HAVE TO BE THIS TALL TO MURDER OUR CUSTOMERS!

Annabeth studied the chicks, which were running in circles, stomping in the straw, and hurling untranslatable insults in our direction. The chick I'd noticed earlier with the pink fluff on her face seemed particularly angry—she was peeping at the top of her tiny lungs.

"Hope I can catch one," Annabeth muttered, mostly to herself.

Before I could say, *For a wise girl, that does not seem like a wise move,* she reached into the coop.

"OWW!"

Li'l Killer had bitten her finger and clamped on. Annabeth yanked her hand back, shaking the fluffy little chick around like a sock with static cling, but Li'l Killer refused to let go.

"Remember not to hurt her," I said.

"Really helpful," Annabeth grumbled.

Blood dripped from her finger, but she cupped her free hand around the chick, holding it against her chest so it wouldn't get away, assuming it ever got tired of the taste of human flesh. "Let's get to the karaoke bar."

"Is one chick enough?" I asked.

"If you're jealous, you can have this one."

"She is kinda cute for a killer chicken."

From across the arcade came a sudden roar of customers cheering, hens screeching *BAWK! BAWK!,* and one panicked satyr yelling, "Incoming!"

How quickly I'd forgotten the herd of holy hens that wanted to tear us apart.

Annabeth and I raced for the karaoke bar, though with

my newly youngified legs, it was more of a waddle. I didn't even have the time or energy to make the diving pool explode as we ran by.

Grover reached the lounge at the same time we did. He had feathers stuck in his fur, and the back of his shirt was shredded like he'd been rolling around on a really dangerous mattress.

"That was super fun," he wheezed.

"Get the doors!" Annabeth said.

Grover and I grabbed the big mahogany panels and started sliding them together. Why the karaoke bar had its own partition, I wasn't sure—maybe to protect the rest of the center from the music, or to create a private event space for birthday parties or intimate interrogation sessions.

We'd just closed the doors when the flock slammed against them.

The hens squawked in outrage. The mahogany panels shuddered and creaked. I couldn't imagine they'd hold for long under a full chicken onslaught.

"What now?" Grover asked, gasping for breath.

He looked so young and terrified that I felt bad for getting a little kid like him into this situation. Then I remembered I was also a little kid like him.

"Now comes the hard part," Annabeth said.

"That was the *easy* part?" I demanded.

Annabeth winced as she yanked Li'l Killer off her finger and set the chick on the floor.

Li'l Killer ruffled her blood-speckled feathers. She looked up at us with her shiny black eyes, peeped in a smug sort of way, like, *Yeah, you best put me down,* then wandered off, contentedly pecking pizza crumbs off the carpet.

Annabeth wrapped a napkin around her wounded finger. "This karaoke bar is Hebe's temple, right? Her inner sanctum?"

I usually didn't associate those words with karaoke bars, but I nodded. "And?"

"On Hebe's holy days, petitioners used to come to her altar," Annabeth continued.

"That's right," Grover said. "They'd ask forgiveness, and Hebe would give them sanctuary."

"But this isn't her holy day, is it?" I asked. "No way we could be that lucky."

"Probably not," Annabeth said. "But we'll have to try."

The doors shuddered, bending inward under the weight of the evil poultry.

"Grover," Annabeth said, "do what you can to barricade the doors. Percy and I will look for the right song."

"Song?" I asked. "You're not really talking about a 'Shallow' duet?"

"No, an *apology* song, Seaweed Brain! We beg Hebe for forgiveness. Once she shows, we ask for sanctuary and a second chance."

"What if she refuses?"

Annabeth looked at Li'l Killer. "Then I hope Plan Chick works. Otherwise, we're dead."

TEN

Ψ

MY SINGING MAKES THINGS WORSE, AND EVERYONE IS TOTALLY SHOCKED

Gotta love those Annabeth pep talks.

They always boil down to

$$\text{If } A = B \Rightarrow \text{Okay; if } A \neq B \Rightarrow \text{Dead.}$$

I didn't know why we'd abducted Li'l Killer, or what Annabeth planned to do with her, but I hoped it wouldn't come to Plan Chick. Unfortunately, that meant I had to pin my hopes on Plan Percy Sings, which sounded just as likely to get us murdered.

While Grover piled furniture in front of the doors, Annabeth and I ran to the stage and fired up the karaoke machine. (There is a statement I never thought I would make.) Li'l Killer made herself at home, rummaging under the tables for crumbs, moldy pizza, or fresh fingers to bite.

Annabeth scowled at the karaoke screen. "Is there a search function on this? Maybe I could cross-reference *apology* and *forgiveness.*"

"'Sorry Not Sorry,'" I suggested.

"Percy—"

"Okay, okay." I racked my brain. "What's the song

where that one dude sings, like, 'I didn't mean to hurt you and make you cry'?"

"We didn't actually make Hebe cry. . . . Oh, wait, you mean the John Lennon song? 'Jealous Guy'?"

"I guess."

"Did you just call John Lennon 'that one dude'?"

"Whatever. See if they have the song!"

The chickens were at the gates, slamming against the panels, rattling the frames, perforating the mahogany with beak-size holes. Grover huffed and puffed as he dragged tables over to block the entrance, but there was only so much one preadolescent satyr could do. I was about to go over and help him when Annabeth said, "Found it!"

She punched a button, and the first bars of "Jealous Guy" started to play.

I wasn't sure whether to feel relieved or not. Now I had to sing the song, and I can't sing. "You want to take the lead?"

"Oh, no," Annabeth said. "You're the one who made Hebe mad!"

"Me? That was all of us!"

"Ninety percent you."

"Only ninety percent, though. I'm improving!"

Grover wedged another table against the doors. "Just crank up the music! We'll both back you up!"

The teleprompter started scrolling, and Annabeth handed me the mic. (That's another statement I never thought I'd make.)

I remembered the song from my childhood. My mom

had played it all the time, even though it made her cry. I hate to see my mom cry, which is why it had stuck in my brain.

Looking back, I'm not sure if the song had made her think of Poseidon, or if she was playing it as a suggestion to my first stepdad, like, *Perhaps you should apologize for being you.* If it was the latter, Smelly Gabe never got the message.

The song started out slow, like a funeral dirge. As soon as I started mumbling the verse, the chickens battered against the doors even harder. No doubt they realized I had to be stopped at all costs before a perfectly good song was tortured to death. It didn't help that I had my squeaky eight-year-old voice back. That was another thing I didn't miss about elementary school.

Annabeth "helped" (full sarcastic air quotes) by warbling all the words half a beat behind me. This is how you know you've found true love: when your significant other is just as bad at singing as you are.

I got to the chorus and yelled, "This one's for you, Hebe!"

(I'd also like to point out that when I typed *chorus* just now, it initially autocorrected to *curse*, which seems right.)

". . . hurt you," I muttered. "Cry. Jealous. Oh, yeah!"

Our chick friend Li'l Killer scurried under the corner booth to hide. She peeked out at me with an offended look as if she was thinking, *I'm two days old and I could sing better than that.*

By the second verse, Annabeth was getting into it. She

threw her arm around me and belted out that she, too, was just a jealous guy. Her enthusiasm improved the song by negative five percent.

Finally, as we launched into the second chorus/curse, a whirlwind of glitter and prize tickets materialized in the middle of the dance floor. Hebe appeared, her fingers wedged in her ears. "Stop it! Stop it, already!"

The karaoke machine died. Li'l Killer disappeared back under the booth. The doors stopped shaking as the army of chickens ceased its assault.

"O great and extremely young Hebe!" I said. "We are so sorry—"

"Especially Percy," Annabeth said.

"I am ninety percent of the sorry!" I agreed. "Please forgive us!"

Hebe glared. "If that song was supposed to be an apology, you should direct it to John Lennon."

"Please, grant us sanctuary from your wrathful hens!" Grover called from the doors.

"And please return us to our proper ages!" Annabeth said.

"Whoa, whoa, whoa!" Hebe T'ed her hands in a time-out sign. "First you desecrate my karaoke machine, then you barrage me with requests? Why should I return you to your former ages?"

"Because . . ." I faltered. "Because you are generous and good, and also super young."

"We are petitioners at your altar," Annabeth said.

"Your holiest of holy karaoke stages!" Grover said. "Most sacred of disco boogie venues!"

Hebe stared at him.

"Too much?" Grover asked. "All we want is to leave here in peace, at our normal ages—so we can spread the word about the wonders and terrors of Hebe Jeebies!"

"And with a little information about the chalice of the gods, please," I said.

Annabeth kicked me in the shin, but it was too late.

Hebe bared her teeth. "There it is again. That insolence. That slander. Perhaps I did not send you far enough back into your childhood."

"Forgive him!" Annabeth cried. I noticed her gaze kept drifting to the corner booth where Li'l Killer was hiding. But if she was waiting for the chick to launch a sneak attack on the goddess, I didn't like our chances.

"We would never try to *run out the clock* on you!" Annabeth added.

That last part was meant for me. Even at eight years old, even being not the sharpest ballpoint pen in the box, I could tell that much. Annabeth was stalling for time. But why?

"It's true!" I said. "Clocks are bad!"

Hebe's hairdo seemed to be curling tighter, as if forming a protective helmet against traumatic injuries like listening to us talk. Was it my imagination, or was she also getting shorter?

"You are spouting nonsense," she said.

"Exactly," Annabeth agreed. "He does that a lot! That's why you must forgive him."

"Must?"

"Should! Might. Could, if you happened to be so inclined. Please, O goddess!"

Hebe stomped her go-go boots, which now came up to her hips like waders. "You are all so—so yucky!"

She was shrinking before our eyes. Her minidress became a maxi dress, the paisley hem puddling around her ankles. Her cheeks filled out with baby fat.

"What is happening?" She shook her now-tiny fists. "I don't like it!"

She looked younger than we were now—maybe seven years old. Her eyes kept their wrathful glare, but her voice had an *I just sucked helium* squeak that made it hard to take her seriously.

"Don't look at me like that!" she cried, her lip quivering. "You're a big dummy!"

But I couldn't help staring. She shrank to kindergarten size, then became a toddler. Even Li'l Killer peeked out from her hiding place to watch.

Finally I understood Plan Chick.

Hebe always had to be the youngest one in the room. Her powers were reacting to the presence of the chick. As a goddess, she should have been able to stop the process, but I guess it caught her by surprise. Or maybe making herself older just went against her nature.

She fell over, unable to walk. She started to crawl toward me like she wanted to grab my ankles, but then she fell sideways, squirming, and began to bawl. The goddess of youth was now the youngest in the room: a cranky newborn with a bright red face.

"What just happened?" Grover asked.

Annabeth strolled over and picked up the baby, swaddling her in Hebe's paisley dress. "Li'l Killer pulled juniority on Hebe." Annabeth tickled the goddess's chin. "But you are so *adorable*."

Hebe squirmed and grunted. She tried to bite Annabeth's finger, but she didn't have any teeth.

"Now hold on," Annabeth told the baby. "I know you're fussy, but I'm sure you're not making an age-based complaint, are you? The chickens wouldn't like that."

Baby Hebe became very still.

"Great," Annabeth said. "Then here's what I suggest. We agree that some young ages are just *too* young. Then we remove Li'l Killer from the room so you can age yourself back up to at least elementary school. Then you accept our apology, put us back to our normal ages, tell us whatever you know about the chalice of the gods, and we all go our separate ways. Gurgle once for yes. Poop yourself for no."

I had never wanted to hear yes so much in my life.

Hebe gurgled. It might have been just a random gurgle, but Annabeth seemed to accept it as a promise.

"Grover," she said, "would you ask Li'l Killer to return to her pen, please?"

Grover made a couple of bleating noises. Li'l Killer peeped at us—probably saying, *Thank you for the excitement and crumbs and blood*—then trotted to the doors and wriggled through one of the beak holes the hens had made.

Judging from the clucking sounds outside, the hens welcomed the chick as a conquering hero. Then their cackling got fainter as they retreated to their pen. I suppose Li'l Killer had spread the word that we'd agreed upon a cease-fire.

Immediately, Hebe began to grow. Annabeth quickly set her down. We watched as the baby fast-forwarded into a kindergartner, then a fifth grader, and finally stood before us as the angriest-looking high schooler I'd ever seen.

"You three . . ." she growled.

"We apologize, Great Hebe," Annabeth said. "And ask for sanctuary."

"And information," I added.

Annabeth elbowed me.

"Please," I added.

The goddess fumed. She snapped her fingers, and suddenly we were our normal ages again.

"You're lucky I like John Lennon," the goddess muttered. "Sit, and I will tell you what I know. But you aren't going to like it."

ELEVEN

⚕

WE WIN ZERO PRIZE TICKETS

"You must go to the farmers' market," Hebe said, as if she were sending us off for a particularly heinous round of standardized testing.

We were sitting around the booth again, enjoying a second serving of pizza. I was actually eating it this time, because I was once again a teenager. Also, there were no boomers singing protest songs, which helped my digestion.

Grover swallowed a mouthful of greasy paper plate. "What's so bad about a farmers' market?"

The goddess wrinkled her nose. "Iris got it into her head that her organic store in California wasn't sufficient. Now she has to share her wares with the whole world! You'll find her hawking crystals and incense and Zeus knows what else this Saturday in front of Lincoln Center."

I was relieved. Another local quest? And on a Saturday? That meant I might be able to spend the rest of the week dealing with school—which wasn't fun, but at least it was better than schlepping across the country to some Farmers' Market of the Damned in Idaho.

But Annabeth narrowed her eyes. She studied Hebe

as if the goddess might attack us with glitter again. "You think Iris took the chalice, then?"

Hebe shrugged. "That's for *you* to determine. All I can tell you is that it wasn't me, and Iris is the only other person who has ever served as divine cupbearer. Perhaps, behind that rainbow peace-and-love facade, she hates Ganymede more than she lets on."

"I've met Iris," I said. "She didn't seem spiteful."

"And I do?" Hebe asked.

I kept my mouth shut. Sometimes, I can learn.

"Thank you for your guidance, Great Hebe," Annabeth said. "We ask your permission to leave here in peace."

"Hmph." The goddess crossed her arms. "Very well. But no prize tickets for you."

Grover cleared his throat, as you do when you've been eating greasy paper plates. "And, um . . . you won't tell anyone about the chalice situation?"

Hebe scoffed. "Of course not. I can't wait to see Ganymede fall on his face at the next feast and get blasted to ashes by Zeus. But mark my words: if you offend Iris the way you offended me, you will *not* escape so easily. You're going to wish you stayed small children."

The last we saw Hebe, she was welcoming a group of millennials who wanted to relive the nineties through the magic of Spice Girls karaoke. I hoped they'd make it out alive.

All the way through the arcade, I felt the eyes of the staff, the customers, and the chickens following us. I feared I'd be turned into a toddler any second.

Somehow, we made it back to Times Square. I'd never been so happy to see the familiar crowds of tourists—now at eye level rather than butt level.

At the subway station, Annabeth, Grover, and I went our separate ways. None of us said much. We were all pretty shaken by our afternoon of youth, chickens, and terror. I wasn't too worried, though. We'd been through post-adventure shell shock together lots of times, and I knew we'd bounce back. Annabeth headed downtown to SODNYC. Grover headed toward the LIRR to Camp Half-Blood. Me, I hiked all the way to the Upper East Side because I needed some air. Every so often, I'd look at my hands, remembering how small they'd been, and how helpless I'd felt not being able to use my own sword. Inside, I still felt eight years old and ready to cry.

That night, I procrastinated on my homework. Huge surprise, I know.

I sat on the fire escape, dangling my legs above the alley. Anxiety hummed through my veins. I'd always had a baseline jumpiness, but this was worse.

I'd been on so many quests where the stakes were higher—where if I failed, cities would burn, the world would explode, bell-bottoms would make a comeback. This was just retrieving some god's cup. Still, it felt as risky as anything I'd ever done.

Maybe that was because I was so close to graduating and hopefully starting a new life in California. Only a few steps to go, but the ground was starting to crack beneath my feet. I didn't trust that the world could hold my weight much longer.

"Hey," my mom said.

I glanced back to see her climbing through the window.

"You need a hand?" I started to get up.

I wasn't sure why I was worried. She'd climbed out that window a hundred times, but tonight I felt concerned—maybe because my whole future felt fragile.

She waved at me to stay seated. "I'm fine," she said. "It just looked like you could use some company."

She sat down next to me, her back against the brick wall. The gray streaks in her hair gleamed like veins of silver.

Weirdly, I'd gotten my first shock of gray before my mom did, thanks to a certain Titan named Atlas, but hers suited her better. She didn't look older so much as more regal. I remembered that, a long time ago, Poseidon had compared my mom to a princess . . . and he hadn't meant the damsel-in-distress stereotype. He meant the warrior princesses of ancient Greece who took no prisoners and knew how to swing a bronze blade.

My mom had that kind of strength. She also had the kindness to notice I was hurting and to climb out a window to be with me.

For a while, we just settled into a comfortable silence, watching dozens of vignettes of city life in the illuminated windows of the neighborhood. A family was cooking dinner, laughing and flinging strings of spaghetti at one another. An old man slumped alone in a chair, his face washed in the blue light of a TV screen. Two kids jumped on a bed, hitting each other with pillows.

I love New York because you can see all those lives side by side, like an endless patchwork of different video game screens inviting you to hit Play and slip into a new reality. I wondered if anyone had ever thought about slipping into my life.

"What was I like when I was little?" I asked.

My mom tensed like this was a trick question. "Why do you ask?"

"I turned eight years old today."

Usually, I don't tell my mom the details of my quests. I don't want to worry her any more than I have to. She already knows how dangerous demigod life is. Tonight, though, I recounted my afternoon with all the heebies and jeebies.

"That's a lot," she said. "I've always liked 'Jealous Guy,' but still. . . ."

I nodded, a lump in my throat.

"You got through it," she noted. "You always do."

"I guess. . . . But it was like all my progress, all those years of getting older and learning how to survive . . . Hebe took it away with a snap of her fingers. I was a helpless little kid again."

"You are a lot of things, Percy. But *helpless* isn't one of them." She put her hand on my shoulder. "When you were little . . . whenever you got scared, you might back away for a second, but then you would march right up to whatever was scaring you. You'd stare it down until it went away, or until you understood it. Thinking about you as a toddler makes me feel . . ."

"Sick to your stomach?"

She laughed. "It makes me feel *hopeful*. You're still moving forward. You've grown into a fine young man, and I'm proud of you."

The lump in my throat was the size of a kiwi fruit.

"It's also okay to doubt yourself," my mom added. "That's completely normal."

"Even for demigods?"

"Especially for them." She pulled me over to her and kissed my head, like she used to do when I was actually eight. "Also, you need to wash the dishes."

I smirked. "All that buttering up just so I'll do my chores?"

"Not *just*. Now give me a hand, would you? Sitting down is easy. Getting up, not so much."

I washed the dishes. Because I guess demigods do what they have to do.

I left Paul and my mom in the living room, cuddling on the sofa, listening to Paul's jazz vinyl. They both thanked me and wished me good night.

But I stayed up. I finished my homework. Somehow, I found the strength for advanced algebra. I even wrote an essay, though the words swam in front of my eyes and half of them were probably misspelled.

That night, I slept the best I had in a long time.

TWELVE

GANYMEDE GETS ME A REFILL

After that, I went three days without any supernatural interference.

Wow. The luxury.

I struggled through my assignments. I met Grover and Annabeth every afternoon for smoothies or a movie or just to walk in Central Park. I gotta say, it was nice.

On Thursday, I had my first swim meet and managed to be impressive but not too impressive. I didn't summon a tidal wave in the deep end or anything.

I almost forgot the weekend was coming up, and with it the farmers' market, until Friday at lunchtime.

AHS is a closed campus. Everybody is supposed to eat together in the cafeteria. Sure, a lot of seniors sneak out at lunchtime, but I stayed put because I didn't want to risk getting kicked out quite so early in the year. It's a small school, so absentees are pretty easy to notice.

I was sitting alone, munching on a peanut butter and banana sandwich (hey, I made it myself, one of my pro recipes), trying to read some short story about a guy who liked to open cans—no idea why. Then someone loomed over me and said, "Here's a refill."

Ganymede poured something from a big glass pitcher into my soda can, which had only been half-empty. He did this with total concentration and precision, not spilling a drop, though the liquid was definitely *not* what had already been in the can.

"Um, thanks?" I said, which wasn't easy with my mouth full of peanut butter.

"You're welcome." Ganymede nodded formally, as if we'd just exchanged gifts as national ambassadors. "I want an update on your quest . . . but I'll be right back."

I had time to finish my sandwich while Ganymede circulated through the cafeteria, refilling the students' drinks without asking permission. Some kids looked at him funny, but most didn't even notice. This was weird, since Ganymede was wearing a Greek chiton and strap-up sandals and not much else. Thank the Mist for obscuring mortal minds, I guess, or maybe the students just figured he was doing a project for drama class.

He came back to my table and sat across from me. "So."

"What are you serving?" I asked. "You're not going to turn the whole student body immortal, are you?"

He sighed. "Of course not, Percy Jackson. I told you, it's the *chalice* that has the magic."

"That's not nectar in your pitcher?" I asked. "Because mortals will burn up if they drink that."

"What makes you think this is nectar?"

"Well . . . it's blue and glowing."

Ganymede frowned at his pitcher. "I suppose it is.

No, this is simply standard Olympian beverage number five. It will refresh and revive, and taste like whatever you desire. It will not turn anyone immortal or make them spontaneously combust. Try it."

I wondered what had happened to Olympian beverages one through four. But Ganymede was staring at me, and offending him was not going to help get me my recommendation letter. I took a drink. It tasted like regular lemon-lime soda, the same as I'd been drinking before, but zippier and crisper. Around the cafeteria, no one was burning up or glowing.

"Okay, great," I said. "Thanks."

Ganymede shrugged. "It's important to stay hydrated. Now, about my chalice."

I brought him up to speed.

When I was done, he knit his majestically sculpted eyebrows. I got the feeling he was not happy, like he might decide to check *somewhat satisfied* instead of *extremely satisfied* on my recommendation form.

"And you trust what Hebe said?" he asked.

"I never—" I stopped myself.

I'd been about to say, *I never trust a god,* but that wouldn't have gone down well with a god. "I never can be one hundred percent sure, but I don't think Hebe took your cup."

"And if she decides to tell everyone?"

"She won't," I said. "At least . . . not until your next feast. She said she'd rather see you fall on your face in front of all the gods."

I did not add *and get blasted to ashes by Zeus.*

Ganymede's forehead darkened to what I imagined was the color of Olympian beverage number two. "That sounds like Hebe. And this flaming marke—"

"Farmers' market."

"This farmers' market happens tomorrow."

"Right."

"Your plan?"

"Talk to Iris. Find your cup. Don't get turned into rainbows."

He nodded. "This is sensible. But if she doesn't have the chalice . . ."

"Let's worry about that tomorrow."

He shifted in his seat. "Forgive me, I so rarely send demigods on quests. Is this the part where I threaten your life if you fail?"

"No," I said. "That comes later."

"Hmm. All right. But do not disappoint me, Percy Jackson. My reputation depends on it. And your college career!" Then he got up and wandered off in his bathrobe to pour more divine Kool-Aid.

I made it through the rest of the day. I have to admit I felt refreshed and hydrated. That night, after dinner, I sat in bed talking to Annabeth. She wasn't actually there—she was across town in her dorm room—but we kept in touch thanks to the cutting-edge technology of Iris-messages.

Demigods don't use cell phones because they attract

monsters. I've never quite understood why. It's just so on-brand for our lives I've always accepted it, like, *Of course they do.* The quickest way to spot a demigod is to hand them a mobile phone. If they're under the age of eighteen and have no idea what to do with it, they're probably a demigod. When the monsters show up and eat them, you can be one hundred percent sure.

Instead of a phone, I had a flashlight, a humidifier, and a bowlful of golden drachmas. You shine light through the water vapor to make yourself a rainbow. You throw a coin into it, say a prayer, and voilà—you've got a shimmering holographic Annabeth sitting next to you. She had a similar setup on her end, but we could only talk like this when her roommate was out. Annabeth had told her the humidifier was for allergies. What she didn't say was that it was an allergy to phones.

She was lying on her own bed, propped up on one elbow, a stack of architecture books in front of her. The droplets of water vapor between us glittered like fireworks.

"So tomorrow," she said. "I have a plan."

Not a surprise. Annabeth always had a plan. That was a trait she got from Athena, but Annabeth took it to a whole new level. I wasn't complaining, though. If she wasn't a planner, I'd be floundering about what to do next year. I'd probably have given up already and gotten a job at Monster Donut.

"Let's hear it," I said.

"Well." She put her dagger across her textbook to

mark her spot. I wasn't sure what her roomie thought about the knife, either. "I was thinking it might be easier if we got someone to introduce us to Iris."

"But I already know her."

Annabeth raised an eyebrow. I got her meaning: having met a god before was no guarantee that they would remember you or treat you well. I'd heard gods grumble that all of us mortals kind of blend together for them . . . like a school of sardines.

"Who do you have in mind?" I asked.

"We don't have a lot of options," she said, "but I thought a child of Iris."

"Butch is home in Minnesota. . . ." I ran through the list of demigods I knew from Camp Half-Blood. "And there aren't any year-rounders in the Iris cabin right now."

"No," Annabeth agreed. "But there *is* a child of Iris who lives locally. Down in Soho."

A knot formed in the pit of my stomach, and all of Ganymede's beverage number five started to drain into my legs. "You can't be serious."

"She's already agreed to meet us at the market."

I wondered how Annabeth had pulled that off. Favors must have been promised. Money. Firstborn children. Something.

"But . . ." I grasped for any idea that might change Annabeth's mind. "Aren't most quests supposed to be three people? Wouldn't a fourth be bad luck?"

"She's not joining our quest. She'll just make the introduction to her mom, and hopefully convince Iris to go easy on us when we tell her . . . well, that we suspect her of being a cup thief."

I shuddered. "Or she could make things worse. You remember what happened at the last campfire?"

Annabeth laughed. "I thought that was kind of funny, actually. Calm down, Seaweed Brain. I've got this under control."

"Hmm."

"Don't *hmm* me." She glanced behind her. "My roommate's coming. Gotta go. Love you."

"You too. Don't love your plan, though."

"Finish your homework."

"Yes, ma'am."

She nodded, satisfied, and blew me a kiss. The Iris connection dissipated into random water droplets.

I looked at my pile of weekend homework and groaned. Another English essay to write . . . this time about that guy who liked to open cans. Plus math, science, and two chapters of history. *And* we had to face Iris and her daughter tomorrow. I wondered if it was too late to apply for the night shift at Monster Donut.

THIRTEEN

⚜

WE LOOK FOR DEAD STUFF AT THE FARMERS' MARKET

Grover was thrilled.

"*Blanche* is coming?" He patted his goat horns as if to make sure they weren't crooked. "Do I look okay?"

He wore cargo shorts with tennis shoes over his hooves—just enough of a disguise so humans would think *That kid needs to shave his legs* and not *That kid is half goat*. His top du jour was a hand-knit green sweater-type thing with little tree designs that I was pretty sure the dryads had made him for Arbor Day.

"You look good," I said.

"Besides, Grover," Annabeth chided, "this is *Blanche*. It's not like she's your girlfriend."

Grover had a girlfriend, Juniper, who would not have been pleased to see Grover acting so flustered.

"No, I know." He blushed to the roots of his goatee. "It's just that she's such an *artiste*."

"Not this again," I muttered.

"She's so *cool*!"

"Are we talking about the same Blanche?" I asked.

"Both of you hush." Annabeth peered down Broadway. "Here she comes now."

Blanche, daughter of Iris, wore a trench coat the color of night, jeans, and tactical boots, all of which matched the makeup that made her eyes sparkle like black diamonds. Her head was shaved except for a white-blond topknot. Around her neck hung a Nikon camera the size of a shoe box.

"Wow," she said, looking around. "Uptown."

She squinted as if she found the Upper West Side too bright, too open, too loud, too everything. Living down in Soho, she probably had to get her passport stamped to come this far north.

"Lots of stuff to photograph!" Grover said, leaning not-so-casually against a mailbox to give her a profile angle.

Blanche seemed more interested in the sick little tree on the median. "This is dying. That's cool." She took the lens cap off her Nikon and started to play with the focus.

Annabeth and I exchanged looks.

Really? I asked her silently.

Be patient, she stared back at me.

I'd heard that Blanche had a one-artist show going on at a Tribeca gallery right now. Her photographs of dried leaves, rotten tree stumps, and roadkill—all in black and white—sold for like a thousand bucks each. She was the Ansel Adams of dead nature. And after our last campfire, Grover had been so impressed with her that he'd decided he wanted her to do his portrait as a present for Juniper.

What happened at our last campfire, you ask?

Ghost stories. It was a tradition. To everybody's

surprise, Blanche had volunteered to tell the last one that night. In front of sixty or seventy campers and holding a flashlight under her face for maximum creepiness, Blanche had launched into a story about this demigod who had died years ago—a son of Morbus, the god of diseases. Supposedly, nobody liked this kid at camp because, well, diseases. Eventually he had wasted away from some terrible plague, but before he died, he laid a curse on the camp so that anyone who walked over his grave would lose all their color, develop a painful rotting sickness, then crumble to nothing. The campers had burned his body and scattered his ashes, trying to avoid the curse.

"But it didn't matter," Blanche had told us. "Because the place where he was burned counted as his gravesite. And that gravesite . . . is right here!"

Then she'd turned her flashlight on us. We'd looked around, startled and half-blind, and realized that all our colors had faded. The entire crowd had turned monochrome like old black-and-white cartoons.

There was screaming. There was crying and running in circles. And that was just me. Some of the other demigods got *really* freaked out, which is not good when you're in a crowd of kids armed with swords.

Meanwhile, Blanche had snapped pictures of us, the flash on her Nikon making a strobe-light effect that only increased the panic.

Finally, our activities director, Chiron, managed to restore order. He'd explained that Blanche had simply drawn all the surrounding colors into herself—a trick that some Iris kids could do. The monochrome effect would pass, and no, we would not die. He'd glared at Blanche, asking her to apologize. She'd just thanked us for the fun evening and strolled away into the dark. For some reason, this made her an artistic genius in Grover's eyes.

Now Annabeth was relying on her to help us.

"Thanks for coming," Annabeth told her.

"Eh." Blanche snapped another shot. "You made me an offer I couldn't refuse. Let's go find Mommy Dearest."

I glanced at Annabeth, wondering what she'd promised Blanche and if it involved selling our internal organs. Annabeth just smirked. Then we followed Blanche into the chaos of the farmers' market.

The day was sunny and mild, so the crowds were out in force. Shoppers milled between rows of produce stands, rummaging through baskets of berries and artichokes. The whole plaza smelled of warm tomatoes and onions. Vendors sold milk, eggs, cheese, honey—all from local farms. It was surreal to have all this country-fresh stuff in the middle of Manhattan, but I guess that was part of the appeal. Grover's nose quivered as he passed the vegetables. I was glad he wasn't a child of Hermes, because I was pretty sure he was tempted to pickpocket some of the rutabagas.

He traipsed along next to Blanche, trying to engage her in conversation. Occasionally he'd throw himself into her line of vision, posing in different dramatic angles, draping himself across tables of vegetables like a lounge singer on a piano. She just ignored him, stopping every once in a while to photograph a dying dandelion or rag-weed growing between the cracks in the pavement.

"Relax," Annabeth told me. "You're grinding your teeth."

"Am not," I said, though I totally was.

She took my hand. "Enjoy the day. Maybe later I'll let you buy me lunch."

"That doesn't make me feel better," I said, though it totally did.

As we got deeper into the market, the stalls started to offer stuff that didn't have much to do with farms. A leatherworker was hawking hand-tooled pouches, wallets, and knife sheaths. (Is there a big market for knife sheaths uptown?) A soap maker offered cruelty-free soap, because nothing is worse than showering with cruel soap. An incense maker displayed a thousand different kinds of smelly stuff to burn.

I was starting to see why a goddess might want to hang out at a farmers' market. Gods loved burnt offerings. They could live on fragrances the way I could live on my mom's seven-layer dip. And this farmers' market was a smorgasbord of smells.

Blanche stopped suddenly. "Okay, there's my mom." She pointed down the aisle, past a linen-towel salesman and a display of macramé plant hangers.

And there was Iris.

She looked nothing like I remembered. That didn't surprise me. Gods can change their appearance the way mortals change clothes. Today, Iris was a plump, grandmotherly woman with long gray hair and a flowing purple-and-white muumuu decorated with . . . well, iris flowers.

Something about the goddess's presence raised the hairs on my arms. My survival instincts were screaming, *Run! She will offer you granola!*

Her booth was decorated with thousands of crystals—some hanging from embroidered cords, some set in bronze holders, all flashing in the sunlight and sending a riot of rainbows across the market. I imagined all of them containing Iris-messages and getting jumbled together as the wrong quests were distributed to the wrong demigods . . . which actually would explain a lot. Maybe my entire career had been a series of Iris-message butt dials.

"Just relax," Blanche told us. "Let me do the talking."

"As long as I look all right," Grover said, turning his face to the sun in his best impression of a dying wildflower.

Blanche paid him no mind. She marched up to the booth with us in her wake.

Iris's eyes lit up as we got closer. "My dear, what a lovely surprise! And you brought . . . friends!"

She said the word *friends* as if it were completely illogical when paired with *Blanche*, like *lobster sandals*.

"They're fellow campers," Blanche said. "They wanted to meet you."

Iris looked us over. Her eyes were multicolored, like oil on water. I smiled and tried to look friendly, but I couldn't tell whether she recognized me.

"How wonderful," Iris said noncommittally. Her mouth

tugged down at the corners as she examined her daughter. "And I see you're still wearing all black. Didn't you like the scarf I sent you?"

"Yeah, it was great," Blanche said. "The pink hummingbirds were totally my style."

Iris winced. "And I don't suppose . . ." She gestured at the camera. "I don't suppose you have started using color film?"

"Black and white is better," Blanche said.

Iris seemed to be trying to smile while a dagger was being twisted into her gut. "I see."

I was beginning to doubt Annabeth's plan. It seemed like we were about to get dragged into some mother-daughter drama that would *not* help our quest. I imagined getting cursed by Iris and leaving the market with my hair permanently blue and my skin decorated with pink hummingbirds.

"So, anyway," Blanche continued, "you said you'd be happy to do me a favor?"

Iris's eyes widened. "Yes, of course, my dear! A new dress? A better camera? A trip to see the northern lights?"

The goddess sounded weirdly desperate to please. It occurred to me that Blanche had found a novel strategy to get a godly parent's attention: complete indifference. It pained Iris to see her child so obsessed with monochrome.

I wondered if that approach would work for me. If I moved to the Sahara Desert and feigned a hatred for water, would Poseidon start shipping me presents: fish tanks, swimming pools, brochures for ocean cruises . . . ?

Nah, probably not.

"I want you to listen to them," Blanche said, jabbing a thumb in our direction. "They're going to sound like they're accusing you of theft."

Iris went dangerously still. "Excuse me?"

"But they just want information. Don't zap them. Don't curse them. Just . . . try to help them, okay? That's the favor."

Iris studied us more carefully. I tried to look unworthy of zapping.

Finally, the goddess sighed. "Very well, dear. For *you*." Her voice took on a sweeter, slightly pleading tone. "And then maybe we could do something together? Binge *WandaVision*?"

"Sounds great, Ma. I'll message you." Blanche turned to us. "I'm outta here, then. Good luck. And remember our deal."

Annabeth nodded. "Grover will be there."

Grover yelped. "Be where?"

"My studio." Blanche handed him a business card. "Next week. For a series of still shots. Been trying to line you up forever, but you play hard to get."

Grover's jaw dropped down to basement level. Blanche trudged off through the market, no doubt looking for sickly weeds and dead rats to immortalize with her lens.

"Well then," Iris said to us, "let's hear what you supposedly think I stole. And I will do my best to help . . . or at least not kill you."

FOURTEEN

Ψ

IRIS GIVES ME A STICK

Color me excited.

We told the goddess about our adventures so far. I'll give this to Iris: she was a good listener. Gods tend to be pretty impatient with mortal problems, but I guess since Iris was a messenger, she'd had to learn to pay attention to what people said.

When I mentioned Ganymede's missing chalice, she grimaced like she'd gotten a crystal shard stuck somewhere uncomfortable. When we described our time in Hebe Jeebies, Iris closed her eyes and sighed like, *Gods, give me patience.* Except, of course, she was one of the gods, and I wasn't sure if praying to yourself would work.

"Obviously, we don't think you took the chalice," Annabeth concluded. "That would be silly."

"Though if you *did*," Grover said, "we'd love to get it back."

Annabeth frowned at him. Grover didn't seem to notice. He had a photogenic glow to him, like now that he was a portrait model for Blanche, he was invulnerable.

"But of course you didn't take it," I said to the goddess. "Did you?"

I didn't mean to put the question mark on the last part. It just kind of slipped out.

Iris pursed her lips. She ran her fingers across the crystal pendants on display, sending fresh bursts of colored light dancing through the market. I had the uncomfortable feeling that with just a thought, she could turn all those light beams into lasers and cut us into demigod mincemeat.

"Do you have any idea how thankless a cupbearer's job is?" she asked.

I recalled Ganymede obsessively walking around my school cafeteria, filling people's cups and cans with Olympian beverage number five.

"Doesn't seem like fun," I admitted.

"No, Percy Jackson. Not fun."

That was the first indication that she remembered me, or at least knew my name. The information did not make me feel any safer.

"So," I said, "the chalice isn't something you'd want back. Like, not even to mess with Ganymede."

This time I managed not to make it sound like a question. But Iris still looked miffed. Nothing is scarier than a hippie grandmother suddenly scowling at you.

"I do not 'mess' with people," she said. "I feel nothing but sympathy for that poor young god. Swept up by Zeus just because he was attractive, used as an eternal party decoration, and having to endure the scowls of Hera and the others as Zeus dotes on him? No. So many young men and maidens have been the victims of Zeus and those other good ol' gods who do whatever they want with impunity. It's terrible."

I looked at my friends. Obviously, we agreed with Iris, but it was a surprise to hear a god say something like that out loud. It was the kind of opinion Zeus might censor with a lightning bolt upside the head.

"I can see we came to the right place," Annabeth said. "You are perceptive, kind, wise . . . all the things we need to find this cup thief. Your advice is as precious as a rainbow."

Iris smirked. "I see what you're doing. Trying to flatter me."

"The rainbow comment was too much?" Annabeth asked.

"Completely over-the-top." Iris curled her fingers in a *Keep it coming* gesture.

"We could use your guidance," Annabeth continued. "You know the gods. You see those who resent Ganymede. Who do *you* think took his chalice?"

Iris spent a moment in silence, thinking. This was another unusual trait for a god. Usually, they just assumed they knew everything and spouted it out.

"I do have a thought," she said. "But I need to look into the idea . . . discreetly."

"Of course," Grover said, his shoulders relaxing. "That's great! Thank you."

"Oh, the information won't be free," Iris added.

I barely managed to bite back a comment. *Of course not.*

"Not because I don't want to help you," Iris said, apparently reading my expression. "I know you think we gods can't resist giving demigods little errands . . . and you're right. You show up on our doorsteps, and we suddenly remember a dozen things we'd love to check off our to-do lists. But it's more than that."

"Knowledge has value," Annabeth guessed. "The more valuable, the more it has to be earned."

Iris beamed. "Spoken like a true daughter of Athena. Also, this will give you something to do while I investigate my hunch."

I didn't point out that we already had lots to do. I suspected that the gods, even the nice ones like Iris, assumed demigods just stood in a utility closet somewhere, deactivated and covered in dust cloths, until we were needed to perform a mission.

"Don't worry," she said. "My quest shouldn't take long. And you still have fifteen days until Ganymede's shame is revealed."

Grover flinched. "Why fifteen days?"

"That's when Zeus is planning to hold his next feast." Iris stared at our blank expressions, then sighed. "But of course . . . Zeus didn't bother to tell Ganymede that, did he?" She turned to Annabeth. "It's the Epulum Minerva— the old Roman feast to honor your mother. Zeus decided to throw her a party, probably because he wants something from her. A new invention. A war. A pit-less variety of olive. Who knows? If the chalice isn't found by the feast date, all the gods will realize Ganymede has lost it. Zeus will be outraged. Ganymede will be . . . probably no longer with us."

Grover's lower lip trembled. His photo-op glow had faded. "What do you need us to do?"

Iris smiled. "That's the spirit."

She turned and started removing crystal pendants from a stand in the back of her stall. As she cleared away the necklaces, I realized the display post wasn't just a post. It was a wooden staff the size of a broomstick, with some kind of fancy metal decoration at the top.

Iris picked up the staff. She laid it on the table between us. Her eyes gleamed, like she was waiting to hear what we'd offer her for it on *Pawn Shop High Jinks*.

Annabeth inhaled sharply. "That's your *kerykeion*!"

"Ah, right," I said. "A kerykeion."

I was going to guess it was Greek for *rug beater*, but I didn't want to be wrong.

Annabeth rolled her eyes. "It's a herald's staff, Percy. Like the one Hermes uses."

"Yes . . ." Iris agreed wistfully. "Another former job of mine. I was the gods' herald."

I studied the staff. Unlike Hermes's caduceus, there were no living snakes coiled around it, but as I looked more closely, I realized the metal headpiece was indeed shaped like a pair of serpents. They had tiny horns and were coiled into a figure eight, facing each other at the top. The metal had gotten coated with grime over the years, so it was hard to make out many details. The wood was also in pretty bad shape, with dark soot stains and grease spots.

I wondered how long ago Iris had been the messenger goddess. . . . Maybe before Hermes was born, which was like, yeah . . . quite some time ago. It looked like this staff hadn't been used as anything but a clearance-rack display ever since.

I also wondered how many times a god could change jobs. Could Iris just decide one day to become the goddess of plant-based proteins? Could Ares give up war and become the god of knitting? I would pay real golden drachmas to see that.

"Percy?" Grover asked, letting me know I'd spaced out.

"Sorry. What?"

"You heard that, right?" he asked. "Iris was just explaining that the top is Celestial bronze, and the base is Dodonan oak."

"Got it." I had no idea what Dodonan oak was, but it didn't look very sanitary. And the headpiece looked more like Celestial grunge than Celestial bronze. "So we're supposed to deliver a message with it?"

"Oh, no," Iris said. "Those days are well behind me. But in ancient times, I used my staff to create wonderful rainbows as I flew through the sky, traveling from place to place. I miss that. . . ." She sighed. "I would like you to give the staff a proper cleaning. Bring it back to its former glory. I admit, I should've done this a while ago, but I suppose . . . Well, I was bitter about losing that job to Hermes."

I thought about what she'd said before . . . that she hadn't held it against Ganymede when she lost the cupbearer's job. But losing the messenger gig *had* left her bitter. It made me wonder how much we could trust this friendly rainbow grandma.

"I'm guessing we can't just use Windex," I said. "Or take the staff to a dry cleaner?"

"Oh, no," she said. "It can only be washed in the River Elisson."

Annabeth blinked. "I don't know that one."

"I do," Grover said. He didn't look happy about it. "Back in the day, the Elisson was known for its crystal-clear magical water. Supposedly it could clean anything, no matter how polluted. And . . . certain creatures took advantage."

"That's true," Iris agreed. "The Furies sometimes bathe there. The River Elisson is the only thing that can get the stench of the Underworld off them when they have to move among mortals."

I shuddered, thinking about my former math teacher Mrs. Dodds, aka the Fury Alecto. I did not like the image of her bathing in a river prior to teaching us pre-algebra.

"Other monsters, too," Grover said, glancing at the staff's snaky headpiece. "Like horned serpents."

"Yes, very good, young satyr," Iris said. "In fact, you must cleanse my staff in the very river where the serpents bathe."

"And these serpents are super friendly," I guessed.

Iris gasped. "Oh, no. They will try to kill you." Like Hebe, she was apparently immune to sarcasm. "But be careful: you must not harm the serpents."

"Because they're sacred to you?"

"Not at all. However, I want this quest to be cruelty-free. You must find a way to accomplish my task without harming any creatures at the river. Good luck, demigods! Now I must return to my duties."

A gaggle of customers descended on Iris's booth and started *ooh*ing and *ahh*ing over her crystals. We were dismissed. I grabbed my rainbow staff of grunge, which did not conveniently turn into a smaller form. As I walked through the market, I felt like a low-rent wizard.

"Cruelty-free," Annabeth grumbled. "I guess that doesn't include cruelty to demigods."

"We'll figure it out," Grover said, surprisingly cheerful again. "I've always wanted to see the River Elisson. There's only one problem."

"Aside from the monsters we can't kill?" I asked.

He waved that away. "I mean the *actual* River Elisson in Greece no longer exists. The mythical river could be anywhere. I heard that the god of the river got so disgusted with all the monsters bathing in his waters, he hid the river so it's almost impossible to find. And Iris didn't tell us where it is."

"I suppose she'd say we have to find it on our own," I guessed. "Because knowledge is valuable, blah, blah."

Annabeth poked me in the ribs. "What we need is

an upper-level water spirit to give us directions. Those Nereids and naiads all know each other. I wonder where we could find a Nereid to ask. . . ." She looked at me pointedly.

I ground my teeth some more. "Fine. I'll wait until Monday and ask my guidance counselor. I just hope she doesn't flush me again."

FIFTEEN

YONKERS!

Reader, she flushed me.

I waited until seventh period to visit the counselor's office, so I wouldn't miss much school if she ejected me into the Atlantic again. At first, though, I was hopeful Eudora and I could just have a nice, calm conversation.

"Welcome, Percy Jackson!"

She seemed genuinely pleased to see me as she ushered me inside and waved me toward a new blue plastic chair. I wondered if she had a stack of them in the closet so she could grab a new one every time she flushed somebody through the floor.

She smiled at me over her jar of Jolly Ranchers. Her eyes floated behind her bottle-glass spectacles. Her scalloped hair glistened like she'd just had it permed with jellyfish goo. "So! How is everything going?"

"I got my first quest," I said. "For Ganymede."

She squealed. "That's wonderful! What exactly is involved?"

I gave her the details, but her gaze was so distracting I mostly kept my eyes on the purple painting of Sicky

Frog. It stared at me miserably with its thermometer in its mouth and didn't judge.

I was working my way up to asking Eudora a favor—the location of the River Elisson—when she stopped me. "Just a moment. Hebe was involved. And now Iris. Did you apply for dual credit?"

"I— What?"

"Oh, dear. If multiple gods are involved, you could have applied for dual credit. Hebe and Iris might have written you recommendation letters as well."

"You mean . . . I could've gotten all three rec letters from this one quest?"

Eudora nudged her Jolly Rancher jar so it made a protective barrier between us. "Well, yes, but—"

"How about I apply for the dual-credit thingy now? I could go back to Hebe. . . ." I mentally slapped myself. "Okay, maybe not Hebe, but I could go back to Iris—"

"Ah, but you have to apply for the dual credit in advance. I'm afraid it's too late."

I glared at Sicky Frog. I felt like punching it in the face, but since it was painted on a brick wall, I figured that might hurt me more than it did the frog.

"Can't we make an exception?" I asked. "I mean, I did the work. I'm *doing* the work."

"Um . . ." Eudora rummaged through her brochures and pulled out the one for New Rome University. "No . . . you see? Right here. It says dual credit cannot be applied for after the fact."

"Is that a general rule? I thought I was the only one who had to do these rec letters."

"You are. See?"

She handed me the brochure. At the bottom of a tiny paragraph about dual credit (which I'm pretty sure hadn't been there before), an asterisk led me to an even tinier disclaimer that read *This applies to Percy Jackson.*

"Okay, that's messed up. I didn't know!"

Eudora sighed. "Well, at least it sounds as if the quest is going well. What's next?"

Next, I thought, *is punching your frog in the face.*

But I didn't say that. I forced myself to exhale. "Next," I said, "I need some guidance."

"Oh!" Eudora sat forward excitedly. "That's what I do!"

I told her about Iris's staff, which was presently taking up space in my bedroom closet. "I'm supposed to clean it, so I need to find the River Elisson."

Eudora didn't stop smiling. (I wasn't sure she was physically capable of that.) But her lips stretched into a grimace as if somebody were tugging her shell-do. "The Elisson. Ah." She shuffled her brochures and shoved them back in her drawer. "Snakes bathe there, you know."

"So I've heard."

"Monsters of all kinds. Not recommended."

"Except I don't have a choice. I need that letter of recommendation. Like you told me."

She winced, probably caught between her job description and her personal feelings. "Yes, but . . . Elisson is touchy. He doesn't like people taking advantage of his clean waters."

"*He?* You mean the god of the river?"

I'd met a few river gods in my time. They tended to be cranky and unfriendly, and they thought of demigods as just another form of pollution, like old tires or cigarette butts.

"If he finds out I gave you directions," Eudora muttered, almost to herself, "he'll never let me into his yoga class again."

"His yoga . . . ? Actually, never mind," I said. "You're telling me you know where I can find him?"

Eudora looked at her watch. "Almost the end of the school day. I suppose if you were to simply wind up at the Elisson's headwaters by accident, that wouldn't be my fault."

The tiles started to bubble and leak around my chair.

"No," I said.

"Good luck, Percy!"

And she flushed me right through the floor.

I could have ended up in Greece or Brazil or who knows how far away. I was fortunate that I ended up in Yonkers, instead—which is the first time in history the words *fortunate* and *Yonkers* have been used in the same sentence.

Okay, sorry, Yonkers, that's not fair, but hey . . . it wasn't a place I wanted to get flushed to right after school, knowing I'd have to take an extra thirty-minute train ride to get back to Manhattan.

My blue plastic chair and I shot out of a drainage pipe, tumbled down a rocky slope, and splashed into a creek. I sat there for a second, dazed and bruised, cold water soaking into my pants. The first thing I noticed was the bottom of my overturned chair, where a metal plate was inscribed:

IF FOUND, PLEASE RETURN TO EUDORA, ATLANTIC OCEAN
REFUNDABLE DEPOSIT: ONE GOLDEN DRACHMA

Great. If I failed to get into college or get a job, I could just wander around New York looking for blue plastic chairs to cash in for drachmas.

I struggled to my feet. The creek meandered through the middle of a gritty small-town business district: low brick buildings, old factories and warehouses repurposed as condos or offices. I knew it was Yonkers because along the riverfront, iron lampposts were hung with weirdly festive banners that yelled YONKERS!

It was the kind of post-industrial area that would've looked better in the dead of winter, under a heavy gray sky and a covering of dirty urban snow. Rough. Grim. A *Deal with it or go home* kind of place.

The riverbed was lined with scrubby bushes and gray boulders—many of them now painted with Percy blood and skin samples from my tumble out of the drainage pipe. The water was what you might politely call *non-potable*— muddy brown and streaked with foam like bubble bath, except I was pretty sure it wasn't bubble bath.

I had landed right next to a marshy area labeled SAW
MILL RIVER MUSKRAT HABITAT.

I saw zero muskrats. Being smart animals, they were
probably vacationing in Miami.

The name Saw Mill River sounded vaguely familiar. I
remembered something in the news from when I was little. My mom had read me this article about how a bunch
of urban rivers had been paved over back in the day and
turned into underground drainage canals, and how people
were now trying to open them up again and make them
nature habitats. What did they call it . . . ? *Daylighting* a
river.

From what I could see, the Saw Mill River didn't
enjoy its daylighting much. Three blocks north, the water
trickled reluctantly from a tunnel large enough to drive a
truck through. The current was sluggish, as if it wanted
to crawl back into the darkness and hide.

I wondered if Eudora had made a mistake.

Oh, you wanted the Elisson, the cleanest waters in the world? I
imagined her saying. *Sorry, I thought you said the Saw Mill, the
cleanest waters in Westchester County! I always get those confused!*

Or maybe she'd intentionally flushed me off-course to
protect the Elisson's location. If so, the river god must
run a really great yoga class.

I waded upstream, slipping and stumbling over mossy
rocks. My head was swiveling for monsters, or Yonkers
police, or ill-tempered muskrats, but no one bothered me.
About halfway to the tunnel, I caught my first whiff of

putrid air from the entrance, like the breath of a sleeping giant who'd been living off moldy fish sandwiches. I doubled over and gagged.

The smell did not make me think of the cleanest waters in the world.

While I was hunched over, praying to the god of not vomiting, something floated by my foot. At first I thought it was a ripped grocery bag: just a shred of milky translucent plastic. Then I noticed the honeycomb pattern on the membrane. Like scales. Like the shed skin of a snake.

That was super helpful for my nausea.

Okay . . . Iris had told us that serpents bathed in the River Elisson. Maybe the water here was not so clean because I was wading through monster bathwater drainoff. Or that snakeskin could be from a normal snake, because nature.

I took a few more steps.

When I looked down again, I saw something else in the water. Snagged in a bed of moss was a curved black pointy thing about the size of my index finger. Some impulse—maybe a death wish—made me pick it up. The broken talon glistened in the sunlight. I'd seen ones like this before on the fingertips of my sixth-grade math teacher, aka the Fury Alecto.

I stared into the dark tunnel. Whatever might be in there taking a bubble bath, I did not want to meet it alone. Also, I didn't have Iris's staff.

Unfortunately, that meant I'd have to come back, with help, and subject Annabeth and Grover to the wonders of the Saw Mill River Fury habitat.

I cursed my guidance counselor, Sicky Frog, and the life of a demigod in general. Then I trudged off to find the nearest train station.

SIXTEEN

Ψ

GROVER BUSTS OUT THE
SNAKE SONGS

The next afternoon, I came back with reinforcements.

When I told Annabeth and Grover where we were going, they looked at me funny, but they didn't ask questions. Downtown Yonkers was well within our standard deviation for weirdness.

I'm not sure what the other passengers thought about me carrying the staff of Iris on the subway train. Maybe they figured I was a shepherd commuting to my pastures. Grover, being Grover, had brought a backpack full of snacks along with his panpipes. Because you never know when you might want to dance a jig while eating sour-cream-and-jalapeno corn squiggles. Annabeth had packed a bunch of practical things, like her knife, flashlights, and a thermos of something that I hoped was more potable than the river water.

By four o'clock, we were standing in the creek bed, peering into the mouth of the tunnel.

Grover sniffed the air. "Cleanest river in the world?"

"This is after the Furies and snakes bathed in it," I said.

"And who knows what else," Annabeth added.

Grover dipped his shoe in the brown water. "I guess we can't just roll the staff around in this muck and call it a day."

I'd had the same thought, but I was glad Grover said it instead of me.

"We'll have to go inside," said Annabeth, distributing the flashlights. "Hope it's cleaner upriver. Let's hug the bank and try to stay out of the water."

That was advice even *I* could recognize as wise. But staying out of the water proved hard to do.

As we forged ahead into the tunnel, the sides turned narrow and slippery. I found it impossible not to slosh around in the stream. My shoes didn't start smoking, and my pants didn't catch on fire, so I guessed the water wasn't that toxic. Still, I added *really hot shower* to my to-do list, assuming I made it home that evening.

About a hundred yards in, Annabeth stopped. "Check it out," she said.

She moved the beam of her flashlight across the tunnel's ceiling, which was coated with moss and lichen so thick I couldn't tell if there was man-made asphalt or natural rock underneath. Wherever Annabeth's light passed, it left behind a streak of blue-green luminescence.

"Cool." I used my flashlight to draw a glowing smiley face on the wall.

"How old are you?" Annabeth asked.

"Eight just last week."

That got a smile. I loved making her smile when she was trying not to. It always felt like a victory.

We spent a few minutes painting light graffiti. Grover wrote *Pan 4ever*. I wrote *AC + PJ*. Annabeth traced concentric arcs until she'd made a blue-and-green rainbow. The moss kept glowing for quite a while, filling the tunnel with a cool turquoise light.

Up ahead, the channel widened into a much larger space. The sound of the current became louder and throatier. We stepped into a cavern so massive it seemed like a different world.

Under a cathedral-high ceiling covered with glowing stalactites, the river wound north between rolling plains of yellow grass. Ash-colored trees dotted the landscape, leafless and stunted, their branches curled like arthritic fingers. The scene reminded me of the Fields of Asphodel down in Hades's realm—and the fact that I can make that comparison the same way you might say *Oh, yeah, looks like Midtown* is a really sad statement about my travel history.

Here and there, outcroppings of granite made islands in the grass, but the main attraction was the river itself. It wound lazily through the cavern, making big loops as if it were in no hurry to reach the daylight. Thick stands of reeds edged its banks. The current glimmered darkly in the blue moss light. The water did look cleaner here. The putrid smell was gone. But in a pool about twenty yards upstream, dozens of slithery, slimy whiplike creatures were rolling and writhing in the shallows, making me never want to eat spaghetti again.

"Gross," Annabeth muttered.

"Hey, now, check your mammalian prejudices," Grover whispered. "Reptiles are people, too."

"With poison," I said. "And cold blood. And a nasty bite. And . . . okay, maybe that also describes humans."

Grover nodded. *Thank you.*

"Lights-out," Annabeth whispered.

We switched off our flashlights, though the snakes didn't seem to have noticed us yet. They were too busy frolicking and power-washing their scales.

I scanned the horizon. "You think we can sneak around them, go farther upstream?"

Grover sniffed the air. "This whole place smells like monsters. I can't tell if there's more besides the snakes nearby. Anything could hide in that tall grass."

"Including us," Annabeth said. "If we can't fight the serpents, sneaking around them sounds like our best option."

"Okay," Grover agreed. "Let me go first, though. I might be able to pick out a safe trail through the fields."

It used to be a rare day when Grover volunteered to go first through dangerous territory. I was too impressed to argue. Look at my old friend . . . taking charge and kicking grass. Sometimes I forgot he wasn't a scared junior satyr protector anymore, but a scared Cloven Council elder. I guess we'd both grown up a lot.

At least here, Grover was in his element, assuming this creepy cave still counted as nature.

We waded through neck-high grass as sharp as hacksaw blades. Grover managed to navigate us around the thickest patches, but I winced every time a wisp of yellow snagged my arm. To make matters worse, the field crackled like bubble wrap as we walked through it. I imagined we'd be audible to any monsters hiding in the undergrowth.

Finally, we reached one of the boulder islands. Grover scrambled to the top as only someone with goat legs could do, then peered toward the river. "That's not good."

"What?" I asked.

He helped us up.

From the summit, I could see the whole course of the river stretched out before us. The Elisson poured into the cavern from a crevice in the northern wall, then cascaded down a series of rocky ledges before widening and meandering across the plains. Everywhere you might be able to access the banks, in every shallow pool or swimming hole where you might want to wash off a grungy kerykeion, the water was full of snakes. Hundreds of them.

"At least I don't see any Furies," Grover offered.

"Yeah," I said. "But spaghetti is definitely off the menu this week."

"What?" Grover sounded hurt. He loves spaghetti.

"Nothing," I said.

Annabeth scanned the river. "What about there?" She pointed to the northern end of the cave, where the river carved a ravine through jumbled heaps of granite. "That's where the water will be cleanest. No easy access for snakes. Probably the current is too treacherous for them."

"But not for a Poseidon kid?" I asked.

She shrugged. "Worth a shot."

"Except there's no way we can make it all the way over there without getting spotted. And if the snakes start chasing us . . . how fast do you think they can go?"

Grover shivered. "Through this grass? A lot faster than we can."

"I kind of wish we had Luke's flying shoes," Annabeth said.

Grover winced. "Too soon."

Five years ago, that pair of cursed shoes had almost dragged Grover into Tartarus. Trauma like that can leave a scar. But what surprised me most was that Annabeth mentioned Luke Castellan, our old friend-turned-enemy. Since the Battle of Manhattan, she'd almost never said his name. It seemed like a bad omen that she was bringing him up now.

"I have an idea," Grover said. "It's terrible, but it might work."

"I love it already," I said.

He pulled out his panpipes. "You guys head for the cliffs. I'll keep watch from here. If you make it, great. But if the snakes start heading in your direction, I should be able to see them moving through the grass. Then I'll distract them with my pipes. I know some pretty good snake songs."

Chalk up another talent I didn't know Grover had: serpent entertainer.

"As soon as you start playing, they'll come for you," Annabeth said. "Which I guess is the terrible part."

"It'll be even worse than the chickens at Hebe Jeebies," I guessed.

"Yeah, I don't love it," he admitted. "But like Annabeth said before, I can run the fastest. Maybe I can buy you some time. If you hear the pipes, know that the clock is ticking, and it would be great for you to hurry. Get Iris's staff washed. I'll meet you back at the exit."

Annabeth and I exchanged looks. We'd been on plenty of dangerous missions just the two of us, but we wouldn't be able to move so stealthily without our super-goat nature guide. I also didn't like the idea of making Grover our decoy for the second time.

On the other hand, Grover was on a roll with the courageous-satyr stuff. I didn't want him to think I doubted him.

"Okay," I said. "Be safe." Which was like telling Grover to win the lottery, because we all knew the odds.

Annabeth gave him a hug. "Hopefully it won't come to the snake songs."

She climbed down the rocks and waded through the grass. I followed, because I was the guy with the grungy messenger's staff.

Within a few yards, the grass was over our heads. The jagged reeds tore at my clothes. Every time we moved, the stalks swayed and rustled. If we'd held up flashing signs that read FREE SNAKE FOOD, we might have drawn more attention to ourselves, but not much.

We used the sounds of the waterfall to navigate north. I kept my eyes on the ground, trying to make each step as careful and quiet as possible. We walked so slowly I wanted to crawl out of my skin from impatience. It didn't help that I kept imagining snakes darting out of the grass, sinking their fangs into my ankles.

I flashed back to the time basilisks had chased my buddies Frank and Hazel and me through a similar grassy field in California. Come to think of it, I'd spent entirely too much of my life playing hide-and-seek with deadly reptiles.

It felt like it took us approximately twelve years to reach the river. Then again, since our experience in Hebe Jeebies, I'd stopped trusting my sense of time.

Finally, we emerged from the grass near the base of the waterfall. We climbed a series of boulders until we stood on a slippery ledge overlooking a wide pool twenty feet below. The water was as clear as glass, free of snakes, and just begging to be cannonballed into. On the downside, it was ringed by sheer cliffs, with no obvious way to get out again unless I wanted to ride the rapids downriver through Serpent Splash Town.

"You could jump in with the staff," Annabeth suggested.

"Sure," I said. "The problem is climbing back up when I'm done."

Annabeth pulled a rope from her backpack and smiled.

"You think of everything," I said, trying to sound happy about it. That pool was looking a little *too* inviting . . . and I remembered Iris mentioning an angry river god, which seemed like the sort of detail that would bite me in the podex later. "Maybe we should plan this out a little bit first. That's your thing right, planning?"

Then I heard the music—the unmistakable trill of panpipes in the distance. It was a song I recognized from my mom's LP collection: Duran Duran's "Union of the Snake." The clock had started. Grover was in trouble.

"Time's up," Annabeth told me. "Bon voyage."

And she pushed me over the side.

SEVENTEEN

⟁

I MEET THE MAN BUN OF DOOM

Find someone who loves you the way my girlfriend pushes me off a cliff.

Without hesitation. With full confidence in your abilities, with the rock-steady belief that your relationship can handle it, and with complete faith that when you come out of the water, assuming you survive, you will totally forgive them for the push. Almost certainly forgive them. Probably.

Bonus points if you find someone with enough chutzpah to say *Bon voyage* while they do it.

Somehow, I held on to Iris's staff as I plunged into the pool. The water hit like an arctic blast, freezing the blood in my capillaries and curling my fingers and toes. I could breathe underwater, but the cold in my lungs felt like the worst case of heartburn ever. Is chest freeze a thing?

As the cloud of bubbles dispersed, I found myself floating in the clearest turquoise water I'd ever seen. Light filtered from the surface, casting shimmering blue fish-scale patterns across the walls of the ravine so they looked like they were clad in living chain mail.

I seemed to be alone. No horned serpents. No Furies

lolling around in swimsuits. A cloud of grass, dirt, and sweat was starting to bloom around me, though. The staff appeared to be smoking, its centuries of grunge slowly loosening.

On one hand: hooray, it was getting clean! On the other hand, I felt terrible for polluting this pristine water.

Then a voice said, "Oh, *Hades* no."

The guy floating in front of me was sapphire blue, which made him almost invisible in the water. I could barely lock my eyes on him even though he was within spitting distance. (But I don't spit underwater, because that's just rude.)

He wore a tank top and loose pants and had the most magnificent man bun in the history of man buns. I could see how he might be a yoga instructor, except that he didn't have that calm, meditative energy. With his scowling bearded mouth and his dark angry eyes, he looked ready to sun-salute me right across the face.

"Hi," I said. "You must be the river god Elisson."

"Actually, I'm your pool attendant. Would you like a towel or a beach umbrella?"

"Really?"

"No, you dolt! Of course I am Elisson, mighty *potamus* of this river!"

I had met enough river gods that I could usually stop myself from smirking when they used the term *potamus*, but it was still hard not to think of hippos.

"Sorry to barge into your waters," I said. "I'm Percy Jackson. Son of Poseidon?"

I put the question mark at the end because sometimes my dad's name will open doors—usually watery doors.

Elisson's eyes widened. "Oh . . ." He crossed his muscular blue arms like a genie about to grant me a wish. "Well, in that case, it's fine that you dropped into my pristine private grotto with that filthy staff and without even taking your shoes off."

"Really?"

"No, you dolt!" He flicked two fingers in my direction. My shoes and socks were ripped off my feet and shot out of the water. The staff of Iris leaped from my hand and rocketed to the surface.

I was doing the ethical math here, trying to figure out if fighting a river god in his home river was a winnable situation, and if so, whether Iris would consider it "cruelty-free." My guesses were no and no.

"Um . . . sorry about the shoes," I said, as diplomatically as I could. "But I kind of need to clean that staff. Do you mind if I—?"

"Go after it?" Elisson asked. "Of course not."

He flicked his fingers again, and this time *I* shot out of the water, slamming into the side of the cliff. I landed in a wet, groaning lump on a narrow ledge. Lying next to me, thankfully not broken, was Iris's staff, still pretty grungy. My shoes were nowhere to be seen.

I sat up and rubbed my head. My fingers came back bloody. That probably wasn't good.

Elisson erupted from the pool, the surface boiling around his waist. Orbiting his hair was a tiny galaxy of weightless water droplets centered on the black hole of his man bun.

"I ask for *so little*," he said. "Use the *sign-up sheet*. Horned serpents are Tuesday-Thursday. Furies and other Underworld minions are Monday-Wednesday-Friday. Demigods are *never*. Take off your shoes before entering my waters. And above all, only use the LOWER POOLS. My headwaters are off-limits! You have managed to break *all* the rules."

I started to say, "I didn't know—"

Elisson pointed at a bronze plaque riveted to the cliff wall next to me. POOL RULES.

I hate written instructions. Especially those posted where you can't see them until you've already broken them.

"Okay," I said. "But—"

"Let me guess." Elisson's water galaxy began to swirl more rapidly, his man bun bending time and space. "The rules don't apply to you."

"Well, I wouldn't—"

"You're an exception. *Your* need is important."

"I mean—"

"It's bad enough I'm being daylighted," Elisson grumbled. "My water quality has turned abysmal downstream. Now you want to pollute my last pristine pool because you need some stick cleaned?"

"It's Iris's staff, if that helps."

"Oh, in that case—"

"You're going to shut me down with sarcasm again, aren't you?"

"So you're not a complete idiot!" Elisson smiled. "That was sarcasm, by the way."

Just my luck. I'd brought sincerity to a sarcasm fight. I guess Iris and Hebe had dulled my natural defenses.

I glanced up at the ledge, where Annabeth was standing perfectly still, wisely not drawing attention to herself. She was giving me that look of alarm I knew well: *Percy, don't you die.*

Elisson hadn't seemed to have noticed her yet. I wanted to keep it that way. I also didn't want to die, but at least if I got killed down here, Annabeth would feel really bad about pushing me. Then I could tease her about it forever.

Except I'd be dead. Never mind.

In the distance, Grover's pipes sounded frantic and weak. I wondered how many snakes were chasing him, and how long he could outrun them while playing a melody. As far as I knew, he had no experience with marching bands.

I raised my hands in surrender.

"I get it," I told Elisson. "I met the Hudson and the East Rivers one time. They *hate* getting polluted. And your waters are much, much cleaner."

Elisson's mouth twitched. I couldn't tell if he was disgusted, or surprised, or pleased . . . but he hadn't killed me yet, so I decided to keep talking. (This is a mistake I make a lot.)

"Rivers have a tough life," I said. "I wouldn't want people turning me into a drainage ditch, or dumping sewage in me, or building a dam generator on me, or a dam anything, really." My hand crept over to the staff of Iris, all stealthy-like. I gripped the handle.

"I should have asked you for permission," I continued. "Rookie mistake. But there has to be a way I can make it up to you and get this staff washed, because it's really important to Iris. She was insistent that it *had* to be your waters, because . . ." I gulped. My head was throbbing, making it hard to think.

What would Annabeth do? I looked up and saw her tapping an imaginary watch on her wrist. Not helpful. Grover's music was getting farther and farther away.

"Because Iris admires you," I told the river god. "Oh, wow, the way she talks about you. And your yoga classes! I think she's your number one fan."

I looked for any sign that my words were having an impact. At that point, I would've taken almost any reaction except sarcasm. Who knew a neat-freak yoga instructor could be so bitter?

"You want to make it up to me," Elisson said.

"Totally."

"I suppose you can snap your fingers and undo all the damage to my river, leave it cleaner than you found it."

"Um—"

"Which you would only do *after* you've gotten what you wanted," he guessed, "and I'd have to take your word for it."

"Well . . ." I gripped the staff tighter. This was not going the way I wanted. I wondered if I'd have better luck riding the rapids back to Yonkers. "I mean, I'm happy to try."

"How did that work out with the Hudson and the East Rivers?" he asked, sweet as acid. "Are they all nice and clean now?"

"Oh. I mean . . . no, but they're harder to clean. They're a lot bigger than you."

Wrong thing to say. Elisson's eyes narrowed. "I see. You find me small. Inconsequential. Even though there's a six-month waiting list to get into my vinyasa flow class."

Up on the ledge, Annabeth was digging through her backpack, no doubt looking for something that might bail me out of the situation she'd been so confident I could handle. I imagined her drawing her knife and yelling *Kowabunga!* as she jumped onto Elisson's back. As much as I would've enjoyed seeing that, I didn't want to see the consequences when she faced the wrath of the sarcastic man-bun god.

I tried to think of another solution, which wasn't easy with my pounding headache. In the future, I'd have to remember not to crack my skull until *after* I was done using the brain inside it.

"There has to be something," I pleaded. "Maybe a visit to Poseidon's palace? He's constructing this amazing infinity pool. You could do your . . . flow-class thing overlooking the continental shelf. Like, with whales."

This sounded like a sweet deal to me, because whales are cool. But apparently, whale yoga was not a fad Elisson was into.

"I'm afraid not." His smile turned a few degrees colder than his water. "But I do have a way you can make it up to me."

I nodded eagerly, which made my vision blur. "Anything, sure."

"Anything? Perfect. I've always wondered how long it would take a son of Poseidon to drown. Let's find out!"

The river surged over me like a wall of liquid bricks.

EIGHTEEN

Ψ

ANNABETH CONQUERS ALL
WITH HERBAL TEA

I wished Elisson would make up his mind.

Throw me out of the water. Drag me into the water. Pummel me with sarcasm. There were so many interesting ways to kill me, he couldn't decide.

To be clear, I'm not an easy person to drown. But when there's a river god tossing me around at the bottom of his grotto, flushing gunk through my nostrils and mouth, it's like trying to breathe in a sandstorm. I was blind and disoriented, slamming into rocks, unable to concentrate.

And that made me angry.

Demigod powers can be weird. Back when I was ten or eleven, things just happened, and I didn't understand why. Fountains would come alive. Toilets would explode. Controlling water was something I did instinctively, only when I was scared or angry—kind of like the Hulk, except with plumbing. As I've grown older, I've learned to control my powers, more or less. Now I can make your lawn sprinklers explode on command. (I rent myself out for kids' birthday parties. Call me.)

But despite my better control, there are still moments

when my power gets away from me. It's kind of like if you think, *Oh, I'm too mature to cry like a little kid*, and then you see a movie about a cute puppy that gets lost, and you start bawling. Or you think you've got your temper under control, then you get a bad grade and throw a world-class tantrum, so your skateboard ends up sticking out of your bedroom wall, impaling your favorite Jimi Hendrix poster. These are purely hypothetical examples, of course.

Anyway, that's what happened at the bottom of Elisson's pool. As I was tossed around, flipped, and pummeled like laundry on a heavy-duty cycle, my control crumbled. I was a scared kid again, screaming for the big bad world to leave me alone. My rage exploded.

And so did the river. It blasted away from me in every direction, putting me at ground zero of the detonation—curled up alone in a bubble of air, howling so loudly I could hear myself even over the roar of the torrent. Some part of me had reached outward . . . not just into the pool, but to the source of the river, deep down in the Underworld or maybe Yonkers, and I had pulled it up by its roots. Millions of metric tons of water roared through the cavern, flooding the pool, scouring the cliffs, surging over the riverbanks, and probably surprising a whole bunch of snakes bathing downstream.

At last, the water crashed back around me, settling into its normal flow again.

I was trembling, strung out, and terrified by what I'd done. I don't know how long it took me to regain my senses. Seconds? Minutes? As the silt cleared, I looked up and had one clear thought: *Annabeth.* If I had accidentally washed her into the Atlantic, I would never forgive myself.

I shot to the surface.

I shouldn't have worried. On the ledge above, Annabeth sat with her ankles crossed, talking calmly with a very rattled Elisson. The river god leaned against her like a shell-shocked refugee, shivering and completely coated with river silt. His man bun had come unraveled, so his hair now looked like a dying yucca plant.

"I—I had no idea," he said, sniffling.

"There, there." Annabeth put her arm around his shoulders. "It's okay. He can be scary when he gets worked up."

I floated in the pool, wondering if I had surfaced in some alternate dimension. Annabeth was comforting the dude who'd just tried to drown me, and she seemed to be calling *me* scary. Then she looked down and winked at me—a sign that meant, *Just go with it.*

"You have to admit, though," she told Elisson, "Percy did a great job."

A great job? I wondered. What was she talking about?

My head wound seemed to have healed itself in the water, so I probably wasn't hallucinating.

Then I scanned the grotto. My tidal wave had swept the cliff walls right up to Annabeth's feet, leaving the rock sparkling clean. Now that the sediment had resettled, the pool was even clearer than before. The air smelled fresh and crisp, with that "new river" smell restored. The current flowed stronger and colder, rushing through the cavern with a jubilant clamor like an audience unleashed onto the streets after a great performance.

I had apparently given the River Elisson my super-deluxe Poseidon Wash package, complete with triple-foam conditioner, undercarriage rust protection, and extreme shine wax.

I looked around for the staff of rainbows. I didn't see it. With my luck, I'd probably blasted it all the way to Harlem.

Annabeth was still patting Elisson's shoulder, making comforting sounds. When I locked eyes with her, she pointed with her chin, telling me to look downriver, but I still didn't see anything.

Elisson shuddered. "I . . . I didn't know I *had* so much water pressure."

"The flow is great now," Annabeth said. "It should help with your vinyasa."

"You think so?"

"Absolutely. And I've never seen a cleaner river. If you find any spots Percy missed, though, I'm sure he could—"

"No!" Elisson yelped. "No, it's wonderful."

He said *wonderful* as if it meant *extremely painful*.

"Sorry," I blurted out. I couldn't believe I was apologizing for rescuing myself from a guy who had tried to kill me, but I felt bad for him. "I got a little carried away."

He winced. "No . . . no, I asked if you could clean the river. And you did. That will teach me to use sarcasm."

For once, he didn't sound sarcastic.

Annabeth gestured downstream again, like she was telling me, *Right there, dummy*.

This time I saw what she was pointing at. About thirty feet away, Iris's staff had wedged itself into a crevice right above the waterline. The oak shaft gleamed. The elaborate herald's crest glowed with a warm yellow light, not a speck of grime on its Celestial bronze designs.

"Uh, if it's okay," I said, "I'm just going to . . ." I pointed to the staff.

Elisson wouldn't meet my eyes. He only nodded. I had the feeling he would've had the same reaction if I'd demanded he hand over his wallet. Wow, I was such a terrible person.

As I swam downstream, I heard a faint strand of music drifting through the air: Grover's panpipes, somewhere far across the cavern. He'd given up on Duran Duran. Now he was playing the Beatles' "Help!" I took this as a subtle message that he was getting tired of leading the snake parade.

I grabbed Iris's staff and swam back to Annabeth and Elisson. I was hoping that Annabeth might throw me the rope and help me up, but she didn't look like she was in any hurry to say good-bye to the river god. In fact, she had pulled out her thermos and was pouring him a hot beverage.

"So this is a nice rose hip–chamomile blend," she told him. "I think you'll find it soothing."

Elisson sipped the tea. "Lovely."

"What is going on?" I asked.

I wasn't really expecting an answer, which was good, since I didn't get one.

"How often a day?" Elisson asked Annabeth.

"Oh, I'd try morning and evening," she said. "Also, anytime you want to meditate. Here." She handed him a couple of extra packets. "No caffeine. I'd stay away from that green tea. It's stressing you out."

"I suppose you're right," the god sighed. "So, for a new schedule . . . perhaps we could reserve every other Saturday for demigods to clean sacred objects. Is—is that fair?"

"More than fair," Annabeth said.

"Totally," I agreed. "But right now, we've got a friend being chased by snakes."

Annabeth frowned, like I was ruining a nice moment, but Elisson drained his teacup and handed it back to her. "Of course. Good luck saving your friend. And, uh . . ." He swallowed nervously. "If you were serious about a whale yoga course at Poseidon's palace . . ."

"Oh, I never kid about whale yoga," I promised him. "I'll put in a word with my dad."

Elisson wiped his nose. "Thank you, Percy Jackson. And, Annabeth Chase, you've been very kind."

Then, clutching his packets of herbal tea, Elisson liquefied and spilled over the side of the cliff. I moved out of the way because I didn't want to get rained on by his runoff.

Once I was fairly sure he was gone, I looked up at Annabeth. "You brought tea? While I'm down here getting tossed around, you're literally drinking tea?"

She shrugged. "Iris told us he was into yoga. I figured herbal tea might be a good offering."

She said this as if her line of reasoning made perfect sense, like of course $x = 2yz^3$ where x is yoga and y is tea.

"Sure," I said. "Got anything else in there that might help us rescue Grover?"

"Bien sûr," she said, which I think is French for *What do you think, Seaweed Brain?* She dug a paper bag from her backpack and shook the contents. "Snake treats. The guy at the store recommended hamster flavor."

"I have so many questions."

"We should get going. We're wasting time."

"You sure we don't have time for another cup of Meditation Magic? How about you throw me that rope."

"Not necessary." She got to her feet. "Just swim downstream. I'll turn invisible. . . ." She pulled out her magic New York Yankees cap—her favorite *get out of jail free* fashion accessory. "I'll go east and find Grover, distract the snakes with these treats, and get him out of danger."

"While I head west and make myself a new target," I guessed.

"Exactly," she said. "Once the snakes are following you, we'll circle back and rendezvous with you at the cave entrance."

"And, uh, do I get hamster-flavored Snakie Bakies?"

"You won't need them."

"Then what am I supposed to distract them with? And more importantly, how do I get away from them once I've gotten their attention? Because, you know, those are the kinds of details I like to have covered."

Annabeth's smile told me I was going to hate her reply almost as much as I hated getting pushed off ledges. "You've got Iris's staff. You've got the best job of all."

NINETEEN

I TASTE THE RAINBOW AND
IT'S PRETTY NASTY

I can now cross *skipping through a field while making rainbows* off my bucket list.

By the time I got out of the river, a few hundred yards downstream, Grover was playing his song of last resort. Distant strains of "YMCA" echoed through the cavern. I knew this was a signal that he was running out of energy and breath. Because when somebody plays "YMCA," it is almost always a cry for help.

Annabeth had instructed me to skip through the fields while holding Iris's staff. She was pretty sure this would create a beautiful rainbow, which would draw the serpents' attention with a high level of *Ooh, pretty*. Meanwhile, she would turn invisible, find Grover, and escort him to safety, tossing Snakie Bakies as needed to keep the serpents away from them.

"And if I can't get the staff to work?" I asked.

"I have faith," Annabeth said.

I was pretty sure she was trying not to laugh.

"And if I can't lose the serpents once they're following me?"

"Just shut off the rainbow," she said. "Once you go

dark, you should be fine. And whatever you do, don't stop skipping, Skippy."

Being a good soldier, I did what she told me. As soon as I trudged out of the river, I put on my shoes and socks—which had washed up in a nearby clump of reeds—and started skipping through the grass.

That lasted about ten feet. Then I realized Annabeth must have been trolling me.

I could run a lot faster than I could skip. I doubted the staff would care. I took off across the fields. Sure enough, after only a few steps, the staff began to glow.

Shimmering ribbons of light unfurled from the Celestial bronze headpiece, glowing brighter the longer I ran. Soon I was trailing a fifty-foot gossamer rainbow, making the fields glow all the colors of a crayon box.

I had a flashback to when I was a kid—like *actually* a kid, not last week at Hebe Jeebies. My mom had taken me to the East Meadow in Central Park to fly a kite for the first time. I remembered running across the field, grinning with delight as my big blue nylon octopus rose into the air. It kind of made me sad thinking about how long ago that was—and also how the kite had gotten zapped by lightning (in the middle of a sunny day) as soon as it was airborne. Even back then, before I knew I was a demigod, Zeus had been watching me. Because that's what you do when you're the king of the gods. You spend your valuable time being as petty as possible, frying forbidden kids' kites out of the sky for fun.

Anyway, it felt good to have another chance. I sprinted

on, holding up the staff, filling the cavern with my one-man rainbow parade. It wasn't long before I heard the sounds of rustling and hissing in the grass behind me. Snakes—lots of them—were closing in, excited to follow the *Ooh, pretty* and eat whatever was causing it.

That thought helped me run faster.

After another hundred yards or so, I made the mistake of glancing back. The entire field was crashing toward me like a surfer's wave, the grass collapsing under the weight of thousands of slithering serpents.

Somewhere in the distance, Grover's music faltered to a stop on the *Y* of "YMCA." I hoped that meant he was safe and Annabeth was now escorting him out of the cave. If I could just keep running for a while longer, I could shut off the rainbow and veer back toward the mouth of the cave. . . .

Hold on. Where *was* the mouth of the cave?

A bit too late, I realized I'd lost my bearings. I was up to my eyeballs in grass with no other landmarks in sight. All I could hear was the rumbling of the Horned Serpent Battalion behind me. I assumed I was still heading west, directly away from the river, but I couldn't be sure. The rainbow light was playing tricks on my eyesight. And my growing sense of panic wasn't helping me think.

I started veering right, hoping I could lead the snakes in a wide arc back toward the river. I didn't factor in how tired I was, though. Exploding the River Elisson had taken a lot of energy. My legs were getting heavy. My lungs burned.

I was losing speed. The snakes were closing in.

So naturally, I chose that moment to trip on a rock.

I bit the dirt. My ankle screamed in pain. Even after enduring sword wounds, acid burns, and fiery dragon breath, it's a bummer how much a normal thing like a twisted ankle can *hurt*. When I tried to stand, it felt like steel spikes were shooting up my leg.

I hobbled a few more feet, using the staff to support my weight, but I was now a slow-moving target. The snakes swarmed me. I staggered to the nearest outcropping of rocks and started to climb, so at least I could see the serpents. When I reached the top, I wasn't happy about the view.

A sea of snakes completely surrounded my previous resting place. Their eyes gleamed red in the light of the Iris staff. Their horns were terrifyingly adorable: little pink-and-white hooks shaped like goal posts. As the serpents closed in, admiring the rainbow light, their mouths all opened on cue, red throats hissing, black tongues flicking to taste the air. Their tone said *YUM!*

"Hey," I said weakly. "Can we talk about this?"

They hissed back at me: *YUM, YUM!*

I wondered if I should draw my sword. Answer: no. There were too many of them. Besides, if I attacked, this quest would become cruelty un-free, and even if I escaped, it would all have been for nothing. Also, I'd probably die anyway.

I hoped Grover and Annabeth got away, at least. I hoped Elisson would enjoy his nice clean river.

The light from the staff seemed to be the only thing stopping the snakes from attacking. The headpiece still pulsed with rainbow energy, and the serpents' eyes stayed fixed on it, entranced.

I was so tired I could barely keep my balance. I had a feeling that if I stumbled, the staff would stop glowing. Then I would be a buffet lunch. But I had to try something.

I raised the staff. The rainbow brightened. The heads of a thousand serpents rose with it. I waved the staff back and forth. The snakes all followed the light, shaking their heads no.

I moved the staff up and down. A sea of snakes nodded along like cats following a laser dot.

I suppressed a hysterical giggle. I was about to get eaten by horned serpents, but at least I was having fun with them.

I couldn't stand on these rocks forever waving a magic stick. Eventually I would get tired, or the snakes would get bored. Then the snakes would swarm the rocks and bite me to death because my rainbow was so pretty.

I didn't want to wait for Annabeth and Grover to try to rescue me, either. I couldn't imagine how they could distract so many serpents without getting themselves killed.

I thought about all the plans Annabeth and I had made about college and beyond. I thought about all the things I wanted to tell her . . . I wished I could at least let her know how much I loved her.

Suddenly, I felt lighter on my feet. The pressure eased on my twisted ankle. I was raising the staff so high it was pulling my arm out of its socket, and I asked myself, *Percy, why are you doing that?*

I don't know, I answered, because I am not very helpful when I talk to myself.

The snakes watched in fascination as the rainbow grew brighter. I found myself on my tiptoes, desperately trying to keep a grip on Iris's staff. Finally, I realized I wasn't lifting the staff. The staff was lifting me.

My first thought was *Why?*

My second thought was *Wait a minute. . . . This is a messenger's staff. Don't messenger gods fly through the air delivering messages?*

Just before the staff had started pulling me upward, I'd been thinking how much I wanted to tell Annabeth I loved her. That was the message.

I held on with both hands.

"Take me to Annabeth," I told the staff.

My feet left the rocks, and I rose slowly into the dank, dark air. Below me, the snakes watched in amazement.

"Farewell, my friends," I told them. "Be good to one another."

Then I ascended.

I wondered if I was leaving the snakes with a new religion; if they would tell stories to future generations about the strange rainbow god boy who tripped a lot before returning to the heavens. Or maybe they were just thinking, *That kid is really weird.*

As I picked up speed, the rainbow shimmered around me, engulfing me in light. My insides twisted. My limbs lost their substance. I wasn't just flying inside the rainbow . . . I was becoming part of it, which sounds a lot cooler than it felt. All the molecules in my body dissolved into energy. My consciousness elongated, like I existed at each point along the arc of my journey simultaneously. And yet I still had all my physical senses. Don't ask me why, but the light spectrum tasted like copper. It smelled like burning plastic. I began to wonder if this was why Iris had gotten tired of her messenger job and started a business where she could burn incense and apply essential oils.

I rematerialized at the mouth of the cave, right next to Annabeth and Grover. My satyr buddy was wheezing and clutching his knees, but he looked unharmed.

"Greetings, earthlings," I said.

Annabeth nearly leaped out of her shoes. "What? How?"

She's cute when she's startled. It doesn't happen very often, so I have to enjoy it when it does.

"I have a message for Annabeth Chase," I said. "I love you."

I tried to give her a kiss, but it was difficult, because she started laughing.

"Okay, I get it," she said, pushing me away gently. "Messenger's staff. Nice work!"

"Yeah, I totally planned it."

"You totally had no idea."

"Just because you're right doesn't mean I don't resent it."

She kissed me back. "I love you, too, Seaweed Brain."

Grover cleared his throat. "I'm fine. Thanks."

"Love you too, G-man," I assured him. "That was some fine panpiping."

"Hmph." He tried to look grumpy, but from the way his ears reddened, I could tell he was secretly pleased. "Let's just get back to Manhattan before things get weird." He hesitated. "I mean *even weirder*."

Going back on the train, we looked like three normal kids who'd been rolling around in a muddy field in Yonkers all day, except I was carrying the cleanest, shiniest staff in the universe. And every time I burped, I let out a little cloud of violet or chartreuse.

TWENTY

Ψ

IRIS TAKES VENMO

The next afternoon we returned the staff to Iris.

I was glad to get it out of my room, because it tended to glow and shoot rainbows around the apartment whenever I thought of a message I needed to tell someone, or whenever a mail truck drove by. That morning, my mom had gotten a special delivery of books from her publisher, and the staff nearly beat up the FedEx guy. I guess it thought he was competition.

Anyway, I met up with Annabeth after school. Grover wasn't with us, since he was downtown doing his photo shoot with Blanche. Apparently, she was going to dress him in a kilt of withered palm leaves, drape him across a burnt log, and photograph him surrounded by dead insects. Grover planned to frame the photo and present it to Juniper as a gift on her bloom day in January. I don't understand a single part of what I just said, but nobody asked my opinion.

Finding Iris was the easy part. I just willed the staff to take me to her. I was afraid it might turn Annabeth and me into a rainbow and beam us to Wisconsin. Then we'd be coughing in twenty different colors all evening, and we'd also be in Wisconsin. Instead, the staff just pointed north and started pulling me along First Avenue like a dowsing rod.

It led us into lower Harlem, where we found the goddess hawking her crystals among a row of sidewalk produce sellers. I wondered if the dude selling cucumbers and the lady selling dried-pepper wreaths knew that the person between them was actually the immortal goddess of the rainbow. Probably not, but I doubt they would've been surprised. When you're a street vendor in Manhattan, you've seen pretty much everything.

"Oh, my!" Iris gasped when she saw us. She took the staff and gave it a full inspection like it was a samurai blade just back from the sword-repair shop. "Mercedes, you look amazing!"

"You named your staff Mercedes?" Annabeth asked. Then she quickly added, "That's a beautiful name."

"She seems so happy!" Iris gushed, rainbow tears trickling from her eyes. "I'm sorry for all the trouble I've caused you."

Foolish me. I was about to accept her apology when I realized she was talking to Mercedes.

"Oh, my sweet." She cradled the staff and continued weeping. "I should have had you cleaned years ago! I will never use you as a display rack again!"

"The quest went well," I offered. "Completely cruelty-free."

"What?" Iris stirred slightly. "Oh, yes. Cruelty-free. Of course. Good."

I got the feeling that I could have destroyed acres of snakes and Iris never would have known the difference. Then again, I was glad it didn't go down like that, since the horned serpents were cute in a deadly, *eat your face off* kind of way.

"So," Annabeth said, keeping her tone upbeat, "does this mean you'll do some of your Iris-messaging in person again?"

"Hmm?" Iris pulled her eyes away from her beautiful herald's stick. "No, no. Those days are over, though it's wonderful seeing Mercedes in such good condition again. I appreciate your help!" She began humming to herself as she arranged her crystal displays around the table, slowly covering up Mercedes.

I glanced at Annabeth, who gestured for me to be patient.

"Did you have a chance to ask around?" Annabeth prompted the goddess.

Iris looked startled that we were still there. "Ask around?"

My heart sank. If Iris hadn't honored her part of the deal, we really had gone to the River Elisson for nothing—except to start a Percy-based religious cult among the reptiles of Yonkers.

"About Ganymede?" I asked. "The missing cup?"

Iris blinked. "Yes. Of course. I . . . asked around. But are you sure you wouldn't rather have a crystal for your reward? Perhaps a package of cleansing sage bath salts?"

She kept piling merchandise over Mercedes: sashes,

beads, pouches of rocks, as if she wanted to hide the staff as quickly as possible. Why did she seem so nervous?

"Just the information would be great," Annabeth said. "You . . . did get information?"

"Mm-hmm." Iris sighed. "It's just that you seem like such nice young people. I would hate . . ."

She let the thought drift away into the Land of Half-Formed Thoughts About Things That Could Kill Percy Jackson. I spent a lot of my time in that land.

"You found where the cup is," I guessed.

"I have a fairly good idea."

Her grim tone made me wonder if I should just take the bath salts. Then I looked at Annabeth. I remembered this was about going to college with her. Being with her. That was nonnegotiable, no matter how difficult the challenge or how cleansing the sage.

"Tell all," I said.

Iris picked at the macramé bracelet around her wrist. "I have narrowed your search down to Greenwich Village."

Annabeth frowned. "That's a pretty big area."

"He will be there," Iris insisted. "If, indeed, I am right about the thief's identity."

"He . . . ?" I prompted.

I waited for more. It's never a good sign when your informant avoids naming the Big Bad. Especially when that informant is a god. Who could make Iris so nervous?

"I should have guessed," she mumbled to herself. She picked up a bundle of incense and waved it around, maybe hoping to clear the air, which it did not. "He would, of course, hate Ganymede. And the goblet. But . . ." She shook her head. "I hope I am wrong. I am probably not wrong."

"Who is it?" Annabeth asked. "We need a name."

She had more courage than I did. I'd already resigned myself to the idea of searching the entire Village for random dudes carrying chalices.

Iris looked over one shoulder, then leaned toward us conspiratorially. "He will go by the name . . . *Gary*."

I didn't dare laugh, but all I could think about was the cartoon snail from *SpongeBob SquarePants*. Usually, the things that sound the most ridiculous are the ones that kill you the quickest. You laugh, then you get murdered in the silliest way possible.

"Gary," Annabeth repeated.

"Yes," Iris said. "I do not know how he managed the theft. Or what he hopes to achieve. But this information came from a reliable cloud nymph."

"So, we go to Greenwich Village," I summed up, "and start asking around for Gary."

Iris tilted her head. "I suppose you could do that. It would be quicker, however, to use nectar."

She plucked a vial from her display rack of essential oils, then held it up like she was modeling for a television commercial. I'd seen nectar before. I'd drunk my fair share of it whenever I'd needed to heal from cuts, contusions, sick burns, and the other daily injuries of demigod life. But this little vial seemed particularly bright and golden, like sunlight suspended in honey.

Annabeth leaned in. "Is that . . . ?"

"One hundred percent pure concentrate," Iris said with a smug little smile. "Collected from the dew in the groves on Mount Olympus at dawn on the first day of spring. With no additives or preservatives. Do *not* consume this. Unblended nectar would burn you demigods to cinders."

I edged away from the happy golden death juice. "Then what do we do with it?"

Iris swirled the little vial, making the insides glow even more. "The chalice of the gods is designed to mix nectar. All nectar is naturally attracted to it. Release a drop or two of this liquid into the air in Greenwich Village, and if the chalice is anywhere in the vicinity, you should be able to follow the droplets right to Gary."

"That's surprisingly helpful," I admitted. "Thank you."

I reached for the vial, but Iris withdrew her hand.

"Ah-ah," she chided. "There is a price."

I suppressed a groan. I wondered what magic item she wanted cleaned now, or what special crystals she needed us to collect from the depths of the Underworld.

"How much?" Annabeth asked.

Iris gave us her best hard-bargaining stare. "Five dollars."

"That's it?" I asked.

Annabeth elbowed me.

"I mean . . . *five dollars*?" I tried to sound outraged. "Cash?"

"I also take Venmo," the goddess offered.

I dug around in my pockets. I came up with my pen-sword Riptide, a paper clip, and a receipt from Himbo Juice. Annabeth took out her purse and produced a five-dollar bill. Because of course, along with every other strange and archaic ancient tool that she might need, she carried cash.

"Deal," she said.

The exchange was made. Annabeth slipped the golden vial into her purse.

"Anything else we should know?" I asked. "Like who Gary is?"

"No," Iris said. "It's better you do not know. Other-wise . . ." She shook her head, then slipped the five-dollar bill into her embroidered fanny pack.

I got the feeling she wanted to say something else. *Nice seeing you. Good luck.* Something like that. Instead, she just gave us a pained smile and turned to arrange her col-lection of tie-dyed shawls.

I suppose *otherwise* was the only thing you really needed to say when sending demigods out on a dan-gerous mission. That way, all your bases were covered. *Succeed. Otherwise . . .*

Well, you can fill in the blank.

TWENTY-ONE

♆

I OFFER RELATIONSHIP ADVICE. NO, SERIOUSLY. WHY ARE YOU LAUGHING?

Never give a satyr a photo op.

The next afternoon, Grover showed up to my second swim meet wearing a black beret, sunglasses, and a white smock thing. He looked like he was ready to paint watercolors on the street in Paris or something. He cheered for me as I did my first race (I came in second, because I didn't need the attention of winning), then chatted with me in the bleachers while we watched my teammates compete.

Every time there was a break in the conversation, Grover opened his portfolio (since when did he carry a portfolio?) and perused the contact sheets from his photo shoot with Blanche.

"Did I show you this one?" he asked.

"I'm pretty sure you showed me all of them." I tried to be nice about it, but I could only look at so many shots of Grover pretending to be dead, draped over a burnt log.

"See, my hand is slightly higher in this one," he said. "Blanche thought it made a nice shadow across my forehead."

"Uh-huh. It's great." I clapped for my teammate, who was just starting his second lap. "Yeah! Go, Lee!"

"It's Lou," said another teammate on the bench, whose name I thought was Chris but with my luck was probably Craig. Hey, I'd just started at AHS. Most days I couldn't even remember my own name.

"So anyway," Grover continued, "I asked Juniper whether she preferred C-twenty-five or maybe A-six for the final print. They both have advantages."

I didn't want to ask, but I did. "And which one did Juniper prefer? Or have you told her about it yet?"

Grover scowled. "I did. It was weird. She seemed . . . angry."

Oh, boy, I thought. "Why do you think that was?"

Grover scratched his goatee. I could tell he was thinking about his answer, because he momentarily forgot about his contact sheets.

"I'm not sure," he admitted. "I told her Blanche liked the prone pose more, but Blanche liked the light in the side pose, so—"

"How many times did you mention Blanche when you were talking to Juniper?" I asked.

Grover stared at me over the tops of his sunglasses, his bloodshot eyes completely lost. "It's—it's Blanche's photography."

"So a lot of times, then?"

Grover frowned. "You don't think . . . You think Juniper is *jealous*?"

I imagined a chorus of Obvious Angels singing the Obvious Hymn above his head, but I tried to keep my expression neutral. "Could be?"

"But . . . Blanche is a *demigod*. I would never——" He swallowed. "I think I may have said her name a lot."

The whistle blew for the end of the hundred-meter race. Lee/Lou had won. I clapped and cheered for him along with my teammates, but I decided not to call him by name.

When I turned back to Grover, he was scratching his head like there were ants crawling around under his beret.

"Maybe a dozen times?" he muttered. "Oh, no . . ."

"Did Juniper *ask* you for a photo for her bloom-day gift?"

"Well, sure, she . . ." Grover hesitated. "Actually, no. I think . . . maybe it was my idea. Oh. How bad have I messed up?"

I squirmed on the bench. I was the absolute last person who should have been giving advice on personal relationships. Well, maybe the absolute last after Zeus, my dad, and the rest of the Olympian gods. Mostly I just followed Annabeth's lead, and so far that had worked out pretty well. With any relationship that wasn't Annabeth and me, I didn't feel qualified to offer an opinion.

But Grover looked at me with pleading eyes.

"Just be honest with her," I suggested. "Apologize. Tell her you weren't thinking. You were being stupid."

"Right," he said, nodding slowly. "Like you do with Annabeth."

"Um . . . yeah. Maybe ask Juniper what *she'd* like for her bloom day."

"But the portrait . . ." He looked wistfully at his

contact sheets—dozens of takes of fake-dead Grover in fake-dead nature. He pulled off his sunglasses and tucked them into his smock. "I guess you're right. There's no place for her to hang it in her juniper hedge anyway. It's just that Blanche worked so hard. . . ."

I cleared my throat.

"And I'm not going to talk about Blanche anymore," he corrected himself. "Thanks, Percy."

He sounded so miserable, I decided maybe a change of subject would be good.

"What about the cloud nymphs?" I prompted. "You said you were going to ask around for more info?"

He perked up. "Right. Right, of course! So I figured I could maybe narrow things down in Greenwich Village, maybe find out where this Gary might hang out. I talked to Phaloa, who talked to Euclymene, and she said she'd noticed some weird energy around Washington Square Park."

"Weird energy kind of defines Washington Square Park," I said.

"Yeah, but this . . . I dunno. She couldn't give me specifics, but she said a lot of nature spirits have been leaving the place in recent weeks. Grass nymphs, flower nymphs, dryads . . . they've either gone dormant, deep in the soil, or taken a vacation."

I pictured a crowd of nymphs in diaphanous, leafy dresses, lugging their suitcases up the gangplank of a cruise ship, bound for spring break in Cancún.

"Gary is so terrifying he can scare nature spirits away from their own life sources," I mused. "You know any monster or god with a name that sounds like Gary?"

"Geryon?"

I shuddered, remembering the three-bodied rancher I'd met during my one and only trip to Texas. "Been there. Killed him. Anyone else?"

"Gar—gary—gany—Ganymede?"

"That would be a plot twist. Let's assume he didn't steal his own chalice, though. Anyone else?"

Grover shook his head. "Maybe it rhymes with Gary. Larry? Harry?"

Considering that I couldn't even get my own teammates' names right, I decided not to play that guessing game.

Down in the pool, the next race had begun. My teammate Lindsey, or maybe it was Linda, was on her first lap for the five-hundred-meter freestyle.

"Maybe we should hit the park early in the morning," I said. "The fewer people around, the better it will be if we end up in a fight."

Grover nodded. "I wonder if Gary is some kind of nature spirit—a big angry one, scaring off all the little ones. If so, maybe I can get him to listen to me."

I remembered how well things had gone with the big angry river god Elisson, but I didn't mention that. There would be plenty of time for Grover's hopes to be dashed later.

"How's tomorrow?" I asked. "We could meet Annabeth at Washington Square Park."

Grover winced. "I think I'd better get out to camp and spend a long weekend with Juniper. How about Monday?"

I wasn't good at keeping a schedule. I was pretty sure I had a math quiz first thing Monday, but hey . . . surely I would be done with our monster encounter before school, right? And if the Minerva-feast thing on Olympus wasn't until the following Sunday, that technically left us plenty of time to find the chalice and return it to Ganymede. . . .

"Okay," I agreed. "Super-early o'clock on Monday. I'll let Annabeth know. She's coming to dinner tonight."

"Cool," Grover said, though he looked uneasy. "Do you think . . . ?" He didn't seem able to finish his thought.

The satyr seemed so worried, I assumed about Juniper, that I wanted to give him a hug, wrap him in a warm fluffy blanket, and drive him to Camp Half-Blood myself. Since I didn't have time to make the drive, and I also didn't have a warm fluffy blanket, I racked my brain for helpful advice.

I remembered something Annabeth had told me months before, when I was trying to figure out what I could do to make up for disappearing our entire junior year.

"Look, man," I told Grover. "Juniper will forgive you. She probably doesn't want presents at all. She just wants you to be there for her. Listen to how she's feeling. Be with her."

From the pool, my coach yelled, "Jackson. You're up again!"

It was time for me to get ready for the high dive.

"I should go," I told Grover.

"Yeah. Yeah, it's just . . . I've been so stressed about me and Juniper, but honestly, we were fine until I started obsessing about her bloom-day present. What if that's not what's really bothering me? What if I'm worried about you and Annabeth leaving me next summer?"

Leaving him.

That hit me like a cold wave of Elisson water. I looked down at the contact sheets from Blanche's photo shoots—all those images of Grover playing dead in a black-and-white landscape of despair.

"Ah, Grover . . ." I did give him a hug then. I felt a little awkward, since I was only wearing a swimsuit and I was still wet from my last event, but he didn't seem to care. "We're never *leaving* you, buddy. We'll be back to visit. You'll come see us in California. You're like our life source, dude. We can only be away from you for so long before we start to wither, you know?"

Grover managed a faint smile. "Yeah . . . yeah, okay."

My coach yelled for me again.

"Go," Grover told me.

"You sure you're good?"

"I'm good. I'll see you Monday morning at Washington Square Park. You wanna say six thirty?"

I didn't want to say 6:30 A.M., and I definitely didn't

want to be awake then. The thought of how early I'd have to get up to make it downtown by that time made me want to stick my head in the water and scream. But satyrs are morning people.

"Sounds great," I told him.

Then I jogged off toward the diving board. I hadn't practiced my dive at all, but I figured I'd spent so much of my life plummeting downward, I'd be a shoo-in for first place.

TWENTY-TWO

I GET A CUPCAKE AND A SURPRISE

It takes strength and courage to bring dessert to my mom's for dinner. My mom is a famously good dessert maker. Most people would be too nervous to bake anything for fear it wouldn't hold up to comparison. Fortunately, Annabeth is both strong and courageous, which meant I got cupcakes.

"Sweetheart, these look amazing!" my mom said, accepting a tray of Annabeth's latest creations.

Annabeth teared up with gratitude. I have seen her shrug off compliments from gods, but my mom's praise really got to her. I guess it was because she'd grown up with Athena as her distant maternal figure.

Sometimes I wondered if Annabeth was open to the idea of marrying me someday only because she was excited about getting Sally Jackson-Blofis as her mother-in-law. Honestly, I couldn't blame her.

Annabeth had started baking because she literally ran out of classes she needed to take for graduation. Despite having the same crazy demigod problems I did, despite having a miserable junior year while I was missing in action, despite being just as dyslexic and ADHD as I was, she had accumulated so many advanced-placement courses and made such good grades that the counselor at SODNYC suggested Annabeth just take a study hall for her seventh course.

Me, I would have said, *Yes, please, and can I have a pillow with that?*

But coasting was not in Annabeth's nature. She'd signed up for the elective Beginning Culinary Design. So far, she'd only been working on cupcakes (which was totally cool with me), but I was pretty sure by the end of the year she'd be constructing bridges and skyscrapers out of angel food cake.

One thing Annabeth didn't do, however, was make blue food. That was kind of an inside joke between my mom and me. Annabeth considered it sacred and off-limits. Her cupcakes today were green with purple sprinkles, for reasons known only to her.

While she and my mom chatted about frosting, I checked in with my stepdad, Paul, who was clearing stacks of student essays off the dining table. The dude worked nonstop, I swear. It almost made me feel bad I didn't put more effort into my own homework. Almost.

"Hey, Paul." I gave him a fist bump.

"Beat any good monsters lately?" he asked.

"You know. Just the usual."

Paul chuckled. He was still in his work clothes: blue dress shirt, faded jeans, wildly colored tie with pictures of books on it. His gray-flecked hair had gotten grayer and fleckier over the last few years, and I tried not to think it was my fault. He worried for me, knowing my demigod history. He worried for my mom worrying for me. He was a great guy. I just preferred to think the teaching job was aging him rather than the constant life-and-death fights I went through. I tried to keep the worst details to myself, but Paul knew. As much as any mortal could, he had seen my world up close and personal during the Battle of Manhattan.

Tonight, though, he seemed tenser than usual. You would never be able to tell if you didn't know him, but he did this thing where he tapped his fingertips to his thumb when he was nervous, like he was trying to pinch a string that he couldn't quite find.

"Going okay?" I asked him.

"Me?" He smiled. "No monster fights this week. Unless you count freshman essays on *Romeo and Juliet*. Help me set the table?"

There was something else going on, but I decided not to push. I set places for four. In the kitchen, garlic bread was toasting. Lasagna was bubbling in the oven. Annabeth was laughing about something my mom said, and the way they both grinned in my direction, I figured it had to do with me. Annabeth had already seen my baby pictures, so I wasn't worried about what they were saying. I had no dignity left. Annabeth and I were still together. I figured that was good enough.

Some Bob Dylan vinyl was playing on Paul's turntable,

soft enough to be background music, but with Dylan's voice, you can never quite ignore him. Not my jam, but I can deal with it. Paul says Dylan was one of the best twentieth-century poets. I mean, the guy can rhyme *leaders* with *parking meters*. I guess that's something?

Once we were all seated, passing around the salad, I noticed something else strange. My mom was drinking sparkling water.

She wasn't a big drinker, but she usually had one glass of red wine with dinner.

"No vino?" I asked her.

She shook her head, her eyes twinkling like she was still thinking about a private joke. "No. Actually, I wanted to talk to you about that."

"About wine?"

"Ahem," Paul coughed. He was now pinching with both hands, looking for that invisible string. Why so edgy?

Annabeth gave me a look. *Seriously, Seaweed Brain? You don't get it?*

Maybe my mom had told her something in the kitchen, or maybe Annabeth had just figured out what was going on by herself. She notices things. Being with her is like being with somebody who's watching the same movie, but fifteen minutes ahead of where you are.

"Not about wine," my mom said. "More about why I'm not drinking it tonight. But first, I want to be clear that this should not affect your plans, Percy. I don't want

it to distract you from everything you've got going on . . .
especially getting into New Rome University."

My mouth dried up. My first thought was, Oh, gods,
she's got some terrible disease.

"Mom, I—I *live* in distracted. It's my zip code. Whatever is wrong, I want to help."

"Oh, sweetheart." She reached across the table and
took my hand. "Nothing's wrong. I'm pregnant."

She could have hit me upside the head with a rainbow
staff and the message would have stunned me less.

"Pregnant . . ." I repeated.

She gave me a brave smile—the same kind she used
to give me when she found me a new school after I got
kicked out of the last one. *Surprise!*

"Like . . . you and Paul."

I looked at my stepdad, who hadn't touched his lasagna. I realized everybody at the table was holding their
breath. Maybe they were afraid I would make all the
plumbing in the apartment building explode. Which, for
the record, I only did that *one time.*

"Yes, me and Paul." My mom took his hand. I wondered if they'd had some awkward conversations about
whether it was safe to have a human child after having a
demigod. After *me.*

Annabeth was watching me carefully, gauging my
reaction. Concerned for me? Concerned for Paul and
my mom?

A warm feeling washed over me. I started to grin.

"That is *awesome*."

The tension broke, which was a lot better than the pipes breaking. I jumped out of my chair and hugged Paul because he was closer. I think I startled the poor guy. He accidentally dragged one of his shirtsleeves through the lasagna.

Then I rounded the table and hugged my mom. She let out a laugh/sob that was a great sound: total relief, total happiness. There was some crying. I am not going to point fingers at who it was, though. Finally, we got settled back into our places, though I still felt like I was floating a couple of inches off the floor.

"I'm really glad you're happy," my mom said.

"Of *course* I'm happy." I couldn't seem to stop smiling, which is a problem when you're hungry and you have a plate of lasagna in front of you. "Hold up. *When?*"

"The due date is March fifteenth," she said.

Annabeth's eyebrows shot up. "The Ides of March?"

"That's just a best guess." My mom winked at her. "*Percy* came much later than expected."

"I was stubborn," I said. "So this means I'll be here when the baby comes. That's awesome. I'll have a few months before . . ."

My smile finally faded. If all went well and I got into school with Annabeth, I would be leaving for California during the summer. That meant I'd miss so much with the new baby. I wanted to hear the kid's first laugh, see their first steps. I wanted to play peekaboo and teach the little rug rat to make rude noises and eat blue baby food.

"Hey," my mom said, "you will be here for the delivery. And you can come home from California as often as you want. But you also need to stick to your plans. They are excellent plans!"

"Yeah, of course," I said.

"Besides," she said with a mischievous smile, "we're going to need your bedroom for the baby."

I was in a fog for the rest of dinner. I was still floating, partly from happiness . . . partly from a feeling like I'd been cut free from my moorings and was now drifting away. I was thrilled for my mom and Paul. Absolutely. I couldn't believe they were going to have a kid I could watch grow up. That baby was going to be so lucky.

But also, it made my own departure seem even more real. I would be leaving just as my mom and Paul were starting a new chapter. I wasn't sure how I felt about that. . . .

I *did* remember to compliment Annabeth on her cupcakes. They were really good: buttery and sugary, the icing a little too thick . . . just the way I like them.

She and I did the dishes together. By the time I walked her down the street to the subway, it was growing dark.

"I'm glad you were okay with the news," she said. I hadn't realized until that moment how relieved she was.

"You were thinking about your stepbrothers," I guessed.

The arrival of those babies had meant the beginning of the end for Annabeth's relationship with her dad. At least, at the time. She'd run away from home shortly afterward, feeling forgotten and unwanted.

She kissed me. "You're not in the same place as I was, thank the gods. You're going to be a great big brother."

A warm flush of joy washed through me again. "You think?"

"'Course. And I can't wait to see you learn how to change diapers."

"Hey, I cleaned Geryon's stables of flesh-eating horses. How bad can baby diapers be?"

She laughed. "In April or May, I'm going to remind you that you said that. You're going to be begging to leave for college then."

"I dunno," I said. "I mean . . . to be with you, sure. It's just . . ."

She nodded. "I know. Families are hard. Long-distance families are even harder."

That was something we both understood.

She squeezed my hand. "See you Monday, bright and early."

And she headed down the steps of the station.

At least I have Annabeth, I thought. We would stay together. Assuming, of course, we solved this whole chalice issue. Otherwise, I'd be stuck in New York, and I'd have a whole lot more diaper changing to look forward to. At that moment, though, both options felt okay. . . . I could make either one work.

Multiple positive outcomes?

Wow. There was a first time for everything.

TWENTY-THREE

GANYMEDE EXPLODES
ALL THE BEVERAGES

School waits for no one.

That's a famous quote from somebody, I think. And it's true. Friday morning came whether I wanted it to or not. I was still sore from the fight with Elisson. My brain felt like it had been turned inside out from my mom's news. I hadn't studied enough for my science quiz, by which I mean I hadn't studied at all.

On top of all that, I got a PA announcement in third period telling me to report to the guidance office, and I was not in the mood to be flushed.

"Percy!" said Eudora as I walked in. She sounded suspiciously glad to see me, or maybe she was just surprised that I was still alive. "Please, sit!"

I had a plan. If she tried to flush me again, I would command the water to lift me toward the ceiling. Then I would steal her jar of Jolly Ranchers and run back to class, laughing maniacally.

"So!" She laced her fingers and beamed at me. "How is everything?"

"Everything is a lot," I said.

I told her about my mom having a baby. Eudora

seemed delighted, until I explained it was a human baby, not one with Poseidon.

"Oh, I see." She shrugged. "Well, that's nice, too, I suppose. And your classwork?"

"Um . . ."

"And the recommendation letters?"

I brought her up to speed. I told her we would be going Monday morning to search Washington Square Park, and I emphasized that there was no need to flush me there.

"Hmm . . ." She looked at Sicky Frog as if it might want to weigh in. "And what exactly are you searching for in Washington Square Park?"

"Ganymede's chalice," I said. "We think it was taken by someone named Gary."

She paled, like sand when you step on it and all the water is pushed away. "You know, it's not too late to consider community colleges. Did I mention Ho-Ho-Kus? I have a brochure here somewhere."

"Hold up—"

"You could get an associate's degree in mechanical engineering—"

"Eudora."

"Or accounting—"

"New Rome University," I said. "Remember? That's the goal. Why are you suddenly steering me away? And please don't tell me Gary runs a yoga class."

She shifted in her seat. "No, no. And it's not so much steering you away. It's more . . . wanting you to stay alive."

I glared at her, doing my best to channel my dad's Unhappy Sea God look. "I'm going to need more than that. You're my guidance counselor, so guide me. Who is Gary?"

"You know—I just remembered—I have a thing. . . ."

A green whirlpool surged up around her. The curtain of water collapsed, splattering kelp across the floor, and Eudora was gone. I glanced at Sicky Frog and wondered how bad this Gary had to be to get a Nereid to flush herself out of a conversation. Sicky Frog had no answers. I grabbed a big handful of Jolly Ranchers and headed back to class.

Lunch was no better. I sat down with my bag lunch—a leftover lasagna sandwich with a leftover cupcake—and I was just starting to feel like maybe I could relax for a few minutes when I heard the ominous tinkling sound of someone filling my thermos.

"Hi, Ganymede," I said.

He sat down across from me, his glass pitcher sweaty with condensation. The liquid inside was orange today—maybe Olympian beverage number six? He was dressed in the same chiton and sandals as before, but he looked more worn with worry. . . . Not older, exactly. Gods don't get older. But his eyes were ichor-shot with golden veins. His face had an unhealthy sheen, as if he were about to burst into his fiery divine form and vaporize the entire student body into piles of powdered drink mix.

"Please tell me you have news," he said.

It's hard to tell a story and eat a lasagna sandwich at

the same time. So I prioritized the sandwich. I nodded and ate, watching Ganymede get more and more agitated. I wasn't sure how he'd take the news. If he vaporized me, I wanted to have eaten a good last meal.

"So," I said, moving on to the cupcake, "we think the guy who stole your chalice is hanging out in Washington Square Park."

I told him what we knew, and how we planned to find the thief.

"Nectar," Ganymede murmured. "That's good. That could work."

"Any idea who this Gary could be?" I asked. "You have any enemies by that name?"

He shook his head. "I have so many enemies. Some of them could be named Gary. I don't know."

He sounded so miserable I wanted to assure him everything would be okay, but I wasn't sure I should promise that. If I were a god, and somebody told me my precious chalice was in Washington Square Park, I would zap down there in a cloud of righteous fury and start busting heads and turning out people's pockets.

But as I'd been told many times before, gods simply didn't do that sort of thing. It was against the Great Cosmic Rules in Goditude or something. Anybody could steal your divine stuff. Only a hero could get it back for you. And by *hero*, I mean me, the schmuck who needed recommendation letters.

Also, if Ganymede started tearing up Greenwich Village, I suppose the other gods might have noticed.

Then his shame would be revealed to everyone. The video would probably go viral on GodTok or whatever they were using on Mount Olympus these days.

"It would really help," I said, "if I could figure out why this guy would steal your chalice."

"Why would anyone?" Ganymede said. "To become immortal? To embarrass me? To become immortal so he can embarrass me forever? I don't know."

He leaned across the table and grabbed my wrist, his gold rings digging into my skin. "You must retrieve the goblet soon, Percy Jackson. We're running out of time. My drink-pouring senses are tingling. Zeus could call for a banquet at any minute!"

"Oh, yeah . . . about that." I told him what Iris had said about the Epulum Minerva feast a week from Sunday.

Ganymede put his head down. All around us, geysers of juice, soda, and water erupted from people's cups. Cries of "Whoa!" ricocheted around the room as my classmates leaped out of their seats to escape their suddenly possessed beverages.

Ganymede sighed. "I should probably go refill those. But listen to me, Percy Jackson. Zeus is unpredictable. He may not even wait until the Epulum Minerva feast! As soon as he gets it into his head to toast one of his guests, any time of day or night, I must be there with my chalice in hand. Otherwise . . ."

"You're toast," I guessed.

"Very funny," the god grumbled. "You haven't lived for millennia dreading the words *a toast!* Some of my

[179]

worst nightmares . . ." His voice trailed off. "Never mind. Just *don't* fail me."

Then he got up to distribute Olympian beverage number six to all the thirsty and drink-splattered students.

That afternoon, I did something unusual. I visited the library.

Yeah, I know. I could almost hear that turntable needle scratch in your head as you tried to process that idea. If I told you I fell into Tartarus again, or got swallowed by a giant, or had to go bungee jumping in a volcano, you'd be like, *Yeah, that makes sense.* But Percy visiting a library? That's *way* off brand.

Truth is, I have nothing against libraries. They're nice quiet places to hang out in, and all the librarians I've met are cool people. It's just that libraries are full of books. Being dyslexic, I tend to think of *book* as a synonym for *migraine headache.* Sometimes, though, books are the only place you can find information, so you have to risk the headache. This concludes my TED Talk on the importance of reading.

Anyway, I needed a place to think. I wanted to figure out what I was doing Monday morning against Gary the Goblet Ganker. I tried the library computer first, but as usual, the Internet didn't help. I guess all the weird stuff I face is so old and bizarre nobody has bothered to make a fan wiki for Stuff that Kills Demigods. If you *do* find monster info online, it's usually about how to beat it in some video game. In real life, holding Z while pressing left doesn't do much.

So I hit the books.

I found five different collections of Greek mythology. I looked through all of them. I even remembered there was a thing called an index in the back. I checked those for gods or monsters whose names might sound even a little bit like *Gary*.

Geryon again. Gray Sisters. I remembered learning about some Norse wolf named Garm, but I wasn't the Mighty Thor, so I didn't want to cross that particular Rainbow Bridge. I had enough to worry about on the Greek side.

Finally, I set the mythology books aside. I pulled out my textbooks and tried to study.

My foot wouldn't stop shaking. My head wouldn't stop buzzing. I felt like I was watching myself trying to study rather than actually studying.

I cared about graduating. I cared about going to New Rome with Annabeth. But I didn't care about science or American literature or persuasive essays. And although I knew that those things were connected to my overall goal, I had trouble making myself believe it.

I couldn't focus on my reading.

I wrote one sentence of an essay: *In this persuasive essay I will persuade you . . .*

Okay. Half a sentence.

I stared at my science textbook.

I thought about Gray Sisters and gray wolves and scary Garys in Washington Square Park. But the image that kept floating in my mind was Ganymede's face when he'd talked about his nightmares. He looked like a classmate of mine in freshman year who'd gotten mugged on his way to school: eyes like empty windows, a face that had forgotten how to make expressions.

Elisson had looked like that after I made his river explode. I still felt terrible about it. Ganymede had a bigger, eternal tormentor in his life: Zeus, a guy I tried very hard never to be like. I didn't know the full story between the two gods. As usual, the myths basically only told Zeus's side of the story. But it was obvious that Ganymede wasn't doing so great in the mental-health department.

I tried to imagine having my life shattered like Ganymede's—kidnapped as a teenager and hauled up to Mount Olympus because Zeus thought I made nice eye candy, then being stuck in that situation forever. Never aging. Never growing. Never getting sick. Never healing.

I realized why I was trying so hard to find answers. I wasn't seeing this quest as just an inconvenience anymore. I wanted to help Ganymede. If I could've taken the guy to Hebe Jeebies and done ancient Greek songs on the karaoke machine with him until he was able to reverse his life and become mortal again, I would've done it.

Since I couldn't, I had to get his chalice back.

At last, I gave up on the library work. I felt like a failure as I headed home, worried that Monday morning I would be totally unprepared for whatever we faced. Maybe I'd at least catch enough z's the night before.

Turned out, I couldn't even do that.

TWENTY-FOUR

⚓

I BRUSH MY TEETH (IN THE MOST HEROIC WAY POSSIBLE)

After an uneventful weekend, Annabeth broke into my room at 4:30 A.M. Monday morning, which sounds a lot more exciting than it actually was.

I'd been having this weird nightmare about the gods. The Olympians were all sitting around my family's dining table announcing that they were pregnant. Hera was pregnant. Aphrodite was pregnant. Hephaestus was pregnant. Apollo was pretty sure he was having twins. After every announcement, Zeus would raise his Himbo Juice to-go cup and yell, "A toast!" Then all the gods would throw burnt toast at me like we were at a midnight screening of *The Rocky Horror Picture Show*.

I woke to the sound of Annabeth's knife blade sweeping across the lock of my bedroom window. She could have just knocked, but I guess she liked the challenge. She slid the bottom pane up and climbed in from the fire escape.

"But soft," I said, "what light through yonder window breaks?"

She flashed me a smile. "I'm impressed you can quote Shakespeare."

"I can quote SparkNotes." I rubbed my eyes. I still had the smell of burnt toast in my nose. I was really glad I'd woken up before Dream Poseidon could show me his baby bump.

Then I looked down and started to feel self-conscious about the ratty T-shirt I was wearing. I wondered if I had saliva crusted on my chin. As Annabeth had often told me, I drool when I sleep.

"Uh, what's the occasion?" I asked.

Annabeth was wearing cargo pants, a tank top, her backpack, and a pair of running shoes, which made me suspect this wasn't just a social call.

"I couldn't sleep," she said. "Figured we might as well get a head start." She slung her backpack from her shoulder and produced Iris's vial of glowing golden liquid.

"That stuff freaks me out," I said. "It looks like radioactive honey."

"No, it's not radioactive, honey."

"I see what you did there."

She shook the jar, which made it glow brighter. "I wanted to find out more about how concentrated nectar works, so I talked to Juniper."

I sat up. "You went to camp this weekend?"

"Just sent an Iris-message." Annabeth sat on the edge of my bed. "Turns out the Dryadic Coven keeps concentrated nectar in their root cellar for special emergencies."

"The Dryadic Coven? That's a thing?"

I imagined a bunch of ladies in billowy green-and-brown

dresses dancing around a tree hung with healing crystals, like a Stevie Nicks cosplay convention.

Annabeth put a finger to her lips. "You didn't hear about it from me. Apparently, concentrated nectar can heal a nature spirit on the verge of death, but it's risky. One time, this badly burnt oak dryad got revived as a chunk of granite."

I rubbed my eyes. I wondered if I was still asleep, because it seemed like Annabeth was sitting on my bed talking about trees and rocks. "Okay."

"Also, the word *nectar* means *overcoming death*. Did you know that?"

"I'm going back to sleep."

"Wait, this is the important part. Juniper said this stuff is so fragrant that one whiff can put a demigod into a coma."

That got my attention. "Why didn't Iris mention that?"

"She probably didn't even consider it," Annabeth said. "But since we don't have time to go comatose this morning . . ." She dug around in her backpack and brought out a packet of tissues and a jar of menthol rub. "We plug our noses before we uncork this stuff."

"Smart," I said, though I was thinking how great we'd look walking around Greenwich Village with Kleenex tusks sticking out of our nostrils.

"Yeah," Annabeth agreed. "Crisis averted. Anyway, I owe Juniper a favor now."

She looked like she was thinking about how to repay her . . . and whether dryads liked cupcakes.

"How's she doing?" I asked.

Annabeth patted my knee. "You must have given Grover good advice. He apologized to her, spent some quality time with her planting seedlings in the forest. Sounds like they are back on good terms."

"Hey, when it comes to advice on being the perfect boyfriend—"

She laughed, then glanced at the wall self-consciously. "Too loud? I don't want to wake Sally and Paul."

"It's fine," I assured her.

The walls in the apartment were surprisingly thick. And if my mom heard Annabeth in my room, the worst consequence would be that she'd offer my girlfriend a cup of tea.

It's weird what happens when your parents just accept you and support you and assume you will do the right thing. You end up *wanting* to do the right thing. At least that's been my experience, and this is *me* we're talking about. My mom has more reason to worry than most parents. After years of boarding schools, summers at camp, and months fighting monsters on the road, I still wasn't used to being at home full-time, but I had to admit that living with my mom and Paul was a pretty sweet gig.

"Second thoughts?" Annabeth asked me.

I realized she'd been reading my expression. "About what?"

"Leaving New York, with the baby coming and all."

"No. . . . I mean, no. I was just thinking how nice it's been to live at home for a while. And they looked so happy at dinner. I wonder what it'll be like for my mom to have a regular kid."

"I don't think Sally could ever have a regular kid," Annabeth said. "Because she's not regular. Neither is Paul."

"True. The baby's probably going to be born like Batman—no superpowers but still a complete beast with six PhDs."

"Now I'm picturing the kid in a onesie with pointy ears."

"Grover would be pleased."

She snorted. "All I'm saying . . . it's okay if you're feeling conflicted about leaving—"

I leaned over and kissed her. "No conflict. No second thoughts. I told you. I'm not leaving you ever again."

"Okay." She wrinkled her nose. "Although it's fine if you want to leave for a few minutes to brush your teeth. Your breath is a little . . ."

"Hey, you woke me up."

"Which reminds me." She held up her vial of concentrated nectar. "We ought to get going soon."

"It's earlier than early—"

"I know," she said. "But thirty minutes for you to get ready, because you're slow."

"I beg your pardon?"

"Forty-five minutes to make it to Washington Square Park. Then to do our job and get you back in time for school—"

"Ugh with the math."

Annabeth has this magic power where she can look into the future and figure out how long it will take to do certain things. She calls her power "scheduling," which directly overrules my magic power of procrastination.

I went to the bathroom to get ready. Thirty minutes, right. Sure. Quick shower. Grab my clothes. Brush my teeth. Put on my shoes.

It took me thirty-one minutes.

Stupid magical scheduling power.

At five fifteen, we slipped out of the apartment and headed to the train, toward what might be my last chance to find Ganymede's chalice . . . or maybe we wouldn't find Gary, and it would turn out to be just another Monday at school. I honestly wasn't sure which scared me more.

TWENTY-FIVE

⚕

I MEET THE GOBLET GANKER

Grover brought mochi donuts.

Bonus points for the G-man.

The three of us stood under the big white archway at Washington Square Park while we munched our sugary breakfast and scanned our surroundings.

I'd never been to the park so early. The sun was just coming up, pouring rosy light through the streets and washing the brick facades of the buildings around the square. In front of us stretched the main plaza—a giant circle of gray stonework radiating from the central fountain. Annabeth said the design reminded her of a sundial or a wheel. To me, being a born New Yorker, it looked like a massive manhole cover.

The fountain itself wasn't running. In the summertime, it made a great wading pool for kids, but now the basin was dry. I imagined it watching me, thinking, *Oh, great. Here's Percy. Now I'll have to explode or drown a monster or something.* As I may have mentioned, water fixtures don't tend to like me much.

As far as people were concerned, there weren't many

around. A lady was walking her dog down one of the paths. A few commuters hustled across the plaza. A couple of old guys were playing a chess game at one of the tables under the elm trees. The place was about as empty as anywhere in Manhattan ever gets.

"Ready?" Grover asked. He was trying to look brave and determined, but the image was undercut a little by the green sprinkles of matcha in his goatee.

"Let's do it," I said.

I'd eaten the last Cookie Monster donut—obviously the best flavor, being fluorescent blue—so now there was nothing left to do but find Gary.

Annabeth wrapped up the rest of her purple ube mochi, stuck it in her backpack, then passed around the tissues and menthol rub.

"Isn't this what cops do before they examine dead bodies?" Grover asked, plugging up his nostrils.

"Let's not make that comparison," Annabeth suggested. "No dead bodies today, okay?"

"Oh-tay," I said, which was all I could manage with wads of Kleenex up my nose. My eyes watered from the menthol. My throat stung like I was being given mouth-to-mouth resuscitation by a koala, but I supposed it was better than going into a nectar coma.

"Here we go." Annabeth took out her glowing vial and twisted off the cap.

She tipped the vial ever so slightly, and three golden droplets trickled out. Instead of falling, they caught the breeze and floated through the air like soap bubbles. Each one drifted in a different direction.

"That's not helpful," Annabeth observed. "Should we split up?"

"Always a derrible idea," I said.

So that's what we did.

I wasn't too worried about losing Annabeth and Grover, since they could go halfway across the park and still be in my line of sight. Annabeth followed her nectar drop down the main concourse toward the chess tables. Grover's bubble led him cross-country through the trees. Mine wobbled toward the children's play area. I passed a pedestrian hustling along with coffee in her hand, but she gave me a wide berth, as you do when you see a strange kid with tissues hanging out of his nostrils. She didn't seem to notice the glowing nectar. Fortunately, she didn't fall into a coma, either. Maybe the scent didn't work on regular mortals.

As I followed the bouncing ball, I remembered what Grover had said about nature spirits fleeing the park. The place did feel abandoned. No squirrels. No rats. Not even pigeons. Even the trees seemed too quiet, which isn't something you'd notice unless you'd spent time hanging out with dryads. You get used to their comforting presence, like someone humming a lullaby in your ear. When they're gone, you miss them.

The gravel crunched under my feet. The Cookie Monster mochi churned in my stomach. When I reached the edge of the playground, I realized how tranquil every-thing had become. No cars passed on the street. The breeze had died. The tree canopies spread motionless overhead like sheets of green ice.

The nectar bubble drifted toward the play structure. It floated up the climbing chains to the top of the miniature fort, then burst into flames.

Yeah . . . that was probably normal.

I glanced back at my friends.

Grover had stopped next to a big elm tree. His ear was pressed against the trunk as if he were listening for voices. His nectar droplet had vanished.

About fifty yards to his left, Annabeth stood at the first chess table, watching a game. The two old guys were hunched over their board, glowering at the pieces, but neither of them moved a muscle. Annabeth's glowing nec-tar bubble had also disappeared.

Something was wrong.

I wanted to call out to her, to break whatever weird trance she was in, but my voice wouldn't cooperate. The tense silence made me afraid to yell or attract attention.

I felt like something was rewiring my brain, chang-ing the way I perceived time. The last time I'd had this sensation . . . I'd been twelve years old, standing on a beach in Santa Monica, when I first witnessed the power of Kronos.

"It is similar, yes," said a voice behind me.

I turned, reaching for my pen-sword, but I felt like I

was moving through gelatin. Standing on the play structure was an old man . . . or rather, what an old man might look like if he was born old and lived another thousand years.

He was as small as a first grader, his back curved in the shape of a fishing hook. His skin hung off his bones in sagging brown folds like moth-eaten curtains. He wore nothing but a loincloth, leaving me a great view of his bent stick legs, gnarled feet, and concave belly. His head reminded me of a boiled egg that had been allowed to sit and rot for a week. And his face . . .

The man's fleshy nose was webbed with red capillaries . . . the most vibrant color in his whole body. His eyes were milky from cataracts. His mouth looked as if someone had punched in all his teeth with a metal pipe.

"Take a picture," the old man grumbled. "It'll last longer."

I tried to speak. The gelatin air seemed to coat my lungs, making it hard to breathe. I took the tissue plugs out of my nose so I wouldn't suffocate.

"What do you mean?" I croaked.

The old dude rolled his eyes. "I mean pictures last longer than—"

"Not that. What did you mean by *It is similar*?"

"My power," he said. "It's similar to the way Kronos stretches time."

"How did you—"

"Know what you were thinking? Sonny boyo, when

you get to be my age, nothing surprises. Besides, I know who you are, Percy Jackson. I've been watching you."

The hairs rose on the nape of my neck. An old guy in a diaper had been watching me. That wasn't creepy at all.

"I'm guessing you're Gary?"

"Or Geras, if you prefer." He raised a withered hand to stop my follow-up questions. "And, yes, I'm a god. I'll give you a hint what I'm the god of. From my name, you get the word *geriatric*."

My mind raced with all kinds of hideous possibilities. I was facing the god of adult incontinency products, bingo parlors, denture cream, fiber supplements . . . or maybe just yelling at crazy kids to get off your lawn. Then my rattled brain managed to put all those things together into one larger category.

"Oh," I said. "God of old age?"

"Ding, ding." Gary showed off his toothless gums. "Now perhaps you understand why I stole Ganymede's little sippy cup."

He held out his hand. In a flash of light, a ceramic vessel appeared floating above his palm, but it looked more like a flying saucer than a drinking cup. The bowl was wide and shallow with two oversize handles. I was pretty sure my mom had a salad bowl like that.

The exterior gleamed with black-and-gold scenes of the gods at a feast, their silhouettes outlined in threads of Celestial bronze. It was a fancy piece of pottery, but I wasn't sure how anyone could pour nectar out of it.

"The chalice of the gods," I guessed.

I wanted to add that *of course* I understood why Gary had stolen it. Unfortunately, I didn't.

"So . . . since you're already immortal, would the cup make you younger?" I asked. "Or has it been your lifelong dream to serve drinks?"

"Oh, that's disappointing. . . ." Gary closed his fist and the chalice disappeared. "Perhaps I should have started with Annabeth Chase. I understand she's smart."

I couldn't really get angry. If I were looking for someone who could guess my diabolic master plan so I didn't have to do the standard villain monologue, I would have started with Annabeth, too. On the other hand . . .

"Wait a minute," I said. "*You* separated us with the nectar drops."

I glanced across the park. Annabeth was still watching the chess match. Grover was still listening to a tree. They didn't look like they were in immediate danger, but they were moving at super-slow speed, like flies in sap that was rapidly hardening to amber.

"What are you doing to us?" I demanded. "Picking us off one by one? Afraid to take us all at once?"

Gary snorted. "I could turn all three of you into grave dust with a snap of my fingers. Normally I would, because you're trying to spoil my fun. But since Ganymede sent *Percy Jackson* after me . . . well, I thought I would give you a chance. I hoped you of *all* demigods might understand why I took the chalice. If you don't, though, I can just disintegrate you now and move on to your friends. Perhaps they'll do better."

"No!" I yelped—not just because I didn't want to be grave dust, but because I couldn't let him hurt Annabeth or Grover. "I totally get it. Really."

Gary narrowed his eyes. "I don't believe you."

I didn't believe me, either. Curse the smart old guy.

I tried to imagine what Annabeth would do. I wondered what Grover would do. Then, because my brain was weird, I wondered what *I* would do in the situation I was in.

Something in that mass of cerebral seaweed must have clicked, or squished, or at least sloshed around a little.

"You're the god of old age," I said. "And the cup makes mortals immortal."

Gary smirked, nodding at me to go on.

"Which keeps people from aging," I said. "And you don't like that."

"I *hate* that," Gary snarled.

"Right," I said. "Because people are supposed to get old. Not get promoted to godhood like . . ." I thought about Ganymede, all young and handsome and wandering miserably around my school cafeteria, filling people's cups. "You want to humiliate Ganymede to make an example. You figured I would understand, because I once turned down immortality."

Gary gave me a little bow, showing off the dark splotches on his cranium. "Perhaps you are not a total fool after all."

"Thanks," I said. "My goal for the week was not to be a total fool."

"Ganymede has no business being a god!" Gary said. "Any object that grants humans immortality is odious and wrong. You are all meant to wither and die and return to dust. That is your purpose!"

"Yay for purpose."

"You were the first demigod in millennia to turn down immortality," Gary said. "I respect that. You get me."

"This has been a nice bonding experience," I said. "I think you've proven your point. Can I have the cup back now?"

Gary glowered. "You can't be serious. Why would you complete this foolish quest? Walk away! Let Ganymede be punished! Let the gods lose their precious chalice so they have one less way to pass on the curse of immortality to others!"

"I totally would," I said. "Except I need a letter of recommendation for college. And I promised Ganymede. Besides, do you really think he is the one to punish? He didn't ask to get kidnapped by Zeus, right?"

"Oh, please!" Gary said. "You think eternal youth and immortality make him the victim here?"

"I mean . . . have you seen the guy? He's a nervous wreck."

Gary folded his withered arms. "I'm disappointed, Percy Jackson. If you insist on helping Ganymede, I suppose I was wrong about you. Grave dust it is."

"Hold on!" I squeaked. Sometimes when I'm in imminent danger of death, my Mickey Mouse voice comes out. "Look, I get why you're angry. But seeing as we have common ground with the whole *mortals shouldn't be gods* thing, isn't there some way we can reach a deal?"

Gary studied me. The milky splotches drifted across his eyes like clouds on some alien planet.

"Perhaps . . ." His sly tone made me sorry I'd asked. "How about I give you one chance to win the cup? You should feel honored, Percy Jackson. In the history of humankind, I have only made this offer to one other hero."

"Hercules," I guessed, because the answer is almost always Hercules.

Gary nodded. "You must defeat me in wrestling. If *you* win, I will give you the chalice. If I win . . . you will fulfill your purpose sooner than expected, and I will turn you into a pile of powdered bone. Do we have an agreement?"

TWENTY-SIX

I NEGOTIATE THE TERMS OF MY DISINTEGRATION

In the demigod business, we call this a *trick question*.

If I refused, I would get zapped to dust. If I agreed, I'd have to wrestle an old guy. *Then* I'd get zapped to dust. . . .

Looking at Gary, I found it hard to focus—and not just because of his filthy loincloth or his missing teeth. His presence made me feel claustrophobic in my own body. Blood roared in my ears. My hands turned sweaty. I had to fight a sense of panic, like my flesh had already started to crumble.

I understood why even a goddess like Iris might be scared of this guy. Immortality was one thing. Being old forever . . . that was something else. Other gods preferred to look young and beautiful. Gary owned his age, every millennium of it. I imagined that when the Olympians looked at him, they saw just how ancient they really were. He was like the painting in that story about the guy who never ages, but his portrait does. Earl Grey? No. That's a kind of tea. Whatever, the story creeped me out.

None of that helped me come up with an answer.

Gary was staring at me expectantly, so I fell back on my demigod tool of last resort: procrastination.

"I have conditions," I said.

Gary tilted his wrinkly head. "Medical conditions?"

"No. Conditions for fighting you. First, if I lose, you only kill me. You leave my friends alone."

"Old Age never leaves anyone alone."

"You know what I mean. You don't dust them *now*. You let them go."

"Acceptable."

"Next . . ." I faltered. *Come on, Percy. There has to be a next.* "When you say I have to defeat you, what would that look like? You're a god. I can't kill you."

"Obviously, young fool," Gary scoffed. "If you can bend even one of my knees to the ground, I will consider that sufficient. I, on the other hand, will win when I flatten your face against the pavement. That is more than fair."

"That was the first word that came to my mind," I said. *"Fair."*

"Anything else?"

"Yes." I racked my brain, wondering what other demands I should make. Bottled water? A bowl of only blue M&M's in my dressing room? I needed Annabeth here to help me think.

Oh. Right. That was a thing I could ask for.

"Let my friends go," I told Gary.

"You already asked that."

"No," I said. "I mean let them go from whatever

you're doing to them right now." I gestured at Annabeth, who was still frozen at the chess game.

"I just slowed them down," said Gary. "Old Age does that to everyone."

"I want them here," I said. "To say good-bye, if nothing else. Whatever happens to me, I want them to see it."

"This is not a spectator sport," he grumbled, which was the first time anyone had ever said that about wrestling.

"Do you want to fight me or not?" I asked.

I felt like I could risk saying that, because the gleam in Gary's eyes told me he was eager to push my face into the pavement. He wasn't the first person who'd ever felt that way.

"Fine," he grunted.

He snapped his bony fingers. Annabeth and Grover both unfroze. They turned in my direction, removed their super-attractive menthol Kleenex tusks, and ran toward the playground.

By the time Annabeth reached us, she had drawn her knife. Grover was wielding a black-sesame mochi donut like a shuriken.

"What's going on?" Grover demanded, hefting his pastry like he was ready to go full donut assassin.

Annabeth sized up Gary, then cursed under her breath. "Geras, I presume? I should have known we were fighting Old Age."

Gary chuckled. "And I should have spoken to you first, young lady. You're clearly the brains of this operation."

"It's cool," I told my friends. "We've come to an agreement."

Annabeth scowled at the god. "Let me guess. A wrestling match? Excuse me. I need a word with my client."

She grabbed my arm and dragged me to the other end of the playground. Behind us, I heard Gary ask Grover, "You going to eat that?"

Annabeth gripped my shoulders. "Percy, you can't do this."

"Hey, it isn't something I *want* to do."

"You can't beat him."

I wanted to argue that this was our best shot. It was a lot better than all three of us getting turned into grave dust. But I could tell from Annabeth's expression that she had already run the angles. She was way ahead, as usual.

"Hercules wrestled Old Age to a standstill," she continued. "That's the *only* time Geras has been forced to call a draw. Beating him is impossible."

"What was Hercules's secret?"

"No secret. Just brute force."

I rubbed my biceps and tried not to feel offended. I wasn't weak, exactly, but superstrength wasn't on my list of powers. I got *breathe underwater* and *talk to horses* instead, which weren't so useful in a Greenwich Village playground smackdown.

"There has to be another way," I said. "Your mom told me one time at the Hoover Dam, there's always a way out—"

"For those clever enough to find it," she said. "Yeah, I know. But this . . . Geras is a force of nature. He's inevitable. You can't fight Old Age."

Unless you're immortal, I thought.

But that was exactly why Geras had stolen the chalice. It let you cheat the system. And he wasn't wrong about immortality being a curse. The gods were the most messed-up people I'd ever met. They'd had centuries to work out their problems. They just didn't. Sure, they changed their clothes and modernized their lifestyles once in a while, but at heart, they were still exactly who they had been back in the Bronze Age.

A heavy feeling settled in my gut. . . . I wasn't sure if it was despair, desperation, or donut. Was I on the wrong side of this fight? If I walked away and let Gary keep the chalice, Ganymede might get shamed and exiled from Olympus. Would that be so bad? The gods would have to pour their own drinks. They'd have one less way of making new immortals. Ganymede could get a job at Himbo Juice. Maybe Gary would even write me a recommendation letter instead, praising me for embracing my inner cranky old man.

But Ganymede had chosen me for this quest. Putting aside the fact that every god chose me for every quest, I felt obligated to keep my promise. I remembered how nervous the poor cupbearer had looked at Himbo Juice; the way he'd ducked under the table when he thought the golden-eagle-flavored smoothie of Zeus might swoop down to get him.

Yes, he was traumatized and miserable. Maybe he would've been better off getting kicked back into the mortal world. But he hadn't asked me to free him from Mount Olympus. He'd asked me to retrieve the cup. If I chose to wreck his life for his own good, without his permission, I wasn't much better than Zeus. I believed everyone should have the right to ruin their own life without anyone else ruining it for them.

"I need to do this," I told Annabeth. "I think I can find a way. . . ."

She studied my face, maybe wondering whether she should try to knock some sense into me with the hilt of her dagger. Finally, she sighed. "It has to be your call. Just . . . don't underestimate him because of how he looks, Percy."

It made me uneasy when she called me Percy instead of Seaweed Brain. It meant we were *way* beyond the point where she needed to criticize how dumb I was being.

We marched back to the play structure. Gary was gumming a Fruity Pebbles donut while Grover looked on in horror. The rainbow sprinkles around the god's mouth somehow made him look even older.

"Ready to say your good-byes?" Gary asked me.

I shook my head. "No good-byes yet. Let's confirm the rules of engagement. You and I wrestle one-on-one. You push my face to the ground, I lose, get turned to dust, et cetera. I force one of your knees to the pavement, you give me the chalice and leave us in peace. Either way, when this is over, my friends go free."

"That is the deal," Gary agreed. "Although, since you're going to lose, most of those terms are . . . What's the word? *Moot*."

"You're moot," I grumbled, because I am deadly with those quick clap-backs.

"Or . . ." Grover said, "you could trade the chalice for these leftover donuts." He flapped the lid of his box, wafting the scent of mochi toward the god. "Then we can all go our separate ways. I still have two more black sesame and a pistachio."

Gary seemed to consider this. In my book, mochi donuts would be pretty close to magic chalices in any post-apocalypse barter system. I thought Grover might actually be onto something. He was about to make my life much easier and also longer.

Then Gary shook his head. "We'll stick to the original arrangement."

"Fine," I muttered. "When do we start?"

I didn't even have time to breathe. Suddenly Gary was on my back, his hands like steel clamps on my shoulders, his legs wrapped around my rib cage, his heels digging into me like I was an uncooperative horse. My knees buckled. The guy weighed a ton. I threw out my hands and broke my fall, my face only inches from the asphalt.

His sour breath made my head swim. He said in my ear, "Oh, we can start whenever you like."

TWENTY-SEVEN

MY DYING WORDS ARE
SUPER EMBARRASSING

I yearned for the good old days when I'd had to fight one-on-one with the war god Ares—whaling on me with his massive sword/baseball bat, unleashing giant wild boars to trample me, glaring at me with his nuclear eyes.

Yes, those were simpler times.

Now I was locked in a wrestle-to-the-death contest with Gary the diapered god of halitosis.

And I was losing.

I tried to push against him, to force myself upright. It was like pushing against the roof of a tunnel. I twisted sideways, using his own weight to sling him off my back. I crawled away, gasping for breath, and barely had time to get to my feet before he slammed into me again, wrapping his arm around my neck. He pulled me into a side headlock, forcing my face dangerously close to his armpit. I really wished I hadn't taken those menthol tissues out of my nostrils.

"Oh, no," Gary cackled. "You can't run from Old Age."

"Technically not true!" Grover shouted. "Exercises like running can add years to your life!"

Gary snarled, "Quiet, satyr. No interference!"

"It's not interference," Annabeth chimed in. "It's commentary! Every wrestling match has commentary."

Their distraction bought me a few seconds, which I'd like to say I used to formulate a master plan. Instead, my thought process was: *Oh gods I'm going to die help ow armpit armpit.*

This falls short of the criteria for *master plan.*

I tried to shuffle sideways. Gary held me fast. I pushed forward with all my weight. I leaned back, hoping to pull him off-balance. Even though the guy was half my size, he didn't budge.

"Going somewhere?" he asked.

With his free hand, he punched me in the ribs. The sound that came out of my throat would have alerted any walruses within a two-mile radius that I was looking for companionship.

"Flag on the play!" Grover yelled. "Ten-yard penalty!"

"No body blows!" Annabeth agreed. "That's not wrestling!"

"Shut up!" Gary complained.

While his attention was divided, I managed to twist out of his headlock. I wrapped my arms around his chest and squeezed with all my might. I tugged and pushed, but I just couldn't budge the guy.

He laughed. "Having fun?"

I didn't have the energy to answer. At least he wasn't smashing my face into the pavement yet. As long as I amused him, he seemed content to let me make an absolute fool of myself. Fortunately, that *was* on my list of superpowers.

There had to be a trick to beating this dude—something aside from superstrength, which was a ridiculous power only possessed by ridiculous Hercules, who was ridiculous. Maybe Gary had an Off button. Maybe he was afraid of something I could use against him. . . .

What fought off old age? Antioxidants. Crossword puzzles. Fiber supplements. I realized I was getting delirious from the pain and the old-person odors. My teacher Chiron had once told me that in a life-threatening situation, the most important thing is to stay calm. Once you get into fight-or-flight mode, you are too scared to think properly. That will get you killed.

Unfortunately, I was not calm. I couldn't fight or flee. And I was fresh out of fiber supplements.

I tried my ace in the hole. I summoned my anger, channeled it into the pit of my stomach, and reached out for the unlimited power of the sea. We were in Manhattan, just above sea level, bracketed by major rivers, right next to the Atlantic. Surely I could draw on my father's might, summon that great force to fight for me!

I unleashed a primal scream.

Halfway across Washington Square Park, a single manhole cover shot into the air. A geyser sprayed the tops of the trees, then fizzled out.

"That was impressive," Gary said. "Now, shall we end this?"

He plucked me off his chest like I was a tick, then threw me across the playground.

"Percy!" Annabeth yelled.

Her tone of concern was the only thing that saved me. As I sailed through the air, Annabeth's voice electrified every molecule in my body. My senses went into overdrive. Instead of slamming into the play structure, I twisted in midair, grabbed one of the bars, swung around, and landed on my feet. My shoulders throbbed. I'd probably pulled my arms out of their sockets, but I hadn't broken my back, or, you know, died.

I staggered forward. Little globs of light swam in my eyes.

Gary scowled at Annabeth and Grover. "If either of you interferes again, I will declare this match null and void. I will turn all three of you into desiccated husks!"

Annabeth crouched, her dagger in hand. Grover gripped her arm, trying to keep her from leaping into the fight. Not that she could hurt Old Age with a knife, but that wouldn't stop her from trying.

As much as I appreciated the sentiment, I couldn't let her take the risk.

"Over here, diaper man!" I yelled. "I'm your opponent, not her."

Gary turned, narrowing his eyes. "So you are."

Then he charged.

Well . . . I say *charged*. It was more of a determined hobble.

I had time to think, *A plan would be really good now.*

Then he was on me. He tackled me and pushed me backward—right into a tetherball pole. My spine creaked, but the pole kept me upright, even gave me some leverage.

I locked my hands around Gary's biceps. My arms groaned. My vision dissolved into black and white strobe flashes. I managed to push Gary forward one step, then two. I was fueled not by strength but by desperation—and my rally didn't last.

Gary clamped his bony fingers around my shoulders. I am here to tell you: shoulders have a lot of nerve endings. Gary found them all. I screamed as he pushed me back against the tetherball pole. The metal began to bend.

"You have lasted longer than most," the old man conceded. "It was a good try."

A good try, I thought, my mind drowning in pain.

Awesome. I couldn't win, but at least I'd get a participation award from Old Age. After I dissolved into dust, Annabeth could frame the certificate and keep it in her dorm room when she went to New Rome University by herself.

My legs trembled. Pressed between Gary and the pole, my rib cage felt like an overtightened piano frame, ready to snap and implode.

I thought about how much pain I was going to cause Annabeth. I'd promised I would never leave her again. When we left this life, I wanted it to be together, many years from now, when we were old and gray. . . .

Wait a minute.

I felt some strength come back into my legs. I was still in agony, but maybe I was getting crushed a little more slowly?

I remembered something my buddy Jason once told me. In a moment of crisis, he'd had a dream that he was an old man, married to his girlfriend, Piper, with a bunch of grandchildren running around. He hadn't taken the dream as an iron-clad glimpse of the future. When it comes to mortal lives, the Fates never hand out money-back guarantees. But he told me that wasn't the point. When he'd needed it most, that vision had made him feel like there was a way forward—something to live for and fight for.

I dug my fingers harder into Gary's arms. He grunted in surprise.

I thought about a conversation I'd had with Paul a few months back. I'd teased him about how he was getting more gray hair every year. He'd said, "Hey, getting older sucks, but it beats the alternative." I didn't really get that at the time. Were the only choices really dying or getting old?

When you're a demigod, you worry a lot about staying alive. You hardly ever think about old age. I'd been so focused on just making it out of high school, becoming an adult . . . but maybe that wasn't the ultimate goal. Getting old might be scary and difficult. It involved things I didn't want to think about, like arthritis and varicose veins and hearing aids. But if you grew older with people you loved, wasn't that better than any other alternative?

I glanced at Annabeth and Grover. We'd been through so much together. I imagined Annabeth with silver hair and wrinkles, chuckling as she called me Seaweed Brain for the four millionth time in our lives. I imagined Grover with tufts of white hair coming out of his ears, his back hunched as he leaned on a cane, bleating as he complained about his aching hooves, then maybe taking a nap on a bench in our beachside garden while I sat next to him, resting my aching bones as I watched the waves and smelled the sea air. Aching bones weren't hard for me to imagine. Actually, the *rest* wasn't hard to imagine, either.

Gary expected me to wrestle him. And unless I died young, I couldn't beat Old Age. But what if I embraced him?

It was a ridiculous idea. Stop fighting and just hug it out with Geriatric Gary?

My knees started wobbling again. I had maybe one second before he crushed me against the tetherball pole.

I loosened my grip and wrapped my arms around the god.

Then I said what I was pretty sure would go down in history as the dumbest last words ever: "I love you, bro."

TWENTY-EIGHT

IT STARTS RAINING TOYS

Gary froze.

I hugged him so hard he hiccupped.

"What is going on?" His voice quavered as he loosened his grip on my shoulders. He was so surprised, I probably could have pushed him down onto one knee, but somehow, I knew that was the wrong move. I just kept hugging him.

I never knew my mortal grandparents. (I suppose Kronos was technically my grandpa, but I tried not to think about that.)

Now I imagined what it would've been like to know my mom's parents. They'd died when she was really young. In fact, when they'd died, they had been younger than my mom was now. That kind of blew my mind. Did they laugh with the same kind of joy my mom did? Had she inherited her love of cooking or writing from them? Did they hum as they walked in the rain without an umbrella, or was that just a Sally thing? If they hadn't died so young, they could've been there for my mom during her hardest years. They could have gotten to know me. Maybe Geras wasn't such a bad guy, despite his questionable loincloth fashion choices.

As I hugged him, I imagined that I was hugging my grandparents and also embracing the idea of growing older and looking back on a great life, thinking, *Well, we made it. Yeah, we'll die someday—maybe soon—but we had a pretty good run, didn't we?*

I pictured myself holding hands with Annabeth when we were both wrinkly and frail, and I still looked into her eyes and loved her as much as ever. I imagined ruffling Grover's gray hair when he fell asleep on a garden bench, telling him, "Wake up, there, G-man. Food's ready!" I imagined us sitting around a table together, sharing a good meal and laughing about all the crazy things we'd done in our lives. Including that time I wrestled the god of old age in Washington Square Park.

I ignored Gary's musty smell, his baggy skin, his liver spots and weird hairs, and I just embraced him like an old friend. A *very* old, past-his-expiration-date friend.

It was better than the alternative.

Living fast, dying young, and leaving a good-looking corpse is a cool-sounding philosophy—until it's *your* corpse people are talking about. Gary pushed me against the tetherball pole one last time, but I guess his heart wasn't in it.

He relaxed, patted me on the back, then put his head on my shoulder. He started to tremble. I heard a single sniffle. Was the god crying? Was he . . . smearing godly snot on my shoulder?

I didn't know. Still, I didn't push him away.

I peeked at Annabeth and Grover. The satyr looked stunned, but Wise Girl was smiling faintly. Of course she got what I was doing. She was quick to recognize a good strategy. And that twinkle of appreciation in her eyes was the best look I could ever hope for. It meant she was proud of me.

Finally, Gary disentangled himself from my hug. He stepped back and evaluated me anew. His eyes swam with reddish-brown tears. His jawline quivered. I couldn't tell if he wanted to hit me or hug me again.

"Why?" he asked.

"I figured I'll be wrestling with you my whole life," I said. "And I'm okay with that. I just wanted you to know." I took a shaky breath. "But if you really feel like the end of my life should be right now, we can keep throwing each other around the playground."

Gary grunted. His expression was a mix of surprise, irritation, and maybe a little respect.

"Technically, I was throwing *you* around," he said. "I was winning."

I didn't respond. It seemed like the smart choice.

"Old Age is *never* embraced," he muttered. "Do you know the last time I had a hug?" He stared into the sky as if trying to remember. His sad expression reminded me of old people I'd seen in nursing homes, gazing into the distance, trying to figure out where their lives had gone, where their loved ones were, how they'd become so alone.

"So what now?" I asked.

He frowned. "Old Age is patient. I hate that about myself, but I almost never rush to end someone's life. And you're right . . . ending your life now, at age sixteen . . ."

"Seventeen," I corrected.

Grover cleared his throat. *Shut up!*

"Seventeen," Gary echoed. The number seemed to taste bitter in his mouth. "No. It isn't right. This isn't your time."

He tilted his head, turning his liver spots to the morning sunlight. "You really wouldn't drink from the chalice, would you?"

"Nah," I said. "I kinda want to live a whole life, you know? Even the tough stuff. Plus, I've seen what happens to people who are turned into gods." I thought about poor Ganymede, frozen as a beautiful teen, but stuck with all his anxiety, self-doubt, and fears forever. No thank you.

"Interesting." Gary studied my friends, then turned back to me. "I look forward to wrestling you for many years to come, Percy Jackson. Do not think I will go easy on you, just because you have impressed me now."

"I'll keep exercising," I promised. "Do a bunch of crossword puzzles."

Gary curled his lip. "We were having a nice moment. Don't ruin it." He snapped his fingers, and the chalice of the gods appeared, floating and gleaming in the air between us. All it needed was an angelic chorus to complete the effect.

"Take it," Gary said. "I suppose it should stay on

Mount Olympus, among those fools who have already turned their backs on Old Age. You give me hope, Percy Jackson, that not everyone is like them." He sniffed before grumbling, "Crossword puzzles . . ."

Then he poofed into a gray cloud of talcum powder.

I managed to catch the chalice just before it hit the pavement. It felt as heavy as a bowling ball, which did not do wonders for my aching arms.

"Ow," I said.

"You did it!" Grover did a little goat dance of relief. "Hugging him? That was *really* risky!"

"It was perfect," Annabeth said. She marched up and kissed me. "You know what? I think you'll make a handsome old man. I hope one day we'll get the chance to find out. But I'm glad that isn't today."

I smiled. The smell of Gary lingered on my clothes. I was weary and sore and felt like I'd aged a few decades. But those mental pictures also lingered . . . the images of growing older with the people I loved, with my best friends. And that made me feel like I could handle the aches and pains. Maybe the trade-off was worth it.

"So, you think we can send Ganymede an Iris-message?" I hefted the chalice. "I don't want to keep this in my locker until Sunday."

Annabeth looked like she was about to say something, but just then, a Hula-Hoop fell out of the sky.

It was pink with blue stripes and sparkles baked into the plastic. It hit the pavement with a jolly rattling *whack,* bounced twenty feet into the air, then came down again and rolled across the playground, wobbling to a stop like a flipped coin.

Even in a weird morning, this seemed weird.

"Um . . ." I said.

Annabeth walked over to the hoop. She nudged it. When it did not explode or turn into a monster, she picked it up. She looked at the clouds, but no other objects fell from the sky.

"This is a symbol of Ganymede," she said.

"The Hula-Hoop?" Grover asked.

"Well . . . the hoop. It's been a kids' toy for thousands of years. It's a symbol of his eternal youth."

I shuddered. "Yeah, that doesn't make Zeus's abduction of him one bit less creepy. And you think what, Ganymede tossed the hoop off Mount Olympus?"

Since these days Olympus hovered over the Empire State Building, it wasn't such a crazy idea. A good godly throw could probably reach Washington Square Park, no problem. But why?

Annabeth examined the hoop more closely. "Hold on."

She found a section of paper wrapped around one part of the hoop. I had assumed it was a label or something, but Annabeth peeled it off and started to read.

"It's a distress call," she announced. "Ganymede says he's stuck on Olympus, and he needs the cup immediately. He says . . ."

Her face fell. "Oh, gods. Zeus isn't waiting for Sunday to have a feast."

I gulped, remembering what Ganymede had said about Zeus being unpredictable. "So . . . what, he's having one tonight?"

"Worse than that," Annabeth said. "Zeus is having his mom over for a family get-together right now. They're having *brunch*."

TWENTY-NINE

⟁

I TEETER ON THE PRECIPICE
OF MOUNT BRUNCH

Is there anything more terrifying than brunch?

It's an abomination among meals, a Frankenstein hybrid of clashing food choices. It evokes nightmares of soft jazz bands, kids in itchy dress clothes, ladies in strange hats, lipstick smears on champagne glasses, and the smell of croque monsieur. I am sorry. I don't eat food with a name that translates as *Mr. Crunchy*.

Even the word *brunch* gives me the willies. (See, I almost said *heebie-jeebies*, but we don't use that term anymore in this household.) Brunch is the most *non*-elegant term for something that is supposed to be elegant. It's like saying, *Let's get all dressed up and go to a quack-splat.* Like . . . why?

But now I had found something even worse than a mortal brunch: a brunch among the gods. On a Monday morning, no less. And during regular breakfast hours, but, oh, no, they had to make it a brunch anyway.

Also, Zeus was having his *mom* over? I'd never met Rhea, the Titan queen, and I wasn't anxious to find out what the gods served her for her special morning meal. Probably poached demigod on toast with demigod-tear mimosas.

I hefted the chalice of the gods. "I don't suppose we can send this Hermes Express?"

Annabeth frowned. "Percy . . ."

"Don't they have one-hour delivery in Manhattan?"

"Ganymede needs it *now*. And *you* have to bring it. It's—"

"My job." I sighed. I was familiar with the rules of quest completion, which included white-glove delivery by the demigod in charge. It was looking increasingly unlikely that I would make it to school in time for my first-period quiz.

"Fine," I said. "Any suggestions on how I can sneak into Olympus and infiltrate a godly brunch?"

"Um, actually?" Grover blinked like what he was about to say would be painful for me to hear. "I might have an idea."

The easy part was getting a taxi uptown. Normally I wouldn't have sprung for a cab, but after Grover and I said good-bye to Annabeth, it seemed like the fastest way to get to the Empire State Building, and also the fastest way to avoid Annabeth's wrath.

With great reluctance, she had lent me her New York Yankees cap. She *never* does that. The invisibility hat was a gift from her mom, so borrowing it just wasn't something you did without a really good reason. It would've been like me letting another demigod use Riptide in a fight. Nope.

But when Grover pleaded that it was the only way, Annabeth had handed it over. She glared at me and said,

"You *will* bring it back. Good luck. Don't die." Then she ran off to start her school day, since her campus was only a couple of blocks away.

In the cab, Grover tapped his hooves nervously on the floorboard as he explained the rest of his plan. I wasn't too worried about the cabdriver listening in, because this was New York. A plan to break into Mount Olympus was not the craziest thing any cabbie would hear on any given day. Also, Grover had insisted on bringing the Hula-Hoop in the cab with us, and I had a giant chalice in my lap, so we were already unreliable narrators.

"A cloud nymph," I said, just to make sure I'd heard him correctly.

"Yeah." He glanced behind us, though as far as I could tell, we weren't being followed.

"Is this the same nymph who gave you the info on Washington Square Park?" I asked.

"No, no. But cloud nymphs, man . . . they're like school secretaries. They know everyone and everything. This one, Naomi—she's been dating Maron for the past few months. She works in the kitchens of Zeus's palace. If you can get to the side entrance, she should be able to slip you inside."

I shivered. Maron was one of Grover's fellow Cloven Council elders—a nice enough goat dude, but he was only slightly below Gary on the weird-old-man spectrum. The idea of him having a dating profile on Satyr-er was not something I wanted to ponder.

I curled Annabeth's hat between my hands. "I don't suppose the invisibility cap will fool the gods?"

"Not likely," Grover said. "The cap is to fool any spirits or minor gods you might come across. As long as you're not waving your arms and screaming in their faces, you should be invisible to them. But the Olympians themselves? You'd need Hades's helm of darkness for that. The best Annabeth's cap might do is make you look, I don't know, unimportant?"

"Perfect," I grumbled. I wasn't sure how Grover knew this much about Annabeth's hat, but since he was telling me bad news, I figured he was probably right on target. "So I get to the side door of the palace kitchen as fast as possible."

"You do the special knock."

"*Shave and a haircut,*" I said. "Because that is a knock no one would ever use."

"When Naomi opens the door, tell her Grover sent you. And you need her help."

"Okay . . ." Why were my hands trembling? Oh, right, I'd just had a wrestling match with Old Age. I was exhausted. Also, I was about to sneak into an Olympus palace uninvited, where several major gods were founding members of the We Hate Percy Jackson Club. "Then I just have to figure out how to get the cup to Ganymede."

"Right."

We pulled up in front of the Empire State Building. *Wow, that was disappointingly fast.* Looking at the black marble entrance, which I'd gone through too many times, I suddenly thought of another problem.

"What about the sentry guy at the front desk?" I asked. "He's not going to let me go up to Olympus unannounced. Will the Yankees cap work on him?"

"Definitely not," Grover said. "You'll need a distraction. That's me."

He paid the cabbie and got out with his Hula-Hoop. I scooted out after him, lugging the chalice.

"When I start doing my thing," Grover continued, "you slip around to the elevator banks and get to the six hundredth floor. Come on!"

I wasn't sure what Grover's "thing" was, but we'd been friends long enough that I figured I would know when the time was right. Grover could be super distracting when he wanted to be . . . and I was an expert on getting distracted.

I put on Annabeth's cap. Even after I adjusted it to the biggest size, it didn't fit my big head, but it still seemed to do its job. I looked down at my body and saw a vague smoky outline where Percy Jackson used to be. Suddenly I felt like I had termites swarming all over my skin. Annabeth had never told me that her hat generated a bad case of the creepy-crawlies. No wonder she only used it when she had to. Leave it to Athena to make a magical gift with a built-in disincentive.

Inside, the lobby was mostly empty. Ever since they'd moved the tourist lines over to the West 34th Street entrance a few years ago, the Fifth Avenue entrance was a lot calmer, and today it was too early for much foot traffic. The usual guards stood by the doors. A few office workers stumbled toward the elevators, but that was it.

The dark marble walls were probably supposed to feel majestic and grand, but they always reminded me too much of Mount Othrys, the Titans' headquarters. All that gloomy stone closed in on me, weighing on my chest like a hug from Gary. I wondered if the Olympians had designed the building's lobby that way on purpose, so when you got to the magical six hundredth floor and stepped out into the clouds, you would be dazzled by the gleaming towers and temples of Olympus. That seemed like a Zeus thing to do. *See how much prettier we are? We must be the good guys!*

To the right of the main reception desk, the sentry guy I'd dealt with before was kicking back, reading a book as usual. His appearance never seemed to change, and he always read really thick novels. To me, those were two indications that he might not be human.

His security-card lanyard dangled from the arm of his chair. I knew from past experience that I'd need the card to access the special god-evator, but even invisible, even if Grover provided a distraction, I didn't see how I could grab it without the sentry guy noticing.

Then Grover stepped into the middle of the lobby and did his thing.

He pulled out his panpipes, yelled "Hey, folks!" and began to hula-hoop.

I knew satyrs could climb and caper. I did not know

they were absolute demons at the Hula-Hoop. Grover shook his wool-maker. The sacred hoop of Ganymede lit up, flashing and sparkling as Grover moved it up and down his body, looping it around one leg, then the other. He put his panpipes to his lips and blasted out the chorus of "Get Lucky."

The regular security guards' mouths fell open. A commuter dropped a full cup of coffee on the floor. The sentry guy put down his book and rose from his chair.

Then I remembered I was supposed to be using this moment to do something other than stare at Grover.

As the sentry guy came around the reception desk, telling Grover, "Sir, you can't perform in here," I skirted around the edge of the lobby, cradling the chalice under one arm like a football. I grabbed the key card and made a dash for the elevators.

I mashed the Up button. I waited for what seemed like forever, sure that the sentry would chase me down, or alarms would go off and vicious harpies would appear to drag me to the dungeon. (Does the Empire State Building have a dungeon? Probably, right?)

Finally, the black-and-silver doors slid open. I slipped inside, inserted my stolen card, and hit the button for the six hundredth floor. Up I went, to the allegedly soothing sounds of "I Got You, Babe."

I hoped Grover would be okay. I wasn't sure what the penalty was for playing "Get Lucky" while hula-hooping in the Empire State Building's lobby, but it was probably severe. Annabeth and Grover had done their best to help me. Now it was up to me. I couldn't fail after all we'd been through. Could I?

The doors opened with a cheerful *ding!* that seemed to say, *Why, yes, you absolutely can fail! Have a nice day!*

I stepped out onto the floating stone bridge that connected the elevator bank to the city of Olympus. There it stood, just as I remembered: a severed mountaintop wreathed in clouds, domed palaces and terraced gardens carved into its steep sides—an entire unearthly city floating over Midtown like *Nothing to see here; move along.*

The chalice grew heavier in my arms. It seemed to tug me forward, as if sensing thirsty gods who needed a refill. I hoped I wasn't going to have a Frodo moment, where I got to the threshold of Mount Brunch with my magic item and then, instead of handing it over, became visible, yelled *Ha-ha! The cup is mine!* and drank the immortality-flavored Kool-Aid.

Zeus would probably make me the minor god of canapés. Annabeth would be so mad.

I shook off that thought.

Somewhere below in the mortal world, church bells were chiming, marking the hour of eight o'clock. That was an ungodly early hour for brunch, so I figured it was exactly when the gods would have it. I had to hurry. I took off down the path, leaping over gaps in the stone bridge and praying I could get the chalice to Ganymede before Zeus called for a round of demigod-tear mimosas.

THIRTY

Ψ

I INFILTRATE THE LAIR OF
LIGHTNING GOD 3000

Sprinting to Mount Olympus sounded cool and heroic, until I got halfway there and realized I still had like a quarter mile to run with a bowling-ball chalice. By the time I reached the other end of the bridge, I was sweating and gasping. I imagined somewhere Gary was laughing at me and reminiscing about how, when he was a kid, they ran barefoot uphill five miles to Olympus and they liked it.

Twice, I stopped to catch my breath, hugging the side of the road while a group of Olympus-dwellers passed by. I wasn't sure what they were—minor gods? nature spirits?—but they didn't seem to notice me. They just drifted past in their shiny golden robes, tittering and chatting in ancient Greek and basically looking like they lived inside a permanent "supernatural beauty" camera filter.

Annabeth's cap must have been doing its job. I was either invisible to the locals or appeared too unimportant to mess with. That was good, because the longer I wore the hat, the worse the itchy sensation got. My skin felt like it was baking into crispy pork rind. I wondered how

Annabeth dealt with this, and also whether Olympus had any pharmacies that sold cortisone cream.

At least the Olympian streets weren't busy. A couple of chariots were in line at the drive-through window of Sagittarius Coffee. A Hephaestus-made steampunk rhinoceros thing was trundling along the street, power-washing the cobblestones with blasts of steam from its snout. In the park gazebo, a sign read OPEN MIC HOT POETRY WITH ERATO! TONIGHT ONLY! But at the moment, the gardens were empty except for a few pigeons. (Because yes, even Mount Olympus has pigeons.)

I followed Grover's directions to the side entrance of Zeus's palace: Left at the big white oak tree, follow the bed of lilies until I found the two poplar trees. Take a right and look for the wall of jasmine. When your best friend is a satyr, you learn a lot about trees and plants. That's how they see the world, so it's also how they give directions.

The chalice helped, pulling me along ever more insistently the closer we got to Ganymede. At least, I hoped that was where it was leading me, and not to the nearest godly high school cafeteria so I could top off everyone's beverages.

I ended up in an alley at the base of a tall cliff. Far above rose the foundations of an enormous white palace—Chez Zeus, I presumed. Sure enough, the wall in front of me was covered with flowering jasmine, except for a small door inlaid with fancy bronze designs. Even the alleys are high-class on Mount Olympus.

I did the *shave and a haircut* knock.

The door creaked open. The woman who poked her head out had a hairdo like a tornado funnel. Her eyes were gray and stormy, her face ageless, her scent like oncoming rain. She couldn't have been more clearly a cloud nymph if she'd had a name tag that said HELLO! MY NAME IS CLOUD NYMPH.

"Naomi?" I guessed.

"You brought donuts?" she asked.

"Oh, um . . . no."

"You smell like mochi donuts."

"That's because . . . Never mind. I'm actually a friend of Maron's."

She snorted. "No, you're not. Maron doesn't have friends."

"True. But I *am* a friend of Grover Underwood's. He said—"

"Come in." She grabbed my arm and pulled me into the kitchen.

I'm not sure what I expected in a godly kitchen. If I'm being honest, I'd never considered whether the gods even *had* kitchens. I mean, they could snap their fingers and create anything they wanted. Why go to the fuss of having someone cook for you?

Now, as I looked at all the nymphs rushing from oven to stovetop, pulling cloud-stuff out of the air and mixing it into their soups and pies like strands of cotton candy, I realized that the gods would *want* servants fussing around, making things for them, the same way they liked it when mortals burned offerings. It was all about being noticed, attended, *catered to*. Gods ate the spotlight more than they ate nectar and ambrosia. Of course they would insist things be done the hard way.

About twenty nymphs were at work, all wearing white aprons, with black nets around their billowy hair. Their legs were just wisps of cloud, probably so they could move faster. Their nebulous dresses were stained with various soups, broths, and glazes, so they looked like colorful sunsets.

The kitchen itself was bigger than my high school gym, and dryads kept popping in and out of the bronze double doors, carrying platters of food into the dining room beyond. As the doors opened, I heard voices I recognized: Zeus's booming baritone, Hera's laughter. Oh, great. My favorite goddess.

As I had feared, the chefs were cooking up all the usual brunch horrors: eggs Benedict with neon-orange hollandaise sauce, steaks with eggs, soufflés. Yep, there were even a few Mr. Crunchys, along with French toast, bacon burgers, and pineapple pizza, because why not? Let brunch chaos reign.

Naomi studied me with the same distrustful expression I was giving the food.

"So why did Grover . . . ?" Her voice trailed off as I showed her the chalice. "I see. You're not supposed to have that."

"Yeah," I said. "I know."

She scratched under her hairnet. "Are you a god, then?"

A line from an old movie flitted through my head: *When someone asks you if you're a god, you say yes!*

I said, "No."

"Right." She hesitated. "This would explain why Ganymede is out there sweating Greek fire."

"I can't really comment," I said. "But if you could signal him to come in here—"

"Oh, no." Naomi folded her arms. She scowled at Annabeth's Yankees cap in a way that made me think invisibility hats were rude in her kitchen and also ineffective. "I will pretend I don't see you. Nobody will bother you in here. But if you want to get Ganymede's attention, you'll have to do it yourself. He's right through there." She pointed at the double doors. "Can't miss him. He's the one sweating—"

"Greek fire. Got it. I don't suppose I could borrow a waiter's outfit and maybe a fake mustache?"

Naomi grunted. "Friend of Maron. That's hilarious." She marched away to check on her soufflés.

I figured that was a no on the waiter's costume. Since Annabeth's invisibility cap wasn't doing much more than making me look out of place and giving me a skin rash, I needed another plan.

I made my way over to the double doors. I waited for a dryad server to go through, then put my foot in between them, keeping them open just enough to peek through the crack.

I'd never seen Zeus's private palace before. The few times I'd been to Olympus, I'd always made a beeline from the elevators to the gods' council chamber, which is what you have to do when you're delivering doomsday weapons or trying to keep the Titans from destroying the world.

Zeus's dining room looked like an ancient Roman feast hall crossed with a Beverly Hills party pad. In the central conversation pit, gold-embroidered purple sofas surrounded a table laden with platters of fruit. The gold cutlery and dinnerware gleamed so brightly I thought my eyes would melt. Bordering the atrium were alabaster columns etched with gold lightning bolts, just in case you forgot whose palace you were in. I was surprised Zeus hadn't monogrammed them . . . although maybe he had. If his monogram was just a Z, that was basically the same as a lightning bolt, right? Mind blown.

The view was suitably impressive—vast open balconies overlooking the other Olympian mansions where the lesser-schmuck gods were forced to live. But what really got me were the games. Lined up along the outer walls, every conceivable Zeus-themed arcade machine blinked and flashed—*King of Olympus* pinball, *Mighty Zeus* slots, even *Lightning God 3000*, which I remembered playing once on Coney Island. I wasn't surprised that Zeus would collect his own memorabilia. That seemed very on-brand. But the fact that he would display it in his dining room was some god-level narcissism. Like, *Why look at these amazing views when you can select my avatar in multiplayer mode and realize how much your powers suck compared to mine?* I wondered if he sourced his machines from the same wholesaler as Hebe Jeebies.

I forced my ADHD brain to stop obsessing about the blinking lights and focus on the brunch guests instead. Plenty of old friends and frenemies lounged on the sofas. At the head of the table sat the big guy himself, the O.Z., chillaxing in a purple velour toga and gold sandals. Because obviously, if you are a god and you can look like anything you want, this is the look you would choose.

To his left was my buddy Hera, goddess of making Percy miserable. She looked regal in her sleeveless white dress and elegant braided hairdo, as if to make a point of how gross her husband was.

To Zeus's right, with her back to me, was a woman I assumed was Rhea, queen of the Titans, aka Grandma Goddess. I'd expected her to look older than the gods, because she was probably pushing six thousand by now, but of course immortals don't have to show their age. Brown-blond hair cascaded down her back in a waterfall of ringlets. She wore a tie-dyed caftan-style dress with silver bangles on each arm. Curled up asleep at her feet was a lion. Just another apex predator at the table.

Other celebrities in the brunch pit included Athena, Hermes, and Demeter . . . because of course the grain goddess would show up for a morning meal. There were a couple of other guests I didn't recognize, either because they'd changed their appearance or because I hadn't met them yet. And standing behind Zeus, trying to figure out what to do with his empty, chalice-free hands, was Ganymede.

He was literally sweating Greek fire. Every so often, a drop of glistening incendiary liquid would pop and smoke on the back of his neck. So far, no one else in the room seemed to be noticing, or maybe he always did that when he served at the boss's table.

Zeus was holding forth about all the delicacies he had ordered for his mother's special brunch day. Apparently, she hadn't been to Olympus in a very long time, and nobody was allowed to start eating or drinking until Zeus finished his speech about how awesome she was. All their cups were empty.

Good. Now all I had to do was get the chalice into Ganymede's hands without being noticed. It seemed so doable, and yet . . .

I stared at the cupbearer, willing him to look in my direction. Finally, as Zeus was extolling the virtues of phoenix eggs Benedict (they have a spicy kick!), Ganymede glanced at the kitchen doors. After a moment of hazy confusion, he saw me holding up the chalice.

His expression changed from surprise to relief to terrified pleading in less time than it would've taken him to pour a drink. His eyes said, *Oh, thank the gods!* I gestured at him to come to the kitchen.

He shuffled to one side, but immediately Zeus reached back and grabbed his wrist. "Stay, Ganymede. I want you to hear this! Then you can pour our drinks and we'll have a nice toast."

Nobody remarked on the obvious fact that the cup-bearer didn't have his cup. I suppose, being a servant, he was even more invisible than I was in my borrowed hat.

Ganymede looked in my direction again. *Help!*

"I thought," Zeus told the group, "that I would honor our dear mother, Rhea, with a special story about her."

"Oh, baby, you don't have to," Rhea said.

The other gods wore pained smiles as if they agreed that Zeus really didn't have to.

"So, one time," Zeus began, "back when I was just a lad and the rest of you were rolling around in Kronos's stomach . . ."

At that moment, two horrible things became clear to me. First, I would have to listen to this story. Second, if Ganymede could not come to the chalice, I would have to bring the chalice to Ganymede.

THIRTY-ONE

I FACE A DANGEROUS PREDATOR WHO IS POSSIBLY MY FUTURE MOTHER-IN-LAW

I will now sing the praises of pastry carts.

Not only can they transport tasty baked goods to the vicinity of your face, they can also be covered with tablecloths that hide a lower shelf perfect for crouching on when you're a demigod who needs to sneak into a brunch. Yes, I know that's a cliché—I got the idea from old TV shows—but hey, you've got to do what works.

The only tough part was convincing Barbara, my new best friend and dryad server, to push me as close to Ganymede as possible.

Her price?

"I want to meet Annabeth Chase," she said. "I want a selfie and an autograph."

"I— Really?"

"She's my hero!" Barbara said.

"No, I get that. She's my hero, too. It's just . . ." I decided not to elaborate. I'd been prepared for Barbara to demand something much more difficult, like a personal quest or a box of gold-foil collectors' edition Mythomagic cards. "I can definitely arrange a meet and greet."

"Deal!" she said cheerfully. "But if you're discovered, I have no idea who you are or how you got under the cart, and I will scream, 'Demigod! Kill him!' Cool?"

"I would expect nothing less."

So I curled up under the cart with the chalice of immortality in my lap, hidden behind a white tablecloth embroidered with lightning bolts, as Barbara wheeled me into the dining room.

"Anyway," Zeus was saying, "there I was, surrounded by angry llamas. . . . Well, you can imagine!"

"My dear," said Hera, "there were no llamas in ancient Greece."

"Well, there were in Crete!" Zeus growled. "I don't know, maybe Kronos decided we couldn't have nice things and he sent them all to Peru, but at the time, wow! Llamas everywhere! As I was saying, I was all alone. No Amalthea. No Kouretes. Just me in my diapers, a mere mewling babe, if you can picture it—"

"I can picture it, Dad," Athena said dryly.

The cart creaked and wobbled. I was so close to the dining table I could smell wet lion fur. I didn't dare look, but I figured I must be getting close to Ganymede.

Just a few more feet . . .

"Stop that!" Zeus snapped.

The cart stopped.

"I'm telling a story here, Barbara!"

"Yes, sir. Sorry, sir."

There was a long pause. I imagined all the gods staring at the cart, wondering why it seemed so heavily laden and why it was creaking more than usual. I waited for Barbara to yell *Demigod! Kill him!*

Finally, Zeus grunted. "Where was I?"

"Crete," Hermes said. "Surrounded by llamas."

"Right, so . . ."

I had trouble keeping track of the story. Partly, my heart was hammering too loudly. And partly, I just didn't want to keep track of the story.

Zeus rambled on, trying to build sympathy for his poor baby self all alone on Crete. I doubted his audience was feeling the suspense since (spoiler) he was immortal, so the possibility of him getting killed by llamas was quite low. Nevertheless, I hoped everyone had stopped looking at the pastry cart. I risked lifting the bottom of the tablecloth.

I had a great view of Zeus's sandaled feet. Did he polish those toenails or what?

Focus, Percy.

Ganymede stood on the other side of Zeus—only ten feet away, but still too far to slip him the chalice, especially since there was a lightning god between us. I tried to look up to see Ganymede's face, but my angle wasn't good enough. I couldn't tell if he knew I was there or if he was too busy sweating Greek fire to notice.

I wondered if I could crawl from the cart to under the table, past all those immaculately groomed godly feet, without getting noticed. Probably not. Then I glanced to my right and locked eyes with the lion.

Well, that was super. He looked sleepy and surprised,

like he was wondering if he was still dreaming or if the pastry cart really had a human head on the bottom shelf.

Probably the worst thing I could have done was to continue staring at him. So that's what I did. He had pretty gold eyes. I've never been much of a cat person, but I could see the appeal of that big fuzzy face resting on giant fluffy paws, except for the fact that the face had fangs and the paws had claws.

I tried to use my son-of-the-sea-god patent-pending telepathy to send him a message: *I am harmless. Please do not eat me.* But I was pretty sure that 1) the lion was not a sea creature, and 2) even if I could communicate with him, he would not listen to me.

I mouthed, *Okay, bye.*

I slowly lowered the edge of the tablecloth. It would not protect me from the lion, but maybe he would forget about me?

"Then," Zeus was saying, "my loving mother showed up! And you will never guess what she did!"

Rawwwwwr, said the lion.

Everyone around the table laughed.

"That's right, Lucius!" Zeus agreed. "She roared! After that . . ."

I risked another peek, just to see if the lion was about to eat my face. Instead, Lucius had his head tilted and eyes closed in a look of utter bliss as Rhea scratched his ear, probably in an effort to keep him quiet.

I did meet the gaze of someone else, though. Apparently,

she had peeked under the table to see the cute kitty. Now, from across the table, Athena was staring right at me.

Our eye-lock lasted less than a second, but the thing about Athena is that she is so smart, she can just glance at you and you feel like you've gone through a silent inter-rogation under a hot spotlight. The conversation went something like this:

Athena: Why?
Me: Quest. Sorry. Trying to hide.
Athena: Under a pastry cart? That is so clichéd.
Me: Yeah, I know.
Athena: I can't believe my daughter is still dating you.
Me: Love is a mystery. Please don't kill me?
Athena: . . . . . .
Me: . . . . . .

She popped her head back up while Zeus went on with his story. I waited for the goddess to interrupt and reveal my identity.

"So anyway, the *first* llama—" Zeus was saying.

"Ganymede?" Athena interrupted. "Would you be a sweetheart and take that pastry cart back to the kitchen? I don't see any clotted cream for the scones, and that's a deal-breaker."

Ganymede stuttered, "Uh, I—"

"I want Ganymede to hear the end of the story!" Zeus protested.

"But, Father," Athena said, calm and collected, "you know how Rhea loves her scones."

There followed a moment of electric tension—I could imagine storm clouds forming around Zeus's chair.

"Hmph," he said at last. I couldn't see him, but I swore I could feel the moment he let go of Ganymede's wrist. "Hurry back."

"Or don't," Hera muttered. "Take your time."

The cart started to move. I couldn't tell if it was shaking because of the wheels or because Ganymede was coming apart.

Behind us, Zeus mumbled, "I do love watching him walk away. . . ."

"Could you not at the brunch table?" Hera asked through what sounded like clenched teeth.

"So where was I?"

"Crete," Hermes said. "Llamas."

The double doors swung open, and we were safely in the kitchen.

Gasping, I rolled out from under the pastry cart. I realized I'd been holding my breath for way too long.

"Oh, baby!" said Ganymede. "Come to Papa, you beautiful thing!"

Thankfully, he was not talking to me. He made gimme-gimme hands at the chalice. I wondered why he just didn't grab it. Then it occurred to me I had to hand it over. I had to complete the quest and place the cup into his possession.

"Chalice for you, sir," I said, and managed to lift the cup.

Ganymede hugged it, kissed its rim, examined it for dents and dings. "Oh, Percy Jackson! You did it! I don't know how to thank you!"

"How about a recommendation letter?"

Ganymede blinked. "Right! Of course!" A piece of paper floated down from nowhere, straight onto my chest.

I looked at both sides. "It's blank."

"Just dictate whatever you want me to say. The words will write themselves. When you're done, as long as you haven't gone overboard with the praise, my signature will appear at the bottom. It's all completely legitimate and legal."

All this . . . for a blank piece of paper.

I could have laughed or sobbed, but that wouldn't have done any good. And it would have attracted the attention of the other gods.

"Thanks," I said, getting to my feet. "So . . . we're done?"

"Now I have to fill this chalice," Ganymede said. "And clotted cream! I need some clotted cream! But yes. We're done. I won't forget this, Percy Jackson. Good luck in college!"

As Ganymede rushed around the kitchen, Zeus called out, "Ganymede, where are you? I'm getting to the good part!"

"Coming, Lord Zeus!" Ganymede called. "Just . . . filling my chalice, which has been in my possession this entire time!"

He winced, then returned to work. Clotted cream obtained and chalice filled, he rushed the cart back into the dining hall.

I glanced at Barbara the dryad. "Thanks for your help. I'll arrange that meet and greet with Annabeth."

"Awesome! It must be such a thrill to work for her."

"Um, yep."

I turned and nearly jumped out of my jeans. Chef Naomi was standing one inch away, glaring at me.

"Bit of a letdown, doing quests for the gods?" she asked. "Kind of the way I feel every time I make a meal and none of them even says thank you."

"You know," I said, "it's a living."

She patted me on the shoulder. "Would you like a demi bag for the road? Then you can get out of my kitchen."

THIRTY-TWO

GROVER EATS MY LEFTOVERS

The worst part of it all?

Demi bags—as in bags of leftovers for demigods—were a real thing.

Naomi gave me an insulated white sack with DEMI BAG! written in red letters above a sketch of smiling children with their tongues hanging out, waiting for tasty treats.

I'm not sure what I found more insulting—the fact that the gods treated their kids like pets, or the fact that Poseidon had never once brought me any leftovers. Naomi loaded me up with primo pastries, though she didn't include any clotted cream.

Somehow, I made it back across the Olympian bridge without being accosted by minor gods or rabid dryad fans demanding Annabeth's autograph.

As I took the elevator down to the mortal world, "I Got You, Babe" was still playing. Gods almighty, how long was that song? Or maybe the Olympians just had it on a loop to torture their visitors.

I realized I was shaking from delayed fear. All the adrenaline rushed out of my body. I could still see Athena's eyes boring into me, so much worse than the gaze of a lion. Unlike Lucius, the goddess of wisdom couldn't be pacified by a scratch behind the ear—or at least, I wasn't going to be the one to try.

I took off Annabeth's cap, which helped a little. The itching stopped immediately. I expected my skin to be covered in red welts, but my arms looked no different. By the time I reached the lobby, I was feeling almost calm again.

The doors slid open. I took a deep breath and strolled out of the elevator, doing my best to act casual. I dropped my stolen key card near the front desk. There was no sign of Grover, though when I passed one of the mortal guards, she was humming "Get Lucky." The sentry at the front desk didn't try to stop me, but I'm pretty sure he narrowed his eyes when he saw my demi bag.

Once out on Fifth Avenue, I spotted Grover at the end of the block, waving his sparkly Hula-Hoop at me.

"Lobby security let me off with a warning!" he said as he trotted up. "And did you— Ooh, a demi bag! Thanks!"

Grover dove in like a horse with a grain sack . . . which I mean in a completely complimentary and positive way.

"Yum," he said. "You know what these pastries need?"

"Clotted cream?" I guessed.

He got a dreamy look on his face. "I was going to say strawberry jelly. But yeah . . . clotted cream. Anyway, tell me what happened!"

I gave him the rundown on my fabulous brunch experience.

"Llamas in Crete?" Grover frowned. "You sure they weren't vicuña or guanaco?"

"You know, I didn't get the chance to ask while I was hiding under the pastry cart."

"That's a cliché. But you met Lucius the lion! I hear he tells hilarious jokes. . . ." Grover must've registered the blank look on my face. "Which of course you didn't have time for. It sounds like everything worked out, though!"

"Yeah," I said. "As long as Athena doesn't report me to the Olympian border patrol. Or as long as Zeus doesn't find out I sneaked into his brunch. I've decided not to mention this incident to anyone at camp."

His goatee quivered. I worried I'd offended him somehow. Then he sniffled, and I realized he was on the verge of tears.

"I'll be honest, Percy . . . the most scared I've ever been? It was probably in that Cyclops's cave in the Sea of Monsters, when I was all alone. . . ." He wiped his nose, which made the Hula-Hoop sparkle cheerfully. (Because Hula-Hoops have no sense of propriety.)

"But today," he continued, "when I watched you wrestling Gary . . . ? That was a close second. I really thought I was going to lose you."

My heart felt like it was being filled with a particularly heavy Olympian beverage. "Ah, G-man . . . we came through it okay. We always do."

Sniffle. "I know. But every time . . . I feel like we're tempting fate. Like eventually our luck will run out. And if I lost you . . ."

"Hey," I said. "I'm fine. Besides, you've been in a

lot scarier spots than today. I mean, Medusa's lair, the Underworld—"

"Nah," he said. "Nothing is scarier than watching your friend struggle and not being able to help."

I put a hand on his shoulder. "But you did help. You know how I was able to beat Gary?"

I told him about the daydream that got me through the wrestling match—of Annabeth and me and him, dozing in the sunshine at a cottage on the seashore.

He listened intently, like he was almost as hungry for the story as he was for the demi-bag goodies. "I had white ear hair?" he asked.

"Yeah."

"That makes sense. And what was cooking for lunch?"

I thought about it. "Probably enchiladas."

He sighed with contentment. "Okay. That's good. I can believe in enchiladas."

He gave me a hug that reminded me how much my ribs hurt, but honestly, I didn't mind. We probably looked strange standing there on Fifth Avenue, just two guys hugging it out with a Hula-Hoop between us. I didn't mind that, either.

"I'm keeping you from school," Grover said, releasing me from the satyr hug of steel. "Haven't you already missed, like, two classes?"

Oh, right . . . school.

"Maybe I should find Annabeth first," I said hopefully. "Tell her what happened. Return her hat."

"I can do that," Grover said. "You get to class!"

That's the advantage of having a friend who does not attend school—he can do things for you while you're stuck in lectures. The disadvantage is that you have one less excuse for skipping those lectures.

I readjusted the cap for Annabeth's size and handed it to Grover. Then I gave him another hug.

"Thanks for everything, G-man," I said. "I couldn't have done it without you."

"Aww." He blushed to the base of his horns. "Just make good grades! Otherwise . . . well, I'm sure you'll do great."

On that happy note, we headed in different directions—him downtown toward SODNYC, me to the subway for Queens.

I tried not the dwell on the fact that I was taking the F train to school. It seemed like a bad omen. Still, it felt weird being back in a mortal commute after my trip to Olympus. In the seat next to me, some guy was on his phone complaining about stock options. The lady across the aisle was rummaging through bags of produce, pulling out turnips and scowling at them. Meanwhile, up on Olympus, Zeus probably hadn't even finished his llama story yet. I preferred hanging out with Stock Option Guy and Turnip Lady. They were more entertaining.

By the time I emerged in Queens and walked a half mile, I'd just about stopped shaking from my morning quest and instead had started shaking thinking about the unexcused tardy I'd have to explain.

Alternative High was right where I'd left it—on a tree-lined block of 37th Avenue between a used-car dealership and a wholesale store called (I kid you not) Hephaistos Building Supplies. I hadn't had the courage to visit the store, though I wondered if they sold used bronze dragon parts.

The building itself looked like a deceptively average New York elementary school: a two-story wedge of red brick with white-trimmed windows and a bright blue main entrance. It wasn't until you compared the sign ALTERNATIVE HIGH SCHOOL to the playground—which still had seesaws and paintings of Disney characters on the pavement—that you started to get a sense of disconnect.

I walked into the front office, ready to spill all kinds of wild stories. I was trying to decide between *My dog ate my shoes* and *My alarm didn't go off*, which, given my state of mind, probably would have come out as *Hi, my dog didn't go off, and I ate my alarm shoes.*

Before I could say anything, the secretary looked up from a phone call. She practically beamed with delight. "Oh, Mr. Jackson! I'm talking to your father right now. He explained that you would be late."

I blinked. "He did?"

She put her hand over the receiver. "What a lovely man! Here, you can tell him you arrived safely while I write you a pass to third period. We've already resched-uled your first-period quiz. Not to worry!"

She handed me the phone and floated back to her desk, humming a cheerful tune.

I stared at the receiver. Had Paul called the school? That didn't make sense. He wouldn't even know I was running late, and he was careful never to misrepresent himself as my father. But who else . . . ? Surely not . . . ?

"Hello?" I said.

"Congratulations," said Poseidon. "That was nicely done with the chalice."

I braced myself against the counter to keep from falling over. Hearing the god of the sea on a mortal landline was beyond strange. Usually, I heard his voice underwater, or echoing through the council chamber on Mount Olympus. On the phone, he sounded like Poseidon the same way I sounded like myself when I heard a recording of my own voice—which is to say, not at all.

"You called my school?" I asked.

I didn't mean to sound rude. I was just in shock. How did Poseidon find the school's number? How did he know what to say? How had he even learned to operate a phone? I pictured him in an air bubble, sitting poolside at the edge of the continental shelf, his line plugged straight into the undersea transatlantic cable. No wonder he had such a clear connection.

"It was the least I could do," he said. "Margaret was very understanding."

Margaret? I guessed that was the secretary. Grover was right: school secretaries really *did* know everyone and everything. I wasn't sure how I felt about Poseidon being on a first-name basis with her, though.

"Uh, thanks . . . *Dad.*" I said that last bit for Margaret's benefit, since she was smiling at me as she wrote out my hall pass. She was probably thinking how lucky I was to have a father who was so active in my life.

"Can I ask . . . ?" I lowered my voice as I cradled the receiver. "And don't take this the wrong way, but why help me now? I mean . . . I've been in way worse situations before. Isn't this pretty hands-on for a god?"

The line was silent for a count of three. Except for the faint gurgling sound of water in the background, I would've thought Poseidon had hung up.

"You know," he said, "sometimes it's the smallest waves that knock you off your feet. Tsunamis—everybody knows they're powerful. Tidal waves—big and impressive. But those small waves? They hold a lot of power. They prove what the ocean is capable of, even when no one is paying attention."

Margaret slid a hall pass across the counter. She smiled as if to say, *This is all very nice and your dad sounds great, but I need my phone back now.*

"Okay, Dad," I said. "I understand."

In fact, I had no idea what he was talking about.

"I always keep an eye on you, Percy," he said. "Mostly from a distance, it's true. I've watched you save the world multiple times, conquering enemies that would scare most immortals. But it wasn't until today that I realized how much of a hero you truly are."

A lump formed in my throat. "Because I dared to go to brunch?"

Poseidon chuckled. "No. That was just foolhardy. You'd never catch me at one of Zeus's brunches. I mean when you accepted Geras's challenge. You could have walked away, left Ganymede to his fate, probably even gotten Geras to write you a recommendation letter instead."

The way Poseidon spelled out what I'd been thinking at the time . . . I wondered if he could read my mind. Or maybe he just understood me the way he understood the ocean's moods. Like the sea, I was part of him.

"Instead," he continued, "you honored your promise. You risked your life for a cupbearer you barely know. Not for a letter. Not because the fate of the world was at stake. But because that's just who you are. Today, you created a small wave, and you showed what the ocean is capable of."

My eyes were getting watery. If I wasn't careful, I was going to start a saltwater flood right here in the office.

"Mr. Jackson?" Margaret sounded impatient.

"I gotta go," I told Poseidon. "But hey, Dad? Thank you. Also . . . would you consider letting the river god Elisson do a yoga class at your palace sometime? I think you'd really love it."

I said good-bye and, after handing Margaret the phone, took my hall pass and left. When I glanced back through the office window, she was talking to my dad again, laughing at something he'd said. Were they flirting? I decided I didn't want to know.

Already this morning, I'd wrestled Old Age, survived a godly brunch, and gotten the demi bag to prove it. I'd saved Ganymede's reputation, and even put in a good word for Elisson and his undersea whale yoga classes.

Those were enough small waves for now. My dad was right. If you weren't careful, they could sweep you off your feet.

THIRTY-THREE

Ψ

ONE MORE JOLLY RANCHER
FOR OLD TIMES' SAKE

I was halfway down the hall when the counselor's door opened.

"There you are!" Eudora said. "Come in! Come in!"

I was in too much shock to argue. Besides, a few more minutes of tardiness probably wouldn't make any difference, so I followed her inside.

I sat on the little blue plastic chair and nodded to Sicky Frog, because by this point, I was pretty sure the creature was sentient. Eudora seemed to be making herself at home in the counselor's office. She'd added a collection of seashells to her desk—maybe in case she needed to freshen up her hairdo. On the back wall, she'd tacked up a motivational poster of a smiling sea otter with the message LAUGHTER IS THE BEST MEDICINE!

I thought maybe I should buy her another poster as a thank-you gift, once I was safely graduated and on the other side of the country. One that said: COUNSELING: WHERE CAN WE FLUSH YOU TODAY?

"So!" Eudora rubbed her hands together. "Tell me all about it! I heard you got Ganymede's letter!"

"It's kind of a do-it-yourself letter, but yeah." I told

her about my adventures since I'd last seen her, making sure she understood there was no longer any need to send me anywhere via her magical sewer pipes.

When I mentioned the call from Poseidon, a trickle of seawater leaked from her scalloped hair.

"I—I see! I would have been happy to talk to the office myself. I'm so sorry your father had to be bothered with that." She paused, looking suddenly terrified. "Not that you are a bother, of course!"

"It's cool," I said. "Actually, it worked out great."

Her shoulders relaxed as she realized I wasn't going to yell at her or demand that my father banish her to the Mariana Trench.

"I'm so glad to hear that," she said. "I think this experience would make a great subject for your personal essay on the application. Bravery! Initiative! Self-discovery!"

"Yeah," I said, trying not to cry about the fact that I would have to write yet another essay. "I think we all learned an important lesson here today."

"Sorry?"

"Forget it."

She leaned forward conspiratorially. "And . . . may I ask, were you tempted at all to drink from the chalice of the gods? You can tell me the truth."

I thought about poor Ganymede sweating Greek fire at the brunch, about the way Zeus treated him like a trophy, about the various looks of distaste Hebe, Iris, and Geras had made when I mentioned Ganymede's name.

"The truth?" I said. "I wasn't tempted a bit."

She studied me as if I'd grown a set of tentacles. "Fascinating. May I see your letter from Ganymede?"

I pulled out my blank sheet of paper and slid it across the desk.

"Oh, goodness . . ." Eudora rubbed the edge of the paper. "This is very nice. Arachnean-silk fiber! Eggshell finish. Triple weave. It will make quite an impression on the admissions committee."

"It's blank," I said.

"Ah, details. I'm sure you'll add the right words."

I wondered if I could use that approach for my English class. Maybe I had been looking at this writing stuff all wrong. I could buy some expensive cardstock at the stationery store, fill it with *Blah, blah, blah, blah,* and my teacher would go, *Oh, nice paper! A+!*

Eudora reluctantly slid the blank letter back to me. "Well done, Percy. When you do write your letter, it's not necessary to thank me too much."

I looked at the poster of the smiling otter, who was loving that laughter medicine, then at Sicky Frog, who was not.

"Okay," I said.

"Just a short mention would be sufficient," Eudora said.

"So I guess we're all done for now?" I pointed to the door. "'Cause I'm really looking forward to spending the rest of my day in class."

"Of course you are!" Eudora said, because much like

minor goddesses, Nereids don't do sarcasm. "And I know how proud your father must be!"

I couldn't bring myself to respond. It still felt surreal that I had talked to my dad. He'd called the school. He'd been watching. It almost made up for all the demi bags he'd never brought me, though honestly, I couldn't blame him for skipping those Olympian brunches. He was too smart to subject himself to phoenix eggs Benedict.

"Soon, we'll have to talk standardized testing," Eudora reminded me. "And you'll need those other two letters of recommendation by winter break. But for now, you should relax! What else do you have on your plate today?"

"A discussion about some short story. A math test. A chemistry lab."

She nodded contentedly, as if I'd given her the perfect description of relaxation. "Remember, I am here if you need anything. Now, what color Jolly Rancher would you like? Green? Yellow?"

She really didn't know me very well. She offered me the jar, and I dug around until I found the only blue piece.

Eudora smiled. "You're going to do just fine, Percy. I have a good feeling about this year! Now if you're running late to third period, I could always—"

"I'll walk," I said quickly. "But thanks, Eudora." I saluted her with my Jolly Rancher, then saluted Sicky Frog. "I'm sure I'll see you soon."

I have to admit, it was kind of relaxing sitting in English class. No, I hadn't read the story or done my homework. But I was pretty sure I could bluff my way through a literature conversation today. I could talk about bravery, initiative, and self-discovery. You can get a lot of mileage out of that stuff.

THIRTY-FOUR

Ψ

I WRITE THE WORST LETTER
EVER, DELETE, DELETE

I was relieved to get home that night—at least until dinner turned into a letter-writing party. You'd think that
with an English teacher, a soon-to-be-published author,
and a daughter of Athena at the table, we could come
up with some believable praise that Ganymede might say
about me. You would be wrong.

Annabeth had come over around sunset. She didn't
bring cupcakes this time. She'd been too busy catching up
on schoolwork after hunting the diapered god of geriat-
rics in the park that morning. She and I chopped peppers
for the salad while Paul cooked spaghetti. And, yes, after
the horned-serpent incident, I'd sworn off spaghetti, but
pasta is like a best friend: you can't stay mad at it forever.

Once the table was set and the Dave Brubeck Quartet
was jazzing out on Paul's turntable, we broke garlic bread
and talked about our respective days, just the four of us.
Well . . . four and a half of us. I had to keep reminding
myself that my mom was expecting a little mortal bundle
of Jackson-Blofis.

It was a pretty average dinner for us, which was exactly
what I needed. Paul told funny stories about his classes.

His students were goofs. His fellow teachers and admin-istrators were even bigger goofs. My mom told us that her book had received its first one-star review online, even though the book wouldn't be out for several more months. Apparently, the reviewer didn't like that the title *Love Songs of the Gods* promoted paganism.

Paul chuckled. "Little do they know."

I offered to talk to Hylla, queen of the Amazons and fearsome monarch of online retailing, about removing the review, but my mom said there was no need.

"I'm going to print it and frame it," she said. "I kind of love it."

Finally, Annabeth told them about our latest adven-tures. She played down the most terrifying parts, like almost getting turned into grave dust, but I think my mom filled in the blanks pretty well.

"Wow. Embracing old age?" She smiled at Paul. "I have a smart kid."

"Yes, you do," Paul said. "I think he gets that from your side."

I may have blushed. It's one thing being called the son of Poseidon. Getting noticed for being anything like my mom, though . . . *that's* a compliment.

"What happened on Olympus?" Annabeth asked me. "I didn't get to hear about it."

I hesitated. I was still processing what I'd seen at the brunch—and not just the horror of Zeus's pedicured toe-nails. "It wasn't too bad," I said. "I got Ganymede the chalice just in time. He gave me my letter."

Annabeth waited for more. I gave her a look. *Later, okay?*

"So . . ." Paul broke the silence. "What does a godly recommendation letter look like?"

"I'll show you after dinner," I promised. "Probably best if we don't get spaghetti sauce on it."

Once we'd cleaned up the dishes, I brought out the letter and set it on the living room table. Everybody leaned in like they were looking at a board game.

"It's blank," my mom noted.

"Lovely paper, though," Paul said.

"If you got an essay on this paper," I said, "would you just give it an A-plus without reading it?"

Paul grinned. "I would probably write 'Nice try with the lovely paper, but you still need to provide examples that prove your thesis.'"

"Well, there goes that idea," I grumbled.

My mom picked up the letter and looked at both sides. "Is it written in some sort of invisible ink?"

"I have to do it myself." I explained what Ganymede had told me—that I could say whatever I wanted, within reason, and once I had done a good job, his signature would appear at the bottom.

Paul frowned. "That seems a bit . . ."

"Too trusting?" Annabeth guessed.

"I was going to say lazy on Ganymede's part." Paul glanced at the ceiling. "Though I hope that doesn't get me zapped with a lightning bolt."

"Nah," I said. "The gods would take that as a compliment. They raise lazy to an art form."

"Nice work if you can get it," Paul said.

I knew he was being facetious, but the comment made me wince. I'd been offered that work, and I'd turned it down. But the more I thought about Ganymede, the happier I was with my choice. His job was anything but nice.

My mom set the paper back on the table. "How does it know when to start writing?"

"Dunno," I admitted. "Maybe I just say 'Dear Admissions Office.'"

I should have known better. Fancy calligraphy blazed to life across the top of the paper, each letter forming in fiery bronze ink with a sound like a burning fuse: *Dear Admissions Office.*

"Well, crap," I said.

Well, crap, wrote the fancy calligraphy.

"No! Delete!" I said.

Thankfully, the writing erased itself.

I looked at Annabeth, who was trying hard not to laugh.

"This isn't funny," I said, "Delete, delete. I didn't know it would start. Delete, delete."

My mom stared at the letters writing and erasing themselves. "That is amazing paper. What's it made out of?"

I wasn't about to tell her Arachnean silk, because Annabeth had a major spider phobia. I didn't want to have to peel her off the chandelier.

"Maybe we should help Percy get it written now," Paul said, "so he doesn't have to worry about it."

"Spoken like a true English teacher," Annabeth said.

"It can't be that hard, right? How about, 'I highly recommend Percy Jackson for New Rome University. He is adorable and has nice eyes.'"

"I am not saying that. Delete, delete," I complained, though I did keep the first sentence. That one sounded okay.

"'And his mother is very proud of him,'" my mom chipped in, "'though college would be a wonderful experience, as it might teach him to do his own laundry.'"

"You're all terrible people," I said. "Delete, delete."

Paul cleared his throat, like he was getting ready to launch into a lecture on similes. "'I, Ganymede, cupbearer to the gods, have found Percy Jackson to be an excellent hero—brave, kind, and fantastic at chopping vegetables.'"

My mom and Annabeth were both giggling.

I wanted to say *Just kill me now*, but with my luck, those words would stick on the letter and the admissions office at New Rome would make me fall on my sword the moment I arrived.

I dictated Paul's sentence, minus the vegetables. For the next half an hour, Paul, Annabeth, and my mom offered all sorts of unhelpful suggestions for Ganymede's letter, while I picked out the least embarrassing lines and read them onto the paper. I even managed to get a line in there about how helpful my counselor, Eudora, had been.

By the end, Annabeth was on the floor crying from laughing so hard. Paul looked like he was starting to feel bad for me. My mom came over and kissed me on the head.

"I'm sorry, dear," she said. "But we do love *all* those things about you. Let's see how the letter came out."

She read it aloud, and I had to admit, it wasn't bad.

"How do you get his signature to appear, though?" Annabeth wondered.

Before she could suggest something like *Hugs and kisses*, I said, " 'Thank you for your time. Yours sincerely, Ganymede.' "

The words burned themselves onto the paper, with Ganymede's signature appearing in red.

"You think it's done?" I asked. Then I realized my question was not transcribing itself.

"Thank gods."

"You have to get two more recommendation letters?" my mom asked. "Sounds like fun!"

"Yeah, and if those are do-it-yourself letters, too," I said, "I think I'll do them by myself."

"But you're never alone, Seaweed Brain." Annabeth squeezed my ankle. "We'll always be here to help you."

She didn't even have the decency to put sarcastic air quotes around *help*.

"To Percy!" Paul raised his glass. "Our own family hero!"

My mom and Annabeth both cheered and drank sparkling water to my health.

I appreciated the sentiment, but I didn't join in. Toasts made me think of Ganymede, and it was a little too soon for that.

THIRTY-FIVE

Ψ

PRETTY MUCH THE BEST
GOOD-NIGHT KISS EVER

That night, I told Annabeth the full story.

After dinner, she'd headed back to her dorm, but once I'd had enough of doing homework, I lay down in my bed, fired up my makeshift Iris-message machine, and tossed a coin into the rainbow. I was a little afraid Iris's staff, Mercedes, might fly through my window and beat me upside the head for using another form of messaging, but thankfully that didn't happen.

"Hey," said Annabeth.

She shimmered in the rainbow light, her head propped on one hand, an open textbook on the bed in front of her: some math stuff that was beyond me.

Her smile was the perfect antidote for my long crazy day. Sure, she had smiled at dinner (And laughed at me. A lot.), but this was a warmer, more intimate smile. I liked to think it was just for me.

"I wanted to tell you about Olympus," I started.

She was delighted to hear about Barbara's request for a selfie and an autograph. "Of course! Happy to!"

I was a little surprised by how unsurprised she sounded.

Maybe she got these requests all the time and just didn't talk about them.

"Thanks for the loan of the Yankees cap, by the way," I said. "You never told me it makes you uncomfortable when you wear it."

She gave me a one-shoulder shrug. "All power has a price. Even being invisible. My mom taught me that a long time ago."

She sounded wistful, maybe a little sad, but not resentful. She had apparently accepted the way the world worked according to Athena, even if she didn't always agree, even if it sometimes didn't make any more sense than Annabeth's math homework did to me.

"Speaking of your mom . . ." I told her what had happened at the brunch, when Athena locked eyes with me under the table.

Annabeth's expression was difficult to read. Iris-messages were always a little hazy, but she looked like she was trying to sew my words together in her mind, to make a coherent story out of them.

"Wow," she said at last.

"Yeah."

"She helped you."

"I . . . guess? She didn't kill me, anyway."

"You know what this means?" She stretched her hand toward me. Her fingers dispersed into water and light as they hit the Iris-message, but I reached toward her anyway. When the image re-formed, it looked as if our hands had merged, fused together at our life lines. Annabeth was smiling again.

"My mom gets it," Annabeth said. "It's weird that she didn't before, seeing as she's usually so far ahead of everyone else, but I guess this isn't a battlefield."

"Sorry, she gets *what*?"

She laughed. "How serious I am about you, Seaweed Brain."

My chest tightened, but it wasn't an unpleasant feeling—more like a snug woolly sweater being wrapped around me. "So you think she helped me for your sake?"

As I said it, I realized it made a lot of sense. At least, way more sense than Athena helping me for any other reason.

"She knows I am going to see this through," Annabeth said. "I'm going to make sure we both get to adulthood and have a chance to settle down—hopefully after having a lot of fun while we're in college."

"You had me at *fun*," I said. "Actually, you had me at the whole thing."

I told her what I had thought about while I wrestled Geras, how I'd decided to hug it out with old age because any future that had *us* in it was a future I wanted to live through.

"Oh, my gods." Annabeth brushed away a tear. "You know, sometimes you can be so sweet."

"Only sometimes?"

"Let's stay focused, shall we? You still have two more

letters of recommendation to get before winter break. That means two more quests for the gods."

"Easy-queasy."

"You mean *peasy*."

"No, I'm pretty sure it makes me queasy. But we'll make it, right? I mean, if even your *mom* is on our side . . ."

"I wouldn't press too hard on that point, but it's a good sign. And, yes, we'll make it. Hey, Percy?"

"Yeah."

"I hate to break it to you, but I think I might love you."

"Ah, crud. I was afraid of that. I love you, too."

"Finish your homework. Good night."

"Good night, Wise Girl."

And as we always did, we rolled toward each other, breaking the Iris-message as we came together, but in the mist and the last flecks of light, I thought I could smell her presence, and feel the warmth of her hug.

Honestly, that was enough to make me believe anything was possible.

Except homework. I fell asleep almost immediately. And for once, I had pleasant dreams.

DON'T MISS THIS RECENT ADDITION
TO THE WORLD OF PERCY JACKSON!

THE SUN
AND
THE STAR

A NICO DI ANGELO ADVENTURE

RICK RIORDAN AND MARK OSHIRO

Nico faced the worst decision of his life, and he was certain he was going to mess it up.

"I can't do this," he said to Will Solace, the stunningly beautiful son of Apollo, who stood across from him. But it was Austin Lake—one of Will's half-siblings—Nico chose to focus on. He was pacing behind Will, which only made Nico more nervous.

"Stop moving, Austin," said Nico. "I can't concentrate."

"Sorry, dude," said Austin. "This is just so stressful."

"You gotta choose," Will said to Nico. "Those are the rules."

Nico frowned. "I'm the son of Hades. I don't live by most rules."

"But you *did* agree to these," said Kayla Knowles, another child of Apollo. She twirled a cherry lollipop in her mouth. "Are you a demigod without honor, Nico di Angelo?"

Austin kept pacing. "To be fair, I don't think this task requires any *actual* honor."

"Quiet!" said Nico, running his hands through his hair. What if he made the wrong choice? Would Will be disappointed in him?

But studying Will's face, Nico saw only anticipation. The good kind. Will was ready for whatever Nico would say, and no matter how this ended, Will would still think just as highly of him.

What did I ever do to deserve him? Nico wondered. He asked himself that question a lot.

"Okay, I've made my decision," said Nico.

"I might explode," said Austin.

"The world might end," said Kayla, now holding the lollipop

at her side, her eyes bright with anxiety. "Like, *actually* end this time."

"So," said Nico, "if I had to choose . . ."

"Yes?" prompted Will. "You would choose . . . ?"

Nico took a deep breath.

"Darth Vader."

Will and Kayla groaned, but Austin looked like Nico had just given him a Ferrari as a birthday present.

"Dude!" Austin screamed. "That is the best answer!"

"It is the *worst* answer!" said Kayla. "Why would you choose Vader when Kylo Ren is *right there?*"

"*I* was hoping for a deep cut," Will mused. "Maybe someone like General Grievous or Dryden Vos."

"Hold on," said Nico. "I just finished watching all those movies *yesterday*. I can barely remember what happened in the prequels at this point." He paused. "Were those all actual characters in Star Wars, or are you joking?"

"Don't distract from your truth, Nico," said Kayla. "*Darth Vader?* You'd go on a date with *Darth Vader?*" She crunched on her lollipop. "I've lost all joy, Nico. All of it."

"Welcome to my world," Nico joked. He caught Will grimacing—a brief flicker of one, but he still caught it.

"This is a safe space," said Austin. "No judgment allowed for our answers, remember?"

"I take it back," said Kayla. "It's an all-judgment space."

"You're very quiet, Will," said Nico. "Especially as *the* number one Star Wars fan in the group."

"I'm considering all the reasons why you'd give that answer," he said. "You might be onto something."

"He's powerful," said Nico.

"And decisive," added Will. "He'd always know exactly where to go for your date. No arguing about that."

"Does he take off his helmet to eat?" said Kayla.

Nico laid his hand over his heart. "Imagine Darth Vader

removing his helmet over dinner and then staring longingly into your eyes over the table. Now *that* is romance."

Will laughed hard, then flashed that brilliant smile of his.

Why, oh why, did it feel like such a victory to make Will laugh? For a long time, Nico had assumed he himself did not have a heart. He was the son of Hades, after all. Love didn't find people like him. But then came . . . Will. Will, who could melt Nico's iciness with a smile. Anyone could have guessed which god was Will's father—he radiated energy and light. Sometimes *literally*, as they had learned in the troglodytes' caverns earlier that year. Will was Apollo's son, through and through.

Maybe that whole saying about opposites attracting was true, because Nico didn't know a single person who was more his opposite. Despite that, they were coming up on a year. A year *together*. Nico had an actual boyfriend.

He still wasn't sure he believed it was real.

The four demigods continued their walk through Camp Half-Blood. There was no fire burning in the amphitheater. Maybe, since it was starting to cool down on Long Island, Nico and Will would light one tonight. No campers were rushing off to the armory or the forge; no one was visiting the Cave of the Oracle. The cabins were empty (aside from Hades's and Apollo's), and that was the clearest sign summer was over.

Nico didn't want to admit it out loud, but he was going to miss . . . well, pretty much all the campers, even though it was at times exhausting to be one of their counselors. He especially didn't want to say good-bye to Kayla and Austin.

As they passed through the strawberry fields, Nico sensed Kayla's and Austin's tension growing. They'd had to make a difficult decision about their travel arrangements earlier that day, and as the four of them climbed Half-Blood Hill, Kayla and Austin slowed.

"I'm thinking that maybe we should have chosen differently," said Kayla.

"You sure we'll be fine, Nico?" asked Austin.

"Yeah," he said. "I mean . . . no one has ever *died* or anything."

"That's not nearly as comforting as you think it is!" said Kayla.

"You'll be okay," said Will, and he put his hand on Austin's shoulder. "I've heard it's chaotic, maybe a bit nauseating, but you'll make it home safely."

They reached the summit of the hill, where the Golden Fleece glittered on the lowest branch of the pine tree. Below, Farm Road 3.141 curved around the base of the hill, defining the outer border of camp. On the gravel shoulder, next to a pile of boxes and duffel bags, stood Chiron, the Camp Half-Blood activities director, his equine lower half gleaming white in the afternoon light.

"There you are!" the centaur called out. "Come along, then."

None of them hurried. It was obvious to Nico that Kayla and Austin weren't in a rush to leave camp. Most everyone else had already returned to their "normal" lives, except . . . well, what was normal for someone like Nico?

Epic battles.

Constantly facing the threat of defeat and death.

The dead talking to him.

Prophecies.

The voice from his dreams bubbled up inside him again now, calling out for help.

Rachel Dare's words haunted him, too. Only he and Will had heard what the Oracle had prophesied a few weeks ago, and Nico hadn't shared it with anyone else yet, not even the other counselors. Why should he? It hadn't warned of any doomsday threats to Camp Half-Blood. The world was—as far as he knew—safe for now from angry gods or rebellious Titans. Resurrected maniacal Roman emperors were no longer a thing to worry about.

The prophecy merely concerned that lone voice in his dreams, begging for help.

Specifically, *Nico's* help.

"Some of the satyrs collected your things," said Chiron as the four demigods joined him at the road. "They wish you well on your journey."

"We might need it," Kayla grumbled. "Chiron, just tell us the truth. The Gray Sisters aren't going to kill us, are they?"

"What? No!" He looked aghast. "At least, they haven't killed anyone so far."

"You and Nico!" cried Austin, throwing up his hands. "Both of you think that's an acceptable thing to tell us?"

Chiron's smile lines crinkled around his eyes. "Now, now, you're demigods. You'll be fine. Try tipping them a few extra drachmas at the start of the trip, though. I've heard that helps make the experience less . . . intense?"

He fished in the pocket of his archery vest, pulled out a golden coin, and threw it into the road. "*Stop, O Chariot of Damnation!*"

No sooner had Chiron finished speaking than the taxi arrived.

It did not putter or cruise up to the group. It *appeared*. The coin sank into the pavement, tendrils of dark smoke curled upward, the asphalt twisted, and the Gray Sisters' taxi erupted into being. It *looked* like a taxi all right, but its edges swirled and wafted if you stared at it too long. Nico had heard all about Percy's, Meg's, and Apollo's experiences with this particular mode of transportation. They'd repeatedly told him that they even preferred his shadow-travel to the bumpy, vomit-inducing nightmare that was riding in that car. The Gray Sisters had a long history of detesting heroes, and at this point they viewed *every* inhabitant of Camp Half-Blood as a potential hero to be detested.

Nico didn't want to admit it to the others, but he had met the sisters several times on his own, and he kind of liked them. They were thorny. Difficult. Stuck in their ways. Chaotic, yet weirdly dependable. They wore their darkness on their sleeves. For Styx's sake, they all shared a single *eye*. How could Nico *not* appreciate them?

The sisters were in the midst of an argument as one of the rear doors swung open.

"I know exactly what I'm doing, Wasp," said the old lady sitting shotgun, her stringy gray hair swaying over her face. "When have I ever *not* known what I'm doing?"

"Oh, *oh!*" screeched Wasp, who sat up front in the middle. "That's lush. That's a real *lush* opinion, Tempest!"

"Do you even know what *lush* means?" Tempest shot back.

The driver groaned dramatically. "Are you two *children?* Will you please stop talking?"

Tempest threw her hands up and put on her best imitation of the driver (which confused Nico, since they all sounded identical). "Oh, my name is Anger, and I'm *sooooo* mature."

"I will eat the eye," warned Anger. "I'll do it."

"You *wouldn't*," said Wasp.

"With salt and pepper and a little paprika!" Anger threatened. "I'll do it."

"Hi," said Austin, hoisting his saxophone case. "Is there any way you could pop the trunk? We have some luggage."

All three Gray Sisters spun toward Austin and spoke in unison: "NO!"

They fell back into arguing. Nico decided right then and there that these were his favorite people in the whole world.

Still, he sympathized with Kayla and Austin. As Chiron worked to open the trunk, both demigods looked more frightened than they ever had in the last year.

"You sure you don't want me to shadow-travel you to Manhattan?" Nico offered.

Will sighed. "Nico, you can't use shadow-travel like public transportation. It'll drain you dry."

"It's okay, Nico," Kayla said, sounding like she was trying hard to believe it. "We'll be fine."

"Plus, we're going to different places," said Austin. "My mom's meeting me uptown. I actually got into an academy up in Harlem, and she found an apartment for us close by!"

"Sounds like a good place to end up," said Will. "Not too far from here."

"And there's so much history in Harlem to explore," added Austin. "Apparently, one of the clubs where Miles Davis used to play has reopened!"

Nico nodded halfheartedly. He had no idea who that was. It was one of the downsides of not being in the "human" world for very long.

"What about you, Kayla?" asked Chiron, loading her archery gear into the trunk.

"Back to Toronto," she said. "Dad wanted me to come home, and it's actually been a while. I'm pretty excited, to be honest." Her eyes glinted. "Especially to prove that I'm now better than him at archery!"

Austin turned to Nico and Will. "So . . . you two are really staying here?"

Nico hoped Will would answer first. The sun falling behind the western hills made Will's curly blond hair look like it was aflame. For a moment, Nico wondered if Will was using his glow-in-the-dark power.

Either way, it made Nico a little annoyed. Why did Will have to be so beautiful all the time?

"I think we are," said Will, taking Nico's hand. "Mom's touring for her new album this fall, and I don't know if I want to bounce around the country in the back of a van."

"Could be fun," said Austin. "I hope I get to travel because of my music one day."

Kayla nodded. "I wonder what it would be like to see other places without worrying whether some murderous statue is going to kill you."

"Oh, come on," said Nico. "Where's the fun in that?"

"Are you going to get in the car?" Tempest growled. "Or are you paying us to listen to your boring conversation?"

She was hanging out the window with an open palm extended toward them. Austin paid her with three drachmas, tipping her heavily as Chiron had suggested. Tempest examined the coins for a moment—Nico didn't know how, as she had no eyes behind that thick gray curtain of hair—then grunted. She pulled herself back into the car.

"Get in," she said.

There were quick hugs and cheek kisses, and then Austin and Kayla climbed into the back seat of the Gray Sisters' taxi. All the while, the sisters continued to argue.

Kayla looked around the cab. "We've been on worse adventures," she said to those outside the car.

"*Have* we?" asked Austin.

"Anyway, hope to see you soon," said Kayla. "And don't get into any trouble, you two."

Austin leaned across Kayla to poke his head out the window, a mischievous excitement on his face. "But if there *is* trouble . . ."

Will waved at them. "You'll know. Promise."

"Be safe yourselves!" Chiron called out.

"Drive, Anger! Drive!" screamed Wasp. "Isn't that what you *do*? Honestly, why do you even sit in that seat if you don't—"

Her words were lost as the taxi jerked forward and disappeared in a blur of gray.

Yep. Nico loved the sisters.

"So, that's it," said Will. "They were the last, weren't they?"

"Indeed," said Chiron. "Aside from some of the staff, the satyrs, and the dryads, Camp Half-Blood is actually . . . empty."

The old centaur sounded a bit lost. As far as Nico could recall since he'd started coming here, this was the first time that there were no demigods present. Aside from him and Will, that is.

"This is weird," said Nico. "*Really* weird."

"A lot has happened over the past few years," said Chiron wistfully. "I understand more than ever why campers would want to go home to be with their families, or to see the world."

"I guess . . ." said Nico.

"Now, gentlemen," said Chiron, dusting off the front of his vest, "I've got a meeting with Juniper and the dryads about tree rot. Exciting stuff, I assure you. I'll see you at dinner?"

They nodded, then waved as Chiron galloped off.

"So," said Nico, "what do we do next?"

Will, still holding Nico's hand, guided him back up the hill. "Well, we don't have any monsters to slay."

"Boo. I could raise a skeleton army to perform a choreographed dance. I bet I could teach them 'Single Ladies,' if you like."

Will chuckled. "We don't have any Roman emperors to locate and dethrone, either."

Nico flinched. "Ugh. Don't remind me. If I could go the rest of my life without even thinking Nero's name again, I'd be happy."

"That's a funny joke," said Will as they reached the summit.

"What is?"

"You," said Will. "Being happy."

Nico rolled his eyes.

"My grumpy little ball of darkness," added Will, poking him in the ribs.

"Ew, gross," said Nico, dancing away from him. "We are *not* making that a thing."

"Did you already forget that I was once your—and I am quoting you here, Nico—'significant annoyance'?"

"Oh, you're *still* that," said Nico, and then Will was chasing him down the hill, back into camp. In that moment, Nico allowed himself to enjoy the sensation. Will was right: there were no threats whatsoever on the horizon. No Big Bads. No lurking demigod traitors, no hidden monsters waiting to destroy Camp Half-Blood.

But then dread prickled across Nico's skin. His body was warning him, wasn't it? *Don't get too comfortable*, it was telling him. *He's waiting for you in Tartarus. Or have you forgotten about him like everyone else did?*

Maybe this period of rest wasn't such a good thing. If Nico didn't have some terrible monster or villain to fight, then what excuse did he have to ignore the voice any longer?

The truth was, he couldn't ignore it even if he wanted to. He'd been visited by so many ghosts over the years. The dead wanted to be heard, and who better to listen to them than the son of Hades?

But *this* voice . . . it did not belong to someone who had passed on. And Nico had never heard someone sound as desperate for help.

So his mood was muted by the time he and Will made it to the dining pavilion after stopping by their cabins to freshen up first. It felt strange to be in this place that was normally so alive. Now there were only a few staff dryads and harpies spread unevenly around the various tables. The camp director, Dionysus—Mr. D to all of them—was lounging at the head table with Chiron, who had somehow beaten them to dinner. The two administrators were so deep in conversation that they barely acknowledged Will when he waved.

Even the satyrs who served Nico and Will didn't seem all that thrilled to be doing so. "This whole place feels like my soul," Nico joked to Will. "You know, empty and dark."

Will swallowed some chicken kebab pieces. "You're not empty," he said, then pointed the skewer at Nico. "You are definitely dark, though."

"Dark as the pits of the Underworld."

Will looked down, focusing on his food like it was the most interesting thing he'd ever seen.

"We don't have to talk about it if you don't want to," said Nico.

Will managed a smile. His warmth was genuine—like it always was, since he was basically a *literal* ray of sunshine—and it softened Nico just a bit. "We can," he said. "Just maybe not now, Nico. Austin and Kayla just left. The camp is calm. Serene. *Quiet.* Let's just appreciate the break, okay?"

Nico nodded, but he wasn't sure how he was supposed to do what Will had requested. When had he *ever* gotten a break before? If it wasn't dead Roman emperors, it was his father. Or Minos. Or his stepmother, Persephone. It had been years since that particular incident had happened, but he was *still* annoyed about being turned into a dandelion. A *dandelion*! It was an affront to his aesthetic!

And there were other things he didn't want to remember. Darker things. Ghosts who would probably visit him eventually. Nico stuffed it all down—making a grumpy little ball of darkness inside his chest. Then he forced a smile as he listened to Will talk about all the things they could do that fall while they stayed at camp.

It would be fine. Everything would be fine.